DEDICATION

In memory of my grandparents, who filled my life, and the lives of so many others, with the magic of love: Mathias Louis Meyer, Harriet Louise Meyer.

ACKNOWLEDGMENT

With love and deepest thanks

To my British family, the Gooches: Mary, John, Caroline, Helen Gooch Adam and Thomas Adam. Over the years they have given unstintingly of their time and encouragement, especially regarding MAD PURSUIT.

To my dear friend, author Harriett Trueblood, for reviewing the work in progress and continually cheering me on.

MADPURSUIT

CHAPTER 1

"Raven Hall? I suppose it has ravens?"

"My goodness. I never thought about ravens."

"You haven't seen ravens, then?"

"They must have been here once. Maybe in the Elizabethan period. It's authentic Elizabethan, you know."

Depressed that Gerald hadn't troubled to meet her plane at Gatwick, Maggie hunched further into the scarf that twisted above her raincoat collar and hugged her knees to her, crumpled as she was in a 2CV. The cheesecake she'd carried on the plane so Gerald could have his favourite treat from Hollywood's Farmers' Market lay in its squashed box beside her.

Gerald's secretary turned and drove up a circular gravel drive as Maggie stared, appalled.

"Aren't you just mad for it?" Miss Always was unable to disguise totally an east London accent. She leaned on the steering wheel and squinted up. "I discovered it all by myself. It's a real find."

Maggie brushed a strand of red hair from one eye. Where is Gerald? she wondered. Why am I here with this odd person? Am I having a nightmare? She gazed through rain-spotted windows at the manor house that loomed above them. Ugly, she thought. Monstrous.

"And don't you love the pointed roofs and all those

dark cross beams? It's either sixteenth or eighteenth century, I think. I get the centuries mixed up. But isn't it romantic? And in the Sussex countryside, my favourite spot. And where a medieval convent once stood."

Never before had Maggie felt so disoriented. Why hadn't Gerald met her plane? After the ordeal of selling their beloved contemporary Hollywood Hills home — all glass and view — and disposing of the furnishings, Maggie felt ravenous for Gerald's touch, for his reassurance that this hateful move to England was the right step.

"Wait until you see the inside. There's a huge drawing room with a walk-in fireplace, and a super master bedroom and about eight other bedrooms. Oh, yes, a tennis court. Gerald says he loves tennis."

Gerald doesn't play tennis, thought Maggie. She unfolded herself and exited the car, then dutifully followed Miss Always up the gravel drive.

" 'A house of great character', that's what the estate agent said." Miss Always, rhythmically rotating her hips, toddled stiffly on five-inch heels. She turned her head to be sure Maggie was keeping up. " 'Lovely wooded grounds' he said. 'Exceptionally sound house', he said. 'Just the home for an underwriter at Lloyd's'. "

Maggie stepped inside her new house. Or rather it was an old house, filled with an ancient, musty, though not unpleasant smell, as if thousands of fires had burnt on the grates on cold evenings and thousands of glasses of sherry and mulled wine had been downed for comfort... or courage. She glanced about at the cold, dark entryway.

"I added these two huge carved chairs," Miss Always boasted, shutting the door behind Maggie and removing her own coat. " 'Victorian' the saleswoman said. "Don't you just adore the red upholstery?"

Maggie stared at the honeypot on Miss Always's breast, the small woven token Gerald gave to favoured workers and clients. Maggie remembered how he'd ridiculed such a business approach when he'd first taken the management course that had introduced the idea. But Gerald, anxious to try any new business technique, had applied it and it had worked for him. Now it was part of his style — a honeypot or hummingbird and a smile or hug or slap on the back.

Miss Always cleared her throat.

"I expect it's all a bit overwhelming for you." She fluffed the ruffles above the neck of her jumper, and Maggie caught a heavy scent, similar to those perfumes she'd sniffed in the chemist's when, as a child, she had lived with her maiden aunt in Dorset. She would come home slightly intoxicated then, and felt a little queazy now.

Miss Always minced ahead into the drawing room.

A cheap oriental screen hid the authentic walk-in fireplace. The ceiling beams had been painted white and dreadful thick gold velvet curtains obscured leaded glass windows. Maggie looked at the furnishings and her head whirled from yards and yards of chintz — pink and red roses on a background of yellow, a colour Maggie hated. Chintz covered footstools, ponderous chairs, and sofas, all meant to look like antiques but sadly failing.

"I furnished it myself."

"Cuckoo," a mechanical bird twanged as Maggie glanced up, startled.

Miss Always laughed. "Gerald was so surprised to hear his first English cuckoo, I thought he'd better have a clock."

Maggie suppressed a shudder. She glanced at a pair of yellow fringed lampshades that unmercifully revealed a French shepherd beneath one and his shepherdess beneath the other, both in idyllic eighteenth century attire. Garish black vases with swirls of flowers adorned small tables. On a heavy sofa table sat two green marble urns which looked as if they contained the ashes of Uncle Ian and Aunt Priscilla. Between them, on a stand, stood a grainy Victorian print in which children, tears in their eyes, hugged their St. Bernard.

Stiff portraits of pompous gentlemen from the past, no doubt painted by itinerant painters of little talent, hung on chains from the mouldings. Former owners? Maggie wondered, but before she could ask, Miss Always said, "These were bloody hard to come by, but you can't have an old house without old paintings, can you? Aren't they impressive?

"And now the dining chamber. Mind the beam. Gerald says that in these old houses if you watch your head, you'll stub your toes and if you watch your toes, you'll hit your head." Miss Always pointed to the beams, then to the floor.

It's as if she's demonstrating for a telly commercial, Maggie thought.

But Gerald's secretary didn't look like a telly star. Her nose was neither dainty nor pert as would befit her chirpy personality, but blunt. Blue eyes, smudged above and below with blue shadow, dominated her face. Pink blush on her cheeks matched the gloss on the full lips. Her chin sank in a trifle. In fact, Maggie found it difficult not to stare at that weak chin.

Even in her spiked heels and with tinted blonde hair teased high, forming swirls and bunches about her face, then falling far below her shoulders, Miss Always was too short to worry about low beams herself. Maggie suspected that so much hair served to make the features appear delicate by contrast.

Miss Always giggled. " 'Dining Chamber' is what the

estate agent calls it. Dining Chamber. That's very grand, isn't it? The nobility used to have music played to them while they ate. See up there? That's the music gallery, though it's so small I can't think that musicians would fit."

As Maggie looked up, her eye caught a contemporary wrought iron chandelier. She winced. It hung above a massive table which bore machine-wrought griffins on its lumpy legs.

"All very grand, isn't it?"

On a badly constructed copy of a country French sideboard stood large brass candlesticks, with yellow candles grasped by Rubens-like naked women, who in turn were clutched by rapacious looking satyrs.

Maggie glanced out the window across the green of a side lawn to give her eyes relief. How would she live in this oppressive place? How would she manage to rid the house of these vulgar furnishings? Each room was worse than the one before. And again, the curtains were yellow. Gerald might have told his secretary that Maggie hated the colour. Did he no longer remember? Did he no longer care what she liked?

"Porphyro." Even after thirty years his pet name came to mind. When first visiting Keat's apartment by the Spanish steps in Rome, Gerald had read her "The Eve of St. Agnes," about daring lovers who had stolen away in the dead of night. And she'd become Madeline to his Porphyro.

And such a handsome, appealing Porphyro. Part Italian, partly of English ancestry, he had a magnetic air about him. People were drawn to him, so much so that Maggie sometimes resented his charm. He had a way of parting his thick dark hair, silver now at the temples, so that a lock fell over one side of his forehead, accentuating his dark brown eyes. One could still see a trace of dimples when he smiled, suggesting a sense of fun beneath the now dignified exterior. With just a twinkle in his eyes and a twist to his smile, Gerald could make any woman fall in love with him.

Oh, why wasn't he here now, showing her their house?

As she continued her tour, Miss Always prattled about her daddy and her mummy and laughed with a honey-rich noise, soft and warm. Maggie found herself annoyed with that little girl innocence, especially since the woman might turn forty at any minute.

They climbed upstairs, Maggie absently running her hand over the carved balustrades, enjoying the smoothness of the oak.

Miss Always toddled ahead, her heels tapping ominously on the dark wood floors, and at the first doorway flung her arms wide.

"This is the master bedroom. The estate agent calls it a 'suite'."

She says that with a kind of pride, as if she's spent time here, Maggie thought, feeling her irritation turn to anger.

The bedroom furniture, too, was heavy and out of date, the wood stained in some colour wood had never before known. It sported an Alpine influence, and Maggie wondered that Miss Always had not put the cuckoo clock here. The bed, with massive headboard, displayed a gold velveteen spread and pillows embroidered with kittens, playing with balls of yarn. The curtains were gold as well.

"I embroidered the pillows myself," Miss Always said. "Bloody hard work, but Gerald really likes them."

Maggie felt uneasy. She didn't think she could sleep in this room. It was bad enough returning to a country she resented and moving into a house she detested, but to live with Miss Always's taste was too humiliating. She glanced at the giant armoire and saw herself and Miss Always, side by side, reflected in the mirror on its door.

Maggie thought about her blue bedroom at home, her blue Diebenkorn Ocean Park painting, her clean, clear sparkling view of Hollywood, all sunny, all light. She remembered sitting in her nightgown and plucking at a satin-covered bed pillow as Gerald told her about the new job and the move.

"I love Hollywood and this house," she'd told him. "And the view. How can I leave? And my friends? I can't go off just like that and start life all over again."

When he didn't answer, she'd said, "You know I hated England as a child."

"Now darling..." Gerald sat on the bed and put his feet into his trousers legs. Then he stood up, pulled them over his lean hips, zipped the fly, threaded the belt through the loops, and fastened it. He put on his shirt, buttoned it, opened his belt and fly, stuffed in his shirt, then redid his fly and belt.

He had put his pants and shirt on like this for thirty years. Maggie had thought his movements amazingly inefficient the first time she had watched. Now, thirty years later, she could still not accept them. They said something about Gerald, but she wasn't sure what.

He always said *she* was the inefficient one — wasting time, wasting effort, forever collecting strays as he called the people she gathered about her. Filling vacant time with volunteer work — another wasted effort. He didn't want her to hold a job — wasted effort as well — so she could be free to travel with him on business, entertain his associates. Yet here he was, wasting any number of motions; and she was rather sure he and his fellows did the same at work each day. It was as if *their* motions, the motions of the system of life, however trivial, were important in themselves, while hers — the motions of the nurturer —

were not.

He remained silent, so she accused him.

"You didn't discuss it with me." She felt lost, betrayed.

"It's the job I want," he stated, the hurt look of a little boy in his brown eyes. "I've waited for this! You always want me to get what I've aimed for.

"By the way, Madeline," he used her pet name automatically, as if all memories were long since forgotten, "you've ruined that pillow."

"Mrs. Featherstone? Do you like the house?" Miss Always unconsciously patted the small woven honey pot on her breast. "Gerald just loves all I've done." She took out a little plastic compact of pressed powder, put a hand beneath her swirling curls and bounced them. Then she used the mirror to redo her face as Maggie looked about the other upstairs rooms.

When Maggie returned, having decided all the rooms were equally dreadful, Miss Always held out her lipstick to show its colour.

"I like this shade, don't you? I just hated last year's lips. So bright."

Maggie glanced at the tube of pale pink. She had somehow missed the fact that there had been a style of lips last year.

"And now, downstairs to the kitchen," chirruped Miss Always. "I don't much like it so saved it for one of the last. Though it has been remodelled."

When Miss Always talked, Maggie noticed, she appeared young and dynamic because of her youthful, energetic way of moving. However, when she was in repose, the deep lines about her eyes and chin became noticeable, and her eyes looked sad.

In the kitchen, Maggie found a blue and white tiled counter. Along its back hung tiles decorated with scenes of

Holland. In the center of the room stood a pine table and four chairs. Maggie found the room fresh, sparkling, and smart. That Miss Always didn't like it pleased her.

Yet even here something old and... and... what was the word Maggie wanted...? Not crumbling, not infected... Aware? Perhaps that was it. Something old and aware lay beneath.

Something knew Maggie and Miss Always were here. Didn't really want them here. Probably resented any occupants. No wonder the house was a "find". Maggie was curious to know what the house thought of Miss Always's contributions.

Miss Always led Maggie back to the drawing room.

"Last, this funny little room. Imagine, it's right off the drawing room. I couldn't think what to do with it."

The oak door stood ajar. Maggie pushed it open, snapped on the light, then walked the distance of the narrow room to the window and slid back grey brocade curtains, obviously left by the previous owner. She wiped dust from her hands as her eyes searched the room. To the right sat an old spinning wheel and three little stools that the former tenants had discarded.

"These are delightful. I'll put them in the drawing room."

"Oh, no. Gerald says they're too quaint," said Miss Always sweetly. "Now come and I'll fix us a nice cup of tea."

"No, thank you."

"Oh, I simply must have something. I'm positively parched." Undaunted, Miss Always led the way from the narrow room, through the drawing room and hallway back to the kitchen. "You sit here," she pointed to the pine table. "I'll have tea ready in a jiff."

Maggie slumped down, furious, but undecided about

how to handle the situation.

Miss Always filled an electric kettle and pulled down blue and white striped mugs from the cupboard. When the kettle boiled, Maggie was surprised to see her pour water over tea bags rather than steep the tea properly in a pot.

Mugs in hand, Miss Always toddled to the table, where a tin of biscuits stood alongside a bowl of sugar. From the fridge she fetched a pitcher of milk. Then she took a chair opposite Maggie's.

"Let's get to know each other," she chirruped. "I want to be just as close to you as I am to Gerald."

How could Gerald possibly have ended up with such a twit of a secretary? But, of course, she was a *find* of Gerald's syndicate.

"I'll bet you're thinking how grand it all is."

Maggie fished out the soggy tea bag and put it in a dish beside the sugar bowl. She poured milk into her cup and stirred diligently. She and Gerald would have a laugh over this silly woman later. And the furnishings. Maggie could imagine Gerald's longing for her to come and remove all this clutter. She'd have to check what agency would cart it off.

In the next weeks, Maggie would acquire authentic pieces that complemented the house. And her crystal collection should arrive shortly.

She warmed to the idea of furnishing Raven Hall. She and Gerald would haunt antique stores on weekends as they had when they were first married. They'd go to Sotheby's auctions for paintings.

It would be just like their Italian period, or so she called it. Then Gerald had been casual, relaxed, extremely fit, extremely witty. They had travelled, staying in inexpensive pensions, and had discovered the world together, especially Italy.

Walking the streets of Florence, they'd bought small engravings and ancient ceramic pots and odd pieces of silver. After every spree they'd sipped wine at sidewalk cafés, examining their finds and exclaiming over their cleverness.

Later in their room, Gerald, his Italian blood on fire, would stroke her as if she were the most prized art object of all, igniting her ardour until together they moaned their bliss.

After several years of marriage and life in California, Gerald had gradually turned that earnestness away from Maggie. He no longer accompanied her on sprees or shared interests with her. She didn't know when they had stopped climbing together.

Before she even realized it, Gerald had left the warm Italian sun, had conquered the arctic peak of his profession, and had planted the flag. She was left in a way station far below.

She took a sip of orange pekoe tea and looked across at Miss Always, who munched on a digestive biscuit. She longed for Gerald's reassurance that this move was the right thing. But maybe he needed Maggie's assurance just as much. She felt a sudden spurt of warmth for the strange little person opposite her. She could almost bless Miss Always for showing her the obvious: Gerald still needed Maggie.

Elizabethan or not, Raven Hall would be a Renaissance house. Here Maggie and Gerald would have their renewal, their fresh beginning.

CHAPTER II

"Ham and eggs, Mrs. Butterfield. And corn flakes. Oh, and don't forget the orange juice."

"Cutting down, he says." Mrs. Butterfield, her broad shoulders bent and her great lugubrious horse face frowning, wiped her nose with the end of a checkered apron and looked askance at Maggie.

"And the marmalade."

"Won't eat it."

"Nonsense. He looks positively pale. He'll love a good, solid breakfast. He has always been proud about how I look after him."

But Gerald, hurrying downstairs at the last minute, in a new dove grey suit and crimson and grey striped tie, sat at one end of the long table and refused even to glance at the steaming contents of chafing dishes on the sideboard.

"Dry toast, darling. Dry toast." He patted his waist. "Keeps me trim."

"But you hate dry toast." Maggie took the place set for her at the other end of the table. "Damn," she muttered as she hit her knee on a griffin leg.

"Two slices of dry toast and black coffee."

"And you hate black coffee."

Ignoring her remarks, Gerald opened the morning paper.

Maggie had dressed in smart off-white wool trousers and a bulky forest green Amish jumper, a cream scarf about her neck, but Gerald hadn't really looked at her either. She felt bewildered, as if she weren't actually living these moments. Her imagined scenario for last night had started with Gerald's gazing at her with his adorable dimpled smile and exclaiming that he couldn't do without her.

Instead, he had claimed exhaustion after arriving by late train from the City, and they'd both gone to bed early. And this morning she felt like an old fixture that is no longer noticed.

She watched Gerald as he read, and admired as always his strong features — cheekbones high and nose decidedly Italian.

He did look older than she. Her own fair skin had been tooled by a finer hand, with only minute etching around her eyes and chin. She ran a finger lightly over her face. At least the skin on her nose and cheeks, though freckled, was still good. And her bone structure was pronounced.

He glanced up from his reading and adjusted his horn-rimmed glasses.

"I hope you appreciate Miss Always and all she has done, darling."

Maggie detected a gleam in his eyes. He's teasing me, she thought. Gerald could be so droll.

"Yes, indeed, I appreciate what Miss Always has done," she said, hardly able to keep a straight face. Gerald was much better at this. "The cuckoo clock is so charming. I'm thinking of moving it to the bedroom."

"Oh, I don't agree, my angel. I think we should leave everything in place. Miss Always has created a certain... atmosphere."

Gerald was too wonderful.

"I prefer the marble urns myself. I fancy Aunt Priscilla and Uncle Ian reside in them."

"Really, Maggie!"

"But my favourites are these priceless candlesticks." She jumped up, careful to watch out for the griffin legs, went to the sideboard and pointed out the candlesticks as if she were touring at the museum. "Solid brass, we're told, attributed to the school of Rubens, whose artists understood, as no artists have since, the multi-curvaceous female form. The satyrs, representatives of an earlier mythology, grasp their subjects in such a way as to complete a cylindrical motion that leads the eye to the yellow candles. Yellow, of course, symbolizing..." Death, she thought, but wouldn't say that and let her voice trail off.

She sat back down.

Gerald stared at her blankly.

"Really, darling. You've always been there, supporting me. And now you seem to be letting me down. That's not like you. Not like you at all."

Maggie felt terrified. She refused to give up her scenario: Gerald and Maggie's chuckling over Miss Always's furnishings; Gerald's relief that Maggie had come to sort him out; Gerald's calling Maggie his saviour; Gerald and Maggie's gliding subtly to a deeper plane in their relationship, the sharing plane they had once known.

"I mean it's all very humourous, Gerald. As if we could live with those dreadful portraits in the drawing room. Or this atrocious dining room table." Maggie gave an empty little laugh. "Gerald?"

He put down his paper slowly, deliberately.

"Darling, Miss Always has worked like a trooper. She's the best secretary I've had. Completely loyal. How can you not appreciate her?" He leaned forward, taking off his glasses and rubbing the bridge of his nose. "Why, she's been my salvation."

Maggie bit her lip. She felt a sharp pain in her stomach. Slowly she added more cream to her coffee. She didn't want a scene. Not now. Maybe Gerald thought if he upset his secretary it would disrupt things at work. But couldn't he just say that? He could be so uncommunicative.

"Did I tell you," Gerald again buried his face in the

paper, "we'll be having twenty from Lloyd's for dinner Saturday night?"

"Gerald, I can't possibly. I don't know where anything is."

"Don't worry. Miss Always has seen to everything."

"But I don't want her to. And I might get jet lag."

"You never do."

"What kind of impression will I make if I'm feeling rotten?" She wasn't up to telling him how uncomfortable she felt about meeting his associates in these hodgepodge surroundings, at being under scrutiny. She supposed her memories from childhood got in the way here: the little Irish girl in hand-me-down clothes.

"Miss Always has hired the caterers and intends to come early to take charge. So you'll have nothing to do."

"Gerald, no. I'm not ready for this."

"My angel." He put his paper down, stood up, and came to her end of the table. Leaning down, a lock of dark hair falling on his forehead, he smiled his most charming, dimpled smile as he put an arm round her shoulders. "Don't get in the way of my business plans. Please don't. You've understood, put yourself out. You'll come through for me now. I know you will. You always do."

He kissed her on the forehead, "That's my girl," then walked to the door. "Oh, I'll be late getting home tonight. About ten, I think. You'll be fine, won't you, darling?"

But I've only just arrived, Maggie wanted to say. Couldn't you have taken the day off to be with me? We have so much to discuss. Yet she didn't say these things. She didn't want to hear his answer.

That afternoon, after unpacking and trying to sort out ideas for her party, Maggie sat at the kitchen table, running her hand along its smooth pine and sipping Darjeeling tea. She had fetched a pad and pen but seemed to have no party plans to jot down. She felt tired and sad. What had got into Gerald? Perhaps he'd wanted her to be as effusive, as breathless as the ubiquitous Miss Always; as little girl excited over each new pillow with a kitten on it. Maybe Maggie's own cool, more precise manner was too thin, too brittle for him in his honeypot stage.

She felt relieved that Miss Always's *find,* the lugubrious Mrs. Butterfield, had taken to her bed this afternoon, no doubt to listen to her favourite radio program. Where Miss Always had found the woman, Maggie couldn't imagine.

She reached for a biscuit from the tin on the table, then crumbled it absently. Raven Hall did have an old world charm, Maggie consoled herself, and it had more rooms than she cared to count. True, she was rather tall for some of the low beams, but she could learn when to stoop.

Even so, had she chosen the house herself, she would have known immediately the mood was wrong; she'd have felt she was intruding on the soul of the house.

She took another biscuit and nibbled it absently.

A knock sounded at the back door. Reluctantly, Maggie answered it. At the moment, she was not up to dealing with anyone.

Cautiously opening the door, she saw an olive-complexioned boy of about twelve, who carried a tall silk hat. She drew in a breath. The god who had fashioned this child knew everything about perfection, Maggie thought. She had never before been so taken with the beauty of a face. The underlying bone structure was strong, but not too much so for the face. The nose was slim, the lips sensitive. Yet it was the eyes that mesmerized Maggie. She felt they should have been black to go with his unruly blue-black hair. Instead, they shone a pale green with any number of deeper green striations, rather like a marble she had once treasured as a child. He lowered his lids, taking in all of Maggie as she studied him, and his dark lashes swept his cheeks, giving him a delicate appearance. This he soon erased as his eyes met and penetrated hers. She felt as she had with the marble, that the longer she gazed into it the deeper she would go, until she lost herself entirely.

Glancing down, Maggie's attention was attracted to a thick gold necklace, twisted like a narrow rope, which he wore about his neck. Hanging from it appeared to be a gold medallion or coin, but she couldn't tell what it depicted. If this were pure gold, it was valuable indeed. Even if it were imitation, it was obviously a designer piece. She wondered if his mother knew that with his open-necked blue shirt and jeans he wore her necklace.

"Magic," he said, flourishing a tall silk hat. Before Maggie could utter a word, he repeated with aplomb, "Practitioner of magic."

As he brushed past her, entering the kitchen, Maggie felt strangely frightened of the knowing look in those startling green eyes.

"A... actually, I'm b,busy now..." Maggie surprised herself by stammering. Was that contempt she saw now in his eyes?

Ignoring her comment, he moved her teacup, pad, pen, and biscuit tin to the sink.

"Are you... are you with the Gypsy camp I saw at the edge of town when I arrived?" Maggie asked, quickly following him. What if he had stolen the hat, the gold necklace? What if he were here to steal? Were others outside waiting? What if she were murdered in her new kitchen?

Setting down his hat, he produced a deck of cards and spread them across the table.

"Pick one."

Maggie again felt his pale impenetrable green eyes taking her measure. Against her will, she stepped closer to the table, reached forward, hesitated, then slowly drew a card from the fan. Perhaps if she co-operated he'd go away.

"Do I look at it?"

"Of course. Remember it, and put it back in the pack."

Maggie watched her hand shake as she did his bidding.

Seeming not to notice, though Maggie was sure he observed everything, he expertly reshuffled the pack.

"Is this it?" He held up the jack of diamonds.

She nodded dumbly. Maybe now he'd go. She hated his insolence.

"And this?" another jack of diamonds. "And this? And this?" another and another. He laughed, throwing his head back, as he tossed the jacks carelessly onto the deck.

Angry, Maggie swept up the fan of cards and spread it face up on the table, revealing… an ordinary deck of cards, except without jacks.

"But where are the jacks? I saw you put them back."

He gave a little shrug and chuckled. Then he stared down at the deck, and the faces on all the cards turned to jacks.

"But you can't do that. That's… that's… magic."

He made no reply, only looked at her with those unfathomable striated eyes, a haughty smile revealing even white teeth.

This is not believable, Maggie thought. I'm under some kind of a spell. Then she realized she must have jet lag.

"Another trick?" He teased her with his smile.

"Oh, no. Truly, I…"

He picked up his tall silk hat.

"May I have a napkin?" he asked, looking about.

"I don't know where they are."

"Don't you live here?"

She'd have liked to say no.

"I just arrived."

"I'll have your scarf then."

"I'd really rather..." but as he looked at her, she began loosening the cream silk rectangle knotted about her neck.

She barely had it untied when he snatched it from her.

She gave a nervous laugh. "I suppose magicians always use scarves?"

"It's more dramatic for the audience." His eyes mocked her. He took the scarf and spread it over the lid of the hat, then pulled a pencil-slim stick from his back pocket, waved it over the hat, "Abracadabra."

Disappointed that he used such a common spell, Maggie nevertheless felt intrigued.

The scarf twitched as if something were alive inside.

He cast the scarf aside, and pulled out — "Oh, my God" — a puppy.

Maggie slouched onto a kitchen chair, surveying the scene in her kitchen.

"I want to know about your trick. I know rabbits and doves are supposed to be pulled out of hats; yet this odd little dog... How did it fit? Where did it come from?" She looked to see if the boy's blue jean pockets could hold the animal.

Though she raised her arms in protest, he plunked the pug-nosed King Charles spaniel in her lap. The puppy, a feisty little bitch, gave a yap, then jutted out her jaw as Maggie tried to cuddle her. Finally, she licked Maggie's finger, and Maggie laughed. As a child, she had admired the Tri-colours, especially, with black spots on white, a white stripe running up the forehead, and ruby markings round the eyes and lining the long spaniel ears.

The boy grinned wickedly.

"Now do you believe in my magic?"

"I think... well..." These tricks suggested sorcery, unless, of course, the puppy had followed him inside. She eyed him suspiciously.

The boy reached out for the puppy, but Maggie objected. "Let me hold her for awhile." She stroked the silky fur, and the puppy lifted her round pug nosed face and gazed at Maggie.

"You can have her but not now. She must go right back." He grabbed the puppy, who gave a yelp, popped her into the hat, shoved her angry face inside the rim, and said "Ar-ba-da-car-ba," without even the decency to cover the puppy with the scarf. Then he held the hat so Maggie could see it was empty.

"The puppy?" Maggie rose and unconsciously took a step backward. "Where's your puppy?" She peered under the table.

"Oh, she's not mine."

"But you do the trick. And the puppy..."

His laugh sounded menacing to Maggie.

"Do you think it's a good trick?"

"What did you say to her? The puppy? You didn't hurt her? The spell, the last one?"

"That's Abracadabra backwards." He looked bored at having to explain. "Any spell will do, you know. And I had to send her back."

"Back where? Look... I, I don't know your name. I don't know you. What are you doing here?"

He chuckled.

"Some magic tricks. You watched me."

"I know. Why here? Why me?"

"I like to do tricks at Raven Hall. Why are you here?"

"I live here. That is," she faltered under his steady gaze, "I'm starting to live here. That is... I don't know why

Raven Hall, not really."

"People who come here have a purpose."

Maggie's temple over her left eye started to throb and she couldn't think where she'd put the aspirin.

"Your name?" she managed. "I don't know your name."

"Robin," he stated simply, holding out his hand.

She hesitantly gave him her hand. What if I were to follow the puppy? she worried. I wonder if Gerald would notice, or if Miss Always would scurry about for a *find* of a wife to go with the house.

Maggie forced her mind to the moment.

"Is there a surname?"

"Macneil. We live down the road." He pointed to the south side of the house where the nearest neighbour was a couple of acres away. "And, yes, my mother is a Gypsy. This," he held out his necklace, "is Gypsy gold, to do Gypsy magic." He glanced down at his treasure, then seemed to forget it. "My father was Irish."

Maggie sighed with relief. A neighbour boy.

"I'm Maggie Featherstone."

"I know. That's why I'm here." He threw his wand into the air and caught it. "Most people around here are farmers. What do you do, Mrs. Featherstone?"

"Me? Well, let me think. I haven't got established here yet. But I taught art at the museum in Los Angeles. Last year I taught boys and girls your age to make masks."

Maggie's mind flew to the museum. Too many teenagers needing too much attention at once. So many masks to finish.

She felt herself bending over the worktables. Hot, she brushed a wisp of red hair from her forehead as sun streamed through the overhead windows, making bars of eerie light on the young people from the halfway house.

"Here." A small black boy called Joey thrust his work at

her. His mouth smiled, but he studied her suspiciously.

She took his mask, she studied it, and felt suddenly cold. The mask was white. Just white. An icy white.

The boys and girls, all one step from juvenile hall, chattered loudly as they daubed at their masks with garish colours. Another volunteer, Trudy, helped at one end of the room as Maggie continued staring at the white.

Taking this for appreciation, Joey gained confidence.

"I'm gonna hang it in my bedroom and look at it every day." He snatched the mask back and put it on, black eyes shining defiantly at Maggie in a chalk white blankness.

Maggie nodded and gave the innocuous smile she reserved for just such occasions, for what could she say? Would he ever be allowed to go home to his parents? And if he got there, would staring at this total rejection of himself bring him any comfort?

She gave a little shiver, in spite of the heat, automatically picked up her flowered scarf, which lay in a heap on one of the stools, and flung it over her shoulders. Once she would have wanted to hug Joey to her, to comfort him, but that would cause the others to scorn him. It had taken her a long time to learn disinterested love for the children, that by being there and being sympathetic, not by being personally involved, she was helping them. She wished she could learn that lesson with Gerald. But after Sean he had needed such care, such mothering.

As she passed along the tables to admire other masks, she was conscious of the guard who had brought the teenagers and now leaned against the wall at one end of the room, rhythmically chewing gum.

The trouble-maker of the group, a white boy, Danny, heavily pock-marked, yelled at Maggie.

"Hey you!" Then he turned toward Trudy. "And you! Look at mine." The two reluctantly walked to where he sat.

"This day's shit!" he muttered as he brandished a mask painted black with a red swastika-like sign. Drops of crimson ran down the mask and dripped onto the workroom floor.

Mask eyes — dark wounds, sticky around the edges with red ooze — stared blankly at Maggie. Revolted, she bit her lip unconsciously, until she could taste the salt in her own blood.

Plump little Trudy began to shake.

Danny's eyes narrowed. His lips twisted grotesquely.

"Pretty, huh?" He forced it under Trudy's nose, and she whimpered. There was violence in his eyes, in his action.

Any second he'll lose control — and Trudy will lose control, Maggie realized.

She stepped between him and Trudy, who backed slowly away, her face ashen. Maggie took the mask, studied it a moment, then stated flatly, "It's very interesting." Her stock phrase to go with her stock expression. Only a nonreaction would settle him down.

These young people, so tough, she thought, yet as fragile as the finest crystal in her collection at home. She watched the light hit them. To her these children, so flawed they could shatter if touched in the wrong way, shimmered exquisitely in their rough form. How sad that the right way to handle them at such moments was the unemotional way, the way of greater distancing.

Danny, his face as marred as the mask with scars, studied Maggie.

"You're not scared like that one," he pointed towards Trudy, who had backed to the other side of the room.

"Certainly not." Maggie couldn't let her fear show. "Your mask is... well... it's dramatic."

Does a dark part of himself scare me? Maggie thought.

How directly he had posed his question. She sighed.

Something that Maggie wouldn't put into words, something far more frightening than these masks, through which the children revealed themselves with a simplistic honesty, had power to fragment Maggie.

"Another trick?"

"What? Oh." Surprised to see Robin rather than Joey or Danny, she murmured, "Not now." Perhaps she should lie down. The throbbing was getting worse.

How different Robin was from those troubled children. How alert he was, how knowing. Too mature, really. She wouldn't have wanted her son Sean to be this precocious.

She stood up and pushed up the sleeves of her jumper. "Would you like some milk and biscuits, Robin?"

"No thanks. I must go." He paused. "I notice you don't have a boy of your own to do magic."

Maggie looked at him, startled.

"No. No, I don't."

"Good. Then I'll come again." At the door, he turned to her, the deep green streaks in his pale eyes blazing. "I hope you feel happier."

Maggie put a hand to her face.

"Oh, dear. Does it show?" I'll have to watch myself for the party tomorrow, she thought.

Robin picked up his tall silk hat, put it onto his head at a cocky angle, and grinned slyly at Maggie.

"Make yourself a mask."

He made an elegant bow, spun about, and was out the door.

Maggie stared after him, astonished. Had he read her mind?

Then she sank onto a chair, rested her elbows on the table and put her head in her hands. *Arbadacarba,* she intoned to the rhythm of the throbbing in her left temple as she concentrated on Miss Always. *Arbadacarba.*

CHAPTER III

Except to the practiced eye, the village closest to Raven Hall appeared non-existent. It was reached by a narrow road, lined with deep green hedgerows, and consisted of a nondescript, temporary-looking schoolhouse and a small white cottage which now served as post office as well as greengrocers and general store.

Maggie, feeling dismally lost after two days of trying to settle into Miss Always's *find,* sauntered along the road, wishing Saturday night's dinner were over.

"So lucky," Gerald had repeated this morning about Miss Always. "She manages beautifully, darling. Just wait until you see her in action at our party. And finding this house! Do let her know how much we appreciate her, that's my Maggie."

"This house sends out bad vibrations which make me miserable!" Maggie had countered.

"You're just being Irish." He removed his glasses and polished them with some slippery paper from a matchbook type folder. He polished his glasses a lot lately, Maggie noticed, or took them off and slipped them into a case in his lapel pocket. "Don't forget about the convent that was here." He smiled mischievously. "Can't get better vibrations than that. And a period house. Everyone will envy us. Miss Always says it's listed."

"I hate the feeling there are spirits from the past here, that we're rejected."

"Past spirits could never afford it in the current price market." Gerald had chuckled at his joke. "Don't worry," he'd added. "We belong."

How fortunate for Gerald, Maggie thought, crossing the road to the country store, that he always knew when and where he belonged. He had once made her feel she belonged, too. But not now. Not here.

A cuckoo mocked her as she turned the handle of the shop's door. She closed the door behind her and a bell tinkled. A tight-lipped woman, brown hair pulled back in a bun, glanced up from where she stood at the fruit stall. Her owl-like eyes, blinking, stared over a small beak of a nose at Maggie. Neither her eyes, nor her mouth gave any indication that she actually saw anyone. A slight raise of one eyebrow, however, revealed that she had taken something in.

She returned to putting strawberries into a bag for a soft, chubby, rosy-cheeked little woman with an upturned nose, who stood silently waiting. Maggie gave a start to see that the chubby woman held two Tri-colour King Charles spaniels on leads. But neither had the feisty face of the little bitch Robin had produced.

"Good morning," Maggie ventured. The shopkeeper ignored her, but the customer gave her a nervous glance, then looked away, her fingers anxiously twisting the leads. Maggie remembered from her childhood that inhabitants of tiny villages like this did not take kindly to strangers. A person could live in an area for twenty years and be the newcomer, still suspect. God forbid Gerald should ever come here slapping honey pots and hummingbirds on these tried and true bosoms.

"Lovely dogs," Maggie added and had to suppress a sigh at the thought of her little Foxtrot, mongrel though the puppy had been. She bent down to pet the spaniels, but with their huge dark eyes they surveyed her as nervously as did their mistress. Wiggling backwards, they would not let her touch them.

Maggie looked to the plump woman for some encouragement with the dogs, but received none. Aware she now exhibited the easy, friendly manner of those from

California, Maggie knew her openness would certainly not ingratiate her with the locals. Furthermore, she was the new resident at Raven Hall, occupied by English noblemen for centuries.

The store's owner went to the back room and the chubby customer, pulling her toy dogs behind her, left without again looking at Maggie, who knew she would be the subject of the woman's gossip for the week.

"Yes?" The shopkeeper returned as suddenly as she had left, yet Maggie was sure she had felt those dark, inscrutable eyes on her right along. Though she knew she was recognized, Maggie introduced herself.

"I'm Maggie Featherstone, the new owner of Raven Hall."

"That's not your house." Those eyes that could not smile could glare, and they did now.

Maggie felt as if she'd been slapped but tried to remain pleasant.

"And you're...?"

"Mrs. Hazlehurst."

"It's good to meet you, Mrs. Hazlehurst," Maggie lied, crushed to have it confirmed that she didn't belong in the village any more than at the Hall. "I wonder if I might buy an airmail stamp to the United States."

"The post office doesn't open for..." she looked at her watch, "three minutes."

"Oh. Well, perhaps I could buy a loaf of bread while I wait?"

"Brown or white?"

"Do you have rye?"

"Brown or white?"

"Brown." As if she spied a field mouse from a branch, Mrs. Hazlehurst studied Maggie.

"One of those health fanatics, are you?" She blinked her

owl eyes. "I don't hold with excess."

"No, quite right." Maggie handed her a five pound note.

"Have you got something smaller?"

"I'm afraid that's all I have."

"Your change will have to come from the post office, then." Her voice sounded flat, as if to conceal the sharpness of her eyes. "I haven't got enough here."

"Is it about time for the post office to open?"

"One minute."

Under the unfriendly stare of Mrs. Hazlehurst, Maggie looked at the rows and rows of staple goods as she waited for whoever would come to open the post office. She knew she shouldn't dread her dinner party, that her parties always went swimmingly. Yet she couldn't get the idea that she was on trial out of her mind, that Gerald would hold her up against his new standard of efficiency, Miss Always. Perhaps if she made a typically Californian dish like a dip with sour cream and onion soup to serve with crisps, it could act as a conversation piece.

"It's time," announced Mrs. Hazlehurst loudly.

Startled from her musing, Maggie looked about to see who had come to open up. But no one had entered. Instead, Mrs. Hazlehurst slowly removed her full length brown plastic apron, folded it carefully, and hid the apron from sight beneath the counter. Then she glanced into a mirror and ran her hands over her head as if she were preening feathers. Finally, she reached into the pocket of her faded housedress, producing a ring with several keys. She unlocked the door to the post office and closed it behind her.

Through the grill, Maggie watched her don a brown jacket. Mrs. Hazlehurst opened the post office drawer beneath the counter, checked its contents, then withdrew the sign that said "closed" from beneath the grill. She leaned her arms on the counter, folded her hands and said, "Well?" as if she'd been kept waiting.

"A stamp to the United States, please." Maggie felt irritated.

"Air or regular."

"But I told you. Oh, never mind. Air."

"That's 31p."

"But you have my five pound note."

"It's change you're wanting." Mrs. Hazlehurst slowly counted out coins.

"You were to take the bread out of my note, Mrs. Hazlehurst."

"Can't mix accounts. Here's the stamp."

"And I realize I must have some sour cream."

"Store's closed."

"When will it open. It's really quite important."

"Come back at one."

"Look, no one else is here. If I could just get the sour cream."

"Don't carry it. Never have. Never will. Something they eat in Hollywood is it?"

Maggie sighed.

"Here, I'll just pay for the bread."

"Oh my, no. You'll have to pay at the store."

"But couldn't you...?"

"This is a post office."

"But my bread?"

"You can come back at one."

"Thank you, Mrs. Hazlehurst. I'll forget the bread."

"Just as you like."

The postmistress didn't say more but blinked her sharp eyes at Maggie, letting her know that foreigners always muddled things.

Maggie left the shop feeling lower than when she'd entered. She knew her loneliness would get worse, that she wouldn't be accepted here. If she'd had her little boy, her Sean, they could ride together and go to dog shows and... but what was she thinking? That was so many years ago. He'd be starting college now.

Once home, she sat by the telephone and pondered. Should she call the Kennel Club? Gerald would be furious, but he had his work and Maggie was left alone. She couldn't stand the silence in the house any longer. Checking the telephone directory, she dialed the Kennel Club and asked for numbers of breeders of King Charles spaniels. Gerald would never reject a rare, pedigreed dog.

After making several calls, Maggie drove the new blue Mercedes down country lanes, deep green in the misty spring morning, to Mrs. Pusey's residence, a giant grey farmhouse.

Standing at the door, and hearing dogs barking from somewhere deep in the house, Maggie felt nervous, like a child who is doing something wrong. After all, Gerald hadn't taken to Foxtrot.

Maggie smiled thinking of Foxtrot and his spots, splotchy tan spots, not the neat trim spots of the pampered pets she'd seen that morning. She'd never forget the odd tan and white puppy that had trotted jauntily towards her as she deposited her groceries in the back of her BMW at a Mayfair store in Hollywood. Though the puppy had looked over its shoulder once, it ran with a sureness of purpose Maggie admired. She'd laughed.

Then her eye caught a coyote, slinking beside a pick-up truck. With a start, she realized it must be stalking the puppy. The coyote moved closer, stopping at the hood of Maggie's car.

"Shoo." She stamped her feet and waved her handbag

at it. The coyote didn't move. She took several steps towards it, shouting, "Hey, Hey, Hey."

The coyote remained immobile, its slanted eyes taunting.

Maggie took off a shoe and threw it at the scruffy animal. It leapt back a few feet, then skulked to the far side of the parking lot and stood behind the garbage dumpsters, still watching the puppy.

Maggie limped to retrieve her shoe, bits of gravel cutting into her foot and slashing her nylons. In what other metropolis, she wondered, would a wild animal stalk a dog through traffic, past early Sunday morning shoppers?

The puppy, which had the head of a smooth fox terrier and the hind end of a beagle, shook itself, then looked up at Maggie expectantly.

Maggie stared back in horror, for under its sparse coat, its skin was a mass of sores. He's probably allergic to flea bites, she thought. She glanced about for a possible owner, although she knew there would be none. Then she walked to an outdoor telephone, the puppy at her heels. Thumbing through the yellow pages until she found some numbers of pet saving agencies, she dropped in two dimes and dialed the first number.

"Furry Friend Finders. We're closed on Sunday," a mechanical voice answered while a recording played in the background, *Where, oh, where has my little dog gone?*

Maggie tried another number.

"Kanine Kennel Krew," a voice sang. "We will find your dog for you. Leave your message, make it sweet, but first be sure to listen for the beep."

No healing on the Sabbath, thought Maggie.

Finally, as the phone ate Maggie's last bit of change, a real person answered at an emergency clinic.

"You'll have to pay Sunday prices," the voice warned.

"All right." She hung up the receiver. "You want to live, don't you?" Maggie whispered to the puppy, who whined, raised his right paw, and looked up, pleading.

"What shall I call you? Something to do with fox terrier, I think. And you have a snazzy trot. How about Foxtrot?"

The puppy jumped on her.

Soon Foxtrot was ensconced in the front seat of Maggie's BMW, the coyote still lurking by the garbage dumpsters, and Maggie drove along Hollywood Boulevard. Early Sunday morning, the street with its gold markers to the stars appeared garish, strewn with litter. She cruised past The Cave's "Live Nude Show", "Peep Show" and "Adult Book Store"; past the Pussycat Theatre, playing "One Night in Bangkok" and "Debbie Does Dallas IV"; past grafitti-marked walls; past fast food joints; past derelicts on bus benches; past the Hollywood Wax Museum; and Maggie sighed for the old Hollywood Boulevard.

Then she caught sight of pink awnings on the purple Frederick's of Hollywood, which housed lingerie in questionable taste, and realized Hollywood had had its indecorous side right along. Maggie still found something fascinating about the Boulevard. She decided it, like Foxtrot, just suffered from sores.

At the vets, the doctor on call, a young woman, wearing a white jacket over her denims and tee shirt, unlocked the office door and led Maggie into the examining room. There she lifted Foxtrot from his box and onto the blond-grained formica counter.

"This is mange," she said, "not fleas. I can do a scratch test to determine if it's contagious."

"Yes, please."

While the vet took the scrapings to be analyzed, Maggie stood rubbing Foxtrot's neck, feeling his short, wiry hair and feverish skin. She glanced around the pale yellow examining room, a colour she detested. As she breathed in the antiseptic hospital smell, she resented the pictures of smug, fat, healthy dogs that decorated the walls.

When the vet, young and pretty in a quiet way, returned, her expression looked serious.

"It's not contagious, but it will be hard to cure. With several dippings and antibiotics, he may recover. If not, you'll have to put him to sleep. No one would think any the less of you if you had me put him to sleep now."

"What would you do?"

"He's such a cute little dog. About five months I'd say." Her voice softened and lost its professional ring. "I'd let him live."

"That's the way I feel." Maggie sighed in relief. I'm no good at playing God, she thought, especially on a Sunday morning. "We'll fight," she said, more to Foxtrot than the vet.

Gerald didn't like dogs, hadn't wanted anything to love in all the years since losing Sean. Maybe Foxtrot could help him a little, Maggie thought as she carried the puppy to the car. How could he not like this little fellow? Foxtrot had a certain flare. And he'd outwitted a coyote. He was special.

"I've got a surprise for you." She greeted Gerald when he awoke around noon.

Still in his pajamas and robe, his dark hair disheveled, he gave her a kiss on the cheek.

"I love a good surprise, my angel."

"Just come see." She took his hand and led him to the service porch, where Foxtrot slept in his box on a bed of towels. "Isn't he adorable."

"A dog? When we travel? Really, darling."

"Just what we've needed, Gerald. We can take up jogging again and he'll run with us."

"But I've always hated dogs. And this is a stray, isn't it?" He bent his head lower and peered at the puppy. "Look, he's got some disease."

"He's been to the vet, and everything is under control."

Gerald sniffed.

"He stinks, darling." Gerald put his handkerchief to his nose, walked into the kitchen, took a bottle of orange juice from the refrigerator, and poured himself a glass. Then he walked back to the doorway of the service porch, where Maggie stood. "He quite literally stinks."

"It's the medication," said Maggie. "The dip they gave him, but he'll be fine in a few days." Mother of God, forgive a white lie.

Gerald bent closer to the puppy and sniffed again.

"It's his skin." He walked into the kitchen and sat at the table. "Maggie we can't have a dog."

She put a plate of sweet rolls in front of him. "I can give him away once he's well. You see..."

"Yes, I see. No one would take him now. My angel, you've got to stop worrying about strays... stray dogs, stray people."

"Somebody's got to care, Gerald."

"It doesn't have to be you, darling."

"Well, I didn't pick Foxtrot; he picked me."

"They all pick you."

"This is different. After all, he came right after Mass and right from the jaws of a coyote. He must be a gift."

"A gift? A bloody, diseased mongrel a gift? What can you be thinking?"

"We don't always know how things are meant, Gerald." Maggie felt bad that Gerald couldn't see Foxtrot as she did. He might have once. Long ago when he hadn't yet converted life into dollars and cents, into objects of value and no value. That philosophy had eventually extended to people of value — winners — and people of no value — losers. "He's a winner, Gerald. He has a will to live."

"He's a loser, darling. He's sick. That smell is driving me crazy."

A sudden flurry of yapping and scratching on the other side of the farmhouse door brought Maggie back to the present. What was she doing? Another dog? She ought to run and hide. But before she could turn to leave, the door opened wide and out stepped a small, energetic-looking woman of about seventy. She wore a marine blue sweater and trousers, white doghairs making a pattern on the wool. Her round face was covered with a fuzz of light hair, and her skin, having succumbed to gravity, creased into folds below a chin that would never yield. Her nose was unusually small, what Maggie thought of as a button nose. A white streak graced the center part of her dyed black hair, which she'd tied in bunches above each ear.

With large, mournful brown eyes she surveyed Maggie. Then she reached forward and grasped Maggie's hand firmly in both of her own as if guessing Maggie's desire to leave.

"You'll be Mrs. Featherstone. I'm Mrs. Pusey." She allowed her vowels to make raspy twists and turns deep in her throat before she spat them out between nearly closed teeth.

"Really, I think..." Maggie felt alarmed.

Mrs. Pusey pulled Maggie inside, through the entranceway, and to a small library.

"Mind the door."

The room's richly carved oak walls, antique tables and blue and rose chintz-covered chairs charmed Maggie. Raven Hall should be decorated like this, she thought. Shelves high on the walls held leather-bound books, and over the fireplace, in which a fire blazed, hung oil paintings of two King Charles spaniels, a Tri-colour and a Blenheim.

"I truly wonder if, if…" Maggie stammered.

"Be seated. I'll bring in the puppies."

"But…"

Mrs. Pusey was out the door, shutting it behind her.

Maggie sank onto a chintz chair. She hadn't known what to expect of a breeder. She had thought to find a motherly sort, someone who made crooning sounds. And she'd anticipated an outdoor kennel, not a seventeenth century showpiece.

She gazed into the fire, marveling at how rarely things turned out the way she'd envisioned.

Listening to the crackles and sizzles of the kindled wood and allowing her eyes to follow the blue in the flames, her apprehension diminished. She could leave without a dog, she consoled herself. She was, after all, just looking.

A log snapped, and she saw Foxtrot's face in the fire. She remembered the dream she'd had after bringing him home. She and Gerald were jogging through a meadow. They were young and laughing, and they began to fly across the chartreuse field sprinkled with daisies. Foxtrot flew with them, healthy and vital. In the dream Maggie had a flash of realization that Foxtrot had brought them to the meadow, had made them young again. Foxtrot was their hope, their joy.

At three that morning, Maggie had awakened, filled with happiness. She'd crept out of bed, slipped on Oomphies and padded downstairs to check on Foxtrot. He'd dragged the towels from his box and made a little nest in an alcove.

"No more coyote, Foxtrot," she whispered.

Foxtrot nuzzled Maggie's hand and whined.

"No more cars to frighten you, no more hunger. You're safe with me." Maggie checked his skin. It felt hot and he shivered a little, so she fetched a soft thermal blanket for him to snuggle into.

Foxtrot made a hole for himself in the mound of towels and blanket, licked Maggie's hand, gave a contented groan, and went back to sleep.

In the morning, Maggie, still in the happy mood of her dream, dressed hurriedly. She planned to attend a museum lecture, followed by a luncheon. She hoped Foxtrot would be all right but supposed he'd be glad of the quiet after all he'd been through.

After the luncheon, Maggie made a quick stop at Farmers' Market to buy Foxtrot a lightweight red collar and a red leash, some rawhide bones, and vitamins.

She hurried home, entered the kitchen, and put her bag on the table, then opened the door to the laundry room.

No Foxtrot. His box had disappeared from the service porch; his towels and blanket, too. She sniffed and caught the faint smell of Lysol spray.

Then Maggie knew. She walked slowly into the kitchen and sank onto a chair. She didn't call Gerald. There was no point. She just sat and waited, she wasn't sure for what. For Gerald. Maybe she did want some confirmation from him. Maybe she wanted to force him to say what he'd done.

Foxtrot was dead. He'd survived the traffic, the wild coyote, the disease. But he couldn't survive Gerald and his belief in winners.

Mrs. Pusey's library door swung open, and at least a dozen miniature yapping King Charles spaniels rushed in, swirling about Maggie's feet, jumping onto the low chairs and tumbling across the carpet. A little Tri-colour bitch flew up and landed on Maggie's lap.

Maggie looked down into the upturned, feisty face. Robin's puppy bitch! The one he'd pulled from his hat. She'd recognize that stubborn jaw anywhere. But how was that possible? Maggie felt terribly cold, and she trembled as she gingerly petted the tiny bitch.

The puppy jutted her jaw out further, making her seem every bit as determined as Mrs. Pusey.

"These are my E and F litters," rasped Mrs. Pusey, crouching cross-legged on a couch opposite Maggie's chair, while several puppies crowded round her. "Never mind the noise. They'll all quiet down once they've settled in."

She picked up a packet from a side-table, offered a cigarillo, which Maggie refused, then lit one herself. "Fabian, Faustina," she pointed out puppies round the room, "Fiona, Fanfare." She motioned to the one in Maggie's lap, "Felicity. All five months."

An ugly old Blenheim pushed the door wider and waddled in. "And here's the father, Leander."

Maggie nodded, overwhelmed.

"The E's are four months. Egerton's here on my lap, and Egbert. That's Eustace over there and Ethelind." Since the puppies kept wiggling about, Maggie couldn't be sure which went with what name.

"Each litter is a letter of the alphabet," Mrs. Pusey explained. "Until I get to N. Then I work back to A." She took a long drag on her cigarillo. "I simply don't like names that begin with the last half of the alphabet. Do you?"

"Oh, but…"

"Well, you shouldn't. They're really not so nice, if you'll just listen. Theodosia, Thelma, Velda. Sound is everything."

Maggie wondered if Mrs. Pusey ever listened to her

own sound.

"Mind you, I won't sell to someone who will rename my dogs. Imagine a poor dog having to live down a name like Olive or Robina. And there's nothing to be said for names starting with Y's or X's. Of course, one could have a Wellington. W's aren't so bad."

She jumped up and searched under some magazines for an ashtray. The puppies on the couch crowded against the arm, watching for her return. "And like everyone else in England," she plunked back onto her seat and was again covered with Toy spaniels, "I've been influenced by you Americans. I've a Minnie Ha Ha and a Minnie Mouse from my last M litter."

The little bitch on Maggie's lap remained gazing up at her. Maggie tickled her under the chin, and she made purring sounds of pleasure.

"Is Felicity... is she special in some way?" Maggie didn't quite know how to ask: does your dog take part in magic?

Mrs. Pusey and Felicity both snorted.

"All my dogs are special."

"Of course. I only meant, is she used in... what I mean is... well... say... magic tricks?"

"What?"

Felicity sat up straight, cocked her head, and gave a low growl.

"Do you know a boy named Robin?" Maggie persisted.

Yapping plaintively, Felicity reared back and almost toppled off Maggie's lap.

"Come, Felicity," snapped Mrs. Pusey. "Let Mrs. Featherstone look at every puppy."

Felicity didn't move.

Mrs. Pusey, cigarillo in her mouth, sprang up and pounced on Felicity, who squealed and grabbed onto

Maggie's arm with her paws.

"Oh, dear," said Maggie, intrigued. "I think she has picked me. But you see, I really didn't intend..."

"Ha!" exclaimed Mrs. Pusey, letting go of Felicity and standing back. "Allow a dog to take charge, will you? Can't have that. Anyway," she sat down again in the tailor's position, puppies crowding back onto her lap, "you'll be happier with Fanfare, the Blenheim playing with the ball at your feet."

As Felicity growled, Maggie glanced at an orange and white male. The center of attention, he looked up questioningly and tilted his head, his puppy ears sticking straight out on each side.

"But, you see..."

Mrs. Pusey stared at Maggie with an expectant grin, making her feel uncomfortable, as if she were supposed to understand some joke.

"Fanfare? Didn't you say on the phone you're from Hollywood? Fanfare?"

"Oh. Oh, yes," said Maggie, thinking she understood.

Mrs. Pusey spilled ashes onto the couch and carelessly brushed them into the ashtray. "I can see you prefer Felicity. But she's wilful. I think, because she's a child of passion."

"Passion? I... a... I didn't know passion applied to dogs. I mean, I know that there's..." Maggie didn't like to say "lust," so let her voice trail off.

"Well, what else would you call it?" Mrs. Pusey snapped. "You see, her father was our noble Leander." She glanced at the fat old dog, who sat, scratching his ears. "Naturally, Hero has always been a little vamp. And Felicity is the only puppy that seems to have inherited a bit of both their temperaments." Mrs. Pusey gave a deep, throaty chuckle at this thought. "You recall Byron's poem?

If, in the month of dark December,
Leander, who was nightly wont
(What maid will not the tale remember?)
To cross thy stream,broad Hellespont!

"Well, one day, as Leander followed me down the hall stairs, he saw Hero lolling in the entranceway. She was in heat for the first time and more flirtatious than ever.

"Just then, Gretchen, my au pair, ran in from the rain and left the front door ajar as she folded her umbrella. And didn't Hero see her chance, trotting — just as coyly as you please — into the rain?

"Leander took out after her, down the steps and out the front door, his little legs churning as they hadn't in years.

" 'Stop him', I yelled to Gretchen, who, silly girl that she is, threw up her hands as he rushed by." Mrs. Pusey jumped to her feet and threw up her own hands to demonstrate. Three puppies landed on the carpet.

"I ran downstairs to the front door to see Leander, dashing across the field in the rain, ears flying, for all the world as if he were swimming the Hellespont."

"Imagine."

"You understand, of course, that Hero was too young, so Gretchen felt guilty." Mrs. Pusey sat down on a puppy, and they all squealed. "The silly goose began to cry, but I said, 'Gretchen'…" Mrs. Pusey gave a cough that came, as did her vowels and chuckles, from deep in her throat, " '…it was meant to be. True love will out'.

"And after that, Hero had this rather perfect F litter. So there you are." Mrs. Pusey grinned at Maggie, then reached down and stroked the old Blenheim's ears. "Anyway, Hero enticed you shamelessly, didn't she, Leander?"

Maggie looked at fat Leander and wondered about choices in love. How did one decide to risk everything for a particular person? Had she risked everything for Gerald? Had she swum the Hellespont? She felt she had. At any rate, she'd flown the Atlantic. Gerald had not flown it for her but for his precious work.

Would the Italian Gerald — her Roman hero — have swum the Hellespont for her?

Mrs. Pusey kept staring at Maggie expectantly, so Maggie murmured, "How romantic."

"Didn't I just say so?" As she lit another cigarillo from the first and stamped that out in the ashtray, Mrs. Pusey glowered at Maggie.

Maggie recalled that Byron's poem about the Greek hero ended, *For he was drowned, and I've the ague.* Sadly, there'd been nothing about a perfect F litter.

"Mind you, Felicity will be trouble. She has the flirtatious habits of her mother and the impetuousness of her father. She'll be passionate, wilful, and difficult. I'm never wrong about these things."

Maggie looked down at the stubborn little face, gazing into hers, and forgot Gerald and Leander. She even forgot her intention merely to look at puppies.

"I'll have her."

"You see, what did I tell you? She always gets her own way, naughty little bitch that she is." Mrs. Pusey jumped up, picked Felicity up by the scruff of the neck, kissed her, then handed her back to Maggie.

Driving home, with Felicity snuggled on towels in a basket beside her, Maggie was not so sure of her choice as she had been moments earlier. Robin's magic prop, she thought. Child of passion, wilful, difficult! Mother of God, what have I done?

Felicity sat up, cocked her head, lifted one ear and one paw, then with gusto howled an eerie primal scream.

CHAPTER IV

Maggie adjusted the pale green scarf on her shoulder. Her flowing chiffon seemed too flamboyant next to the long shirtdress-style formals of the older women, too extreme compared to the high, tight skirts of the younger ones.

A waiter stopped with a tray. Noticing how few shrimp puffs remained, she shook her head and he moved on.

"Are they something you do in California? Hollywood, is it?" A woman in black, her hair pulled into a chignon, looked at Maggie through clouds of boredom, a superior twist to her pale lips.

Ordinarily Maggie would be amused at the woman's attitude, but tonight she resented the critical appraisal. She smiled briefly, nodded her head in recognition, and turned aside to greet other guests.

"Charming dip." Lady Wizzell deposited a half-eaten crisp in an ashtray. "Avocado pear is it?"

Maggie watched the pudgy, bejeweled hand and, fascinated, let her eyes follow up one tiny forearm, past the small elbow to the upper arm which spread across Lady Wizzell's body like an immense white ham. Surely she should not wear a sleeveless gown, and a brown, shapeless one at that.

Maggie smiled at her guest, and found that the sparse, tinted, mousy brown curly bangs that appeared pasted to Lady Wizzell's forehead intrigued her almost as much as did the monstrous arms. Probably close to sixty, Lady Wizzell had all of the self assurance a title should bring yet none of the charm. A peasant rather than a lady, Maggie thought.

Feeling a tap on her shoulder, Maggie turned to look into the cloudy grey eyes of Mrs. Normington, was it? Maggie hated not knowing her guests.

"Maggie, you know Edith Normington," Lady Wizzell said. "Weren't Maggie and Gerald lucky, Edith, to find a house so near the main line? And a period house at that. Why, it took us no time at all to drive down from London. Makes me positively jealous."

Maggie forced a smile as Lady Wizzell's little brown eyes and Mrs. Normington's grey ones agreed someone from Hollywood didn't deserve this spot of English countryside.

"I tried to get Harold to buy here, didn't I, Lady Wizzell," Mrs. Normington lamented, stressing her friend's title, "and now prices are out of sight for us natives." Mrs. Normington brushed a hand across her hair, coiffed in tight, blue-white waves.

"I really must..." Maggie stammered, not sure what she must do but certain she'd like to leave these two.

"The furnishings. How quaint," said the miniskirted wife of a Lloyd's member.

"Gerald's secretary chose them..." Maggie protested.

"We understand," cooed Mrs. Normington, smoothing her tailored pale blue crêpe gown.

"Our youngest daughter is going up to Cambridge next autumn," said Lady Wizzell. "I don't suppose you have any sons or daughters her age?"

"N-no," Maggie stammered, attempting to stop the young, worldly-looking Father Dove, or was it Father Hawk, from bouncing into her mind the way he'd bounced into her hospital room years ago. He'd acted as if he were on his way to a ballgame, too cheerful, too anxious to leave the antiseptic atmosphere. His blue eyes had darted restlessly about the room.

All these years later, Maggie could recall in detail each second of the moment, a moment that had changed her life and Gerald's more than had the death of their baby boy, their Sean. Not a day went by that she didn't try to push the catastrophe from her thoughts.

"So you've lost a baby?" said Father Dove, his exquisite blue eyes never really seeing her as she lay in the pale yellow hospital room.

Does he not know, Maggie thought, that he speaks of Sean, baby of Madeline and Porphyro? That the child of love is dead?

"A miscarriage," said Father Dove. "That's common. We'll have to accept God's will." He patted her hand, still not directly looking at her.

Maggie drew back her hand.

He seemed embarrassed by the silence. "I take it the baby received the Sacrament of Baptism?"

Maggie shook her head, no. She felt exhausted. Why didn't he leave her in peace?

"A blessing, Father, please. I'm so tired."

"A blessing for you, and you didn't give instructions to have your little infant baptized immediately?" He shook his head, raised his eyes heavenward, and said aloud, "Why do people leave the things of God to last?"

"He died in my womb," Maggie whispered the words.

"But he could still have been baptized immediately upon delivery. We don't know the exact hour of death. We don't know when the soul leaves the body. Now your baby will be in Limbo."

Maggie felt dizzy, yet in her fury answered, "Maybe you don't understand, but God understands." She couldn't admit even to herself she'd been carrying a dead child for a month.

"You people who try to write your own rules! An unbaptized baby can never go to heaven or see God." Father Dove turned in disgust and marched out of Maggie's room.

Gerald, his arms laden with spring daffodils and golden iceland poppies, passed the priest in the doorway and found Maggie weeping. If she'd only had time to compose herself! She'd tortured herself with that thought every day since then. It was her crying that had upset Gerald so. She could hear him now:

"Limbo? Where you can't see God?"

"It's supposed to be very beautiful." Maggie wailed.

"Our son?" He sank onto the bed beside her and stared in disbelief.

"They say souls are happy there." She bit her lip and dabbed with a wet handkerchief at her eyes. But when she tried to picture Limbo, she couldn't see any trees or flowers, only a vast, dry, cracked desert space with her little red-headed Sean, alone and frightened, crying for her.

"But no God?" Gerald moaned.

"Original Sin," Maggie mumbled, feeling on the bedside table for a dry handkerchief.

Gerald started to shake as if possessed.

"God, Maggie," he panted. "What have we done? We should never have tried for a child." He clutched at her, sobbing in angry, horrified groans. "Our little boy! Our Sean! We've sentenced him to Limbo!"

Maggie held Gerald tightly, stifling her own cries. "It's all right, Porphyro," she crooned. "The priest is young. He doesn't understand."

Gerald's body heaved in despair. He couldn't answer.

After that he never spoke of the incident. But he never entered a church or spoke to a priest again.

She knew Gerald carried with him the thought of their son in Limbo, unable to see the face of God. Maggie refused that idea. She had put her son in the care of the Blessed Mother, and a mother would never let that happen. But Gerald, who wouldn't come to Mass because he couldn't believe, did believe and lived with his torment.

She had tried to make up to him for the loss, to protect him from any little pains or problems that came along over the years. He still claimed he couldn't do without her, yet recently he seemed to be doing just that.

"Ah, you ladies aren't wearing hummingbirds. We've got to make business hum." Gerald, grinning, nudged Maggie out of her daydream as he pasted a hummingbird on the giggling young mini-skirted wife.

Maggie noted that the *soignée* woman in black looked with scorn at the appliqué. Her glance made Maggie long for home, where sticking hummingbirds on one was jovially accepted. Much as she'd always hated Gerald's insistence on giving out the woven favours, Maggie now appreciated Hollywood's tolerance of all styles.

Then Gerald turned his dark eyes to the woman in black and gave her his most appealing smile. Maggie was pleased to see her blush slightly and look flustered.

Glancing at the other men about the room, Maggie noticed that though they were more solemn than Gerald, they, too, had been caught up in the system of life. She studied their various striking silk ties and decided in reality they all wore one tie, a school tie. Like the whispers of this house that conceal the truth, she thought, my guests wear masks, the masks of that dread system, donned to conceal plans lurking beneath.

She realized that Gerald had worn a mask for a long time now. Would it come off finally, she wondered, or would he be chewed up and swallowed by the system before he could find his way out?

"The happy bee brings home the honey." Gerald approached Mrs. Normington, his eyes and his deep voice playfully teasing her.

A caricature of the modern executive, Maggie thought.

That's what Gerald is becoming. The others — too alike — are caricatures as well, even Miss Always.

Mrs. Normington paled and pulled back just as Gerald tried to stick a honey pot onto her crêpe dress, with the result that it clung right at the nipple.

"A honey pot!" she exclaimed. "Oh, dear." And in her confusion as Gerald gave her his most melting smile, she neglected to remove it.

"The loving boss has the loving worker," said Gerald, laughing, his hornrimmed glasses slipping as he hugged the young mini-skirted wife.

While Maggie tried to hide her disapproval with a smile, he looked into her eyes, and she felt her lips go into a rather sickly grimace.

Gerald released the mini-skirted wife, picked a gin and tonic from a tray a waiter held, and took it over to Lady Wizzell, who had drifted to another group.

Something felt definitely wrong tonight. Usually Maggie's parties went smoothly. But then she planned the guest lists carefully, mixing all ages, a variety of professions, temperaments.

Tonight's list had been handed to her by Miss Always. Everyone except Maggie knew everyone else, knew everyone else's stories and gossip.

Moreover, though she had thought early in the day that everything was ready, she had sensed sabotage. Little things had gone amiss.

First Mrs. Butterfield had taken to her bed, sick, after tea, so she couldn't direct the caterers.

Second, the gardener had watered all the lawn chairs. Gerald had become furious, since he'd wanted to show off their spectacular garden and tennis court. Maggie herself felt disappointed about the wet garden, as she'd planned to serve drinks outside.

And she felt annoyed with Gerald for having come in late last night, giving her no chance to prepare him for Felicity, who remained hidden in her basket in one of the guestrooms.

Then the caterers had come late, and in ill-fitting attire.

Worst of all — she'd been avoiding thinking about it — Miss Always had arrived early and had rushed about, supposedly making herself useful. Why Gerald's secretary must be at her party, Maggie couldn't guess. Miss Always in her short yellow satin dress — as if she were one of the younger women. Miss Always, slouching in that yellow satin which pulled across breasts unnaturally high and pointed, the nipples clearly outlined, a honey pot over one, a hummingbird over the other. Miss Always, tossing swirls of blonde hair, sprinkled with glitter. Miss Always, chatting pleasantly to the Lloyd's men who surrounded her as she fluttered blue lashes, lips parted in a shimmering pink smile.

Miss Always had not brought a man for herself, Maggie noted.

Despite the disappointments, Maggie thought she herself was carrying the evening off well. At least she was maintaining her presence. Her odd little Aunt Maude had always said, "You either have Presence or you don't, rather like a belief in God." Unfortunately, no one in the world had had less presence than her late Aunt Maude, bless her soul. Despite this, to her Aunt Maude, Presence superseded knowledge of any diety; and she said the word with a capital 'P'.

Maggie was finding Presence decidedly trying. Robin was right. A mask was what she needed.

What mask would it be? Endurance? Not very sociable. Delight? Too frivolous.

Cordiality! That was it. Maggie mentally designed her

mask with its understated though warm smile and an encouraging look in the eyes. When she had the image firmly in mind, she placed Cordiality on her face, certain that her mysterious Robin would have been pleased.

"Madeline?" Gerald whispered, coming up and putting an arm about her shoulders.

"Porphyro," she whispered back, hopefully. She looked into his eyes and noticed he'd removed his glasses. He looked so debonair tonight, so warm, so charming, so Italian. They were good together at parties, Maggie had to admit. If they could just go from one party to another with no time in between!

"Darling, have you seen my briefcase? Miss Always said she last saw it in the study." Gerald led her to the group of men he'd been talking to.

Maggie caught the scent of musky shaving lotion, cheap shaving lotion. Where would that have come from? And why would he wear it? She looked from Gerald to Miss Always, who now took little puffs from a cigarette she held in a white plastic holder. Forbearance might have been a better mask for tonight, but she decided Cordiality also suited her purpose.

"Surely no work tonight?"

"Aha, so you've hidden it to keep me from overdoing." Gerald's smile needed a touch of her own Cordiality. "I really must get some papers, my angel."

Barely able to move in her tight skirt and yellow satin high heels, Miss Always minced closer to Maggie.

"Gentlemen, you don't know what Mrs. Featherstone puts up with. My boss is a real… slave driver." The pause before "slave" made whatever Gerald did at the office sound pornographic.

Maggie watched the men's smiles. Miss Always's stock, already high, had just taken another upward swing.

"I haven't seen the briefcase." Maggie knew she sounded dull by comparison.

"Gentlemen, my wife loves her parties to go smoothly."

"The mark of a good wife." Miss Always gave a low, honeyed laugh which took the group's mind off the briefcase and the good wife.

Maggie felt furious.

"I assure you, I haven't seen it." Luckily Cordiality hid her emotions. "I can look for it."

"No, no. You're probably right. We'll leave it till tomorrow." Gerald protested. "She just won't let me overwork, will you, darling?"

Though this was said to Maggie, his eyes stayed with Miss Always, whose shrug caused the satin to pull even tighter across her breasts.

Then Miss Always turned and her tiny steps, as she made her way to the fireplace, caused her hips to rotate in a most alarming fashion. Gerald's eyes followed.

Maggie glanced at Lord Wizzell, the red-faced gentleman next to her, with a large red and white moustachio. His bulging eyes fixed on Miss Always, he bent to small, anaemic-looking Mr. Normington and said, loud enough for Maggie to overhear, "Torpedo Tits."

The two men chuckled.

"If you'll excuse me," said Maggie. But, of course, they would, since they were otherwise engaged.

She moved to the cumbersome old sofa table — she'd hidden the urns in the closet — and absently ran her hand over a Lalique swan, one of the treasured collection of crystals that had arrived that afternoon. Enjoying the coolness and smoothness of it, she thought, Mother of God, give me strength.

"Mrs. Featherstone?" Jeremiah Hoare, the Latin caterer with dark hair and slim moustache, hissed at Maggie from the hallway and motioned nervously for her.

"I can't tell what you're saying."

To Maggie's horror, he rushed up to her.

"Rice, Mrs. Featherstone," he boomed accusingly. "You haven't any rice!"

"Shhh," Maggie hissed as nearby guests looked on amused. Maggie quickly followed him into the kitchen, where she found the catering staff in an uproar.

"I put it out for you. Right here on the counter."

"Yes, it sat right here," said Mr. Hoare, fluttering his hand at the spot as if to conjure up the missing box. "It can't have walked away, but it has." He put the palm of one hand to his forehead and held the pose. "I can't carry on without the rice."

"Can't someone run out for more?"

"Early closing today, Mrs. Featherstone." Again he was accusing Maggie, with his voice, with his little black eyes.

One of the things Maggie hated about living in England was that shops closed at noon two days a week. At home she could have bought rice at midnight. "But it must be somewhere?" Then she noticed grains of rice around the edge of the room. They had spilled it and swept it up. "We'll have to go on without rice."

"But my stroganoff..."

"Can't be helped, Mr. Hoare." Maggie turned and pulled up her mask which had fallen.

From the highest reaches of the house, a howl, chilling and eerie, rent the air. The primal scream. Maggie ran to the drawing room to see Gerald looking about, confused. When he caught Maggie's eye, his expression changed to concern. He pushed past her, running up the stairs.

Maggie started up after him, hesitated, then turned to wave her guests back to the party. "Nothing to worry about. Everything's under control." She had let Cordiality slip again and didn't quite know how to get it back on. Why hadn't she told Gerald sooner? What a time for him to find out. She hurried after him.

"What is it?" He ran down the hall and flung open a guestroom door.

As Maggie caught up to him, he barred her entrance with his arm. He snapped on the light and stepped bravely into the room.

"A dog?" He turned to Maggie in disbelief.

She knotted and unknotted her chiffon scarf.

"I was a little lonely… and you said… well…"

"A dog!"

"Yes. No, a puppy. You always said in the country…"

"But the scream?"

"Likes attention."

"No puppy sounds like that."

"This one does." Maggie entered and picked up Felicity. The puppy stopped screaming the moment she was the center of attention.

"What an ugly dog. That pushed-in nose, that mean chin jutting out. That's not the right kind of dog for you."

"It's a King Charles spaniel. In the seventeenth century the king carried one under each arm. It's a royal dog, rare, pedigreed."

"Oh? Why was it screaming? What's the matter with it? God, I hope it hasn't got mange."

"She wants company, I think." Maggie could somehow understand that scream. She cuddled the puppy to her.

"She? You mean it can have…? Oh, no. Not in this house."

"But the country…"

"Tomorrow get rid of her."

"Her name's…"

Gerald put a hand over Maggie's mouth.

"Darling, I don't want to know."

Maggie pulled away and placed the puppy back in her basket.

"She's a show dog."

"Show dog?" Gerald's eyes widened as he looked at the puppy in surprise.

"She'll win ribbons."

"Ribbons?"

"Yes."

"You're sure about ribbons? And royal?"

"Her body has lovely conformation the breeder told me. 'Cobby'." The Normingtons and Wizzells looked like members of the horsey set. They were probably dog people as well. Felicity might help Gerald bridge a gap he would never be comfortable about but would never quite understand.

"Ribbons!" Gerald smiled at Felicity, stooping and chucking her under the chin. "What does she have to do to win them?"

"Nothing much." She and Felicity were home free now.

"I suppose a show dog is all right." He turned to go, then swung back and scooped up the puppy. "I'll take her downstairs and show her off. A show dog! What did you say you named her?"

"Felicity." Maggie heaved a sigh of relief and readjusted her mask so she could face her guests again.

"Felicity? For a puppy?"

"She was already named, so I suppose we'd better not confuse her by changing it."

Gerald walked proudly downstairs, Felicity cradled in his arms. He passed her from one to the other of the guests, boasting about future dog shows.

At a reasonable hour, couples commenced their parting noises. "So lovely. Charming. We must lunch at my club." A main advantage of life in the country, Maggie thought, was that people often had to leave early to get back to town, starting everyone heading home.

Miss Always was the last. She couldn't find her wrap. Then she missed her evening bag. A scarf, without which she could not face the night air, was eventually discovered in the dining chamber.

"Maggie!" Miss Always took her hostess' hand. "I hope I've been a real help to you this evening. I want so much to be your good friend."

"You were wonderful." Gerald gave Maggie no chance to respond.

"Ta ta." Miss Always called as she slunk down the drive to her taxi.

With the heavy oak door bolted, Gerald flopped onto the couch, his feet stretched before him on the carpet, his arms over his eyes.

Maggie picked up Felicity, kicked off her sandals, and curled close to him.

"You were magnificent tonight, Porphyro," she said in the old way. She had almost forgotten that at home she'd say that after each party, and he'd look, love in his eyes, and with a little smile answer, "You weren't too bad yourself, Madeline." Then he'd kiss her on just the right spot on her neck where she loved to be kissed, and then...

She looked up for the teasing, the grin, the kiss.

Gerald stretched and yawned.

"I'm beat." He stood up. "Darling, I get up so early, I know I disturb you."

"Nonsense, Gerald." Her stomach knotted. This was the wrong scenario. "I'm always up with you."

"Well, now that we're in the country, you could sleep late, my angel. I'm moving my things to one of the spare bedrooms so I won't feel guilty about waking you."

He walked quickly upstairs.

CHAPTER V

Ugh! Cigar ash. The drawing room smelled of stale smoke. Maggie screwed up her nose as she poured the contents of two ashtrays into a third and carried the three into the kitchen. She wouldn't let herself think about Gerald's moving to a guestroom last night, about the death of their renewal. About her fear of Lloyd's swallowing Gerald up.

She rinsed out the ashtrays and left them in the sink. From the master bedroom, Felicity howled her primal scream. Maggie shivered, remembering the screams of jack rabbits in the Hollywood Hills when coyotes chased them through the canyons. Neighbourhood dogs barked frantically and the rabbits screamed in terror. When the kill took place, all became still as death.

Maggie felt that stillness now, the terror of the jack rabbit, paralyzed as it waited for the jaws of Fate to snap out its existence. She understood the cruelty of that moment, the anguish. The anguish of Gerald's changing bedrooms, of loosening a link, a bond. Of threatening to snap apart their union itself. Leaving Maggie shivering in terror, not knowing what loneliness awaited her or if she could handle it. Appalled at Gerald's behaviour, Maggie decided that she needed several masks to see her through, to camouflage her until she could get her bearings, understand where she was and what she was up against.

She went upstairs and carried her puppy down. Felicity lunged at Maggie's every step. If Maggie paused while fluffing and rearranging pillows, Felicity tried to climb up her legs, snagging her stockings.

Unwillingly Maggie sat on an overstuffed chair. "*You* can sit on this furniture, Felicity." She pulled the puppy up beside her, stroking Felicity under the chin. "You must tell me what masks I shall need."

The wilful puppy gave Maggie a haughty glance.

"Arrogance. Quite right." Maggie tried to imagine an arrogant mask for herself, eyes half-lidded, mouth turned down slightly, ready to sneer. No, that had been one of her troubles in life. She had never learned to be arrogant. How fortunate the person born arrogant, she thought. To give others commands and have them carried out without question. To feel just a shade better then everyone else.

"No, Felicity. Arrogance would pinch and constrain." Though, she thought, anything would be an improvement on my usual expression: Kind. "People don't really like Kind, Felicity, even if you are kind to them. Kind appears uncomfortably vulnerable. People want to hurt you if you wear Kind, almost to see if you will say ouch, which, of course, a kind person would never do."

Felicity whined and nuzzled Maggie.

"Sweet? Is that what you're suggesting? It has proved a popular look. But be careful, Felicity. Sweet says with a sweet smile, 'I'll give you anything, do anything for you. But you must then wear Guilt if you fail to come up to my standards while I play Martyr'."

Felicity chewed on Maggie's thumb.

"How does Remote strike you? People can't make you out, so leave you alone."

Felicity sat up and cocked her head, sticking out one puppy ear. "You're right. Interested is a superb look. Alert, listening, yet not committed, and people love it. They sense that you won't disagree. I could have a mask for each occasion." Maggie pictured herself reaching for the mask that matched the moment, just as she reached for the shoes that matched her bag. No longer looking kind or vulnerable in the least, she could carry off any situation with ease. She could ride through any number of luncheons and those dreaded Lloyd's parties behind the right mask. Robin's idea had grown into an ingenious plan.

"But where shall I put the masks once I've created them?" Maggie laughed to think of her masks mentally ready and placed in a row, just as she placed her shoes. Albeit they'd be invisible, she would know just which mask to pull.

"I don't want to be forced to think out the right expression on the spot, Felicity."

Felicity busied herself licking Maggie's palm.

"And I don't have room in my armoire for such an array. If guests stay in any of the spare rooms, I couldn't get to my masks."

What if she were to use the room next to the living room — the dark, narrow place that could belong only to Maggie, since neither Gerald nor Miss Always liked it? There Maggie could escape the ubiquitous Miss Always.

As Maggie put her down, Felicity barked her objection, then trotted behind Maggie, pushing between her legs. At the old oak door, Maggie paused, then shoved it open. A cold draught hit at her. Felicity growled menacingly but remained hiding behind Maggie's legs.

Maggie stepped inside, Felicity's whiskers tickling her leg as the puppy remained within touching distance.

Maggie snapped on the light. Her eyes searched the room. To the right sat the spinning wheel and the three little stools that the former tenants had discarded. She thought she saw the spinning wheel move slightly.

She slid her fingers across the dusty shelves and decided they would be perfect for the masks. Felicity, watchful and growling low, the hair of her neck raised, stood at Maggie's feet. Patting the puppy, Maggie mentally made a list of masks she'd need.

1) Remote.

2) Pleased, though bored enough not to look kind.

3) Superior. No, she wasn't good at that. She changed Superior to 3) Interested.

4) Entertained. She liked Entertained. It would do for happy, humorous, even ecstatic in a pinch, any number of moods. She didn't want to call undue attention to her masks by anything too extreme.

5) Passionate. But Passionate seemed too extreme. She hated to admit the truth. She didn't need Passionate. She was no longer certain how Passionate looked or felt.

She carefully dreamed up her masks, one by one. Imagining the occasions, she applied the make-up, more dramatic for evening, softer for day trips to the city, non-existent for the country.

Momentarily ignored, Felicity started to whimper. Hunched on her little stool, Maggie scratched the puppy behind the ears. As she leaned against the spinning wheel, it creaked with an almost human moan, making her wonder if spinning wheels needed to be oiled.

Perhaps Gerald would no longer be so critical if she could wear the mask that pleased him. She thought long and hard about what role Gerald would most like. Clearly one she had not been playing. He was searching for something besides power but that would complement it. She feared if she could not give it to him, she would lose him, to the system, to another.

She decided to try out all the masks on him, one by one until she discovered what he desired.

"There's one mask I can't make or wear, Felicity." Maggie gave a sigh. "And I fear it's what Gerald wants."

The little bitch snorted contentedly.

"You're wrong, Felicity. Everything's not all right. Even for Gerald, I cannot fashion Youth."

CHAPTER VI

As Maggie stared out the drawing room window, a face appeared upside down, and she felt for a moment that she was looking at a childhood game in which one was supposed to find faces in a tree. She shivered. Had she created a face in her oak?

But when white teeth gleamed in an inverted smile and eyes green as the leaves laughed down at her, she knew this was no apparition.

"Robin," she shouted through the glass. "Come down from there."

He jiggled the branch and laughed.

"You could be hurt," she called, pacing in her desire to reach him.

Lithely, he swung up and was momentarily lost from sight. Then he reappeared, edging forward on the branch, until he perched on it like an elf.

"Robin, come down at once." If he falls, he'll tumble onto the stone walk, Maggie thought, both frightened and furious. Whatever was she to do?

With relief she saw him scramble toward the trunk. In seconds he was sliding down the broad stem without seeming to hold on. Was he using magic, she wondered. When he reached the ground, he waved his wand at the tree, which trembled violently. Then he turned to Maggie and looked at her with his infuriating, superior grin. She motioned towards the kitchen and went to open the door.

Mrs. Butterfield, wiping up with a dishcloth that seemed much too small for such a large, cumbersome person, glanced up mournfully as Maggie hurried past her to the door.

"Anxious is it now?" She slowly spread her dish cloth over the sink to dry.

Maggie stopped and looked at her curiously.

"What?"

"Anxious. And earlier it was Smug, then downright Rebellious. I never seen a face with more changes to it."

Before Maggie could alter her expression once again, Robin opened the door and peered in, a sour Mrs. Butterfield imitation on his face.

"Robin, you mustn't climb that tree. Not ever. If you fall, you could be killed."

"I won't fall." He walked to the kitchen table as if balancing on a tightrope. Once there, he began drumming on the pine wood with his magic wand. "I never fall."

Mrs. Butterfield eyed him.

"Humph!"

"She's right," agreed Maggie. "Pride goeth before a fall."

"Or the reverse," said Mrs. Butterfield in her enigmatic way. "There's a boy, so I've heard, that took a tumble from the oak, and that's a fact."

"Was he hurt?"

"Aye. Killed."

"How dreadful. Who?"

Robin drummed more furiously.

"Him as had no business there. Him as was too curious." She glared at Robin, who glowered at her in return, his eyes shooting vibrant greens in the morning light.

"Robin, do stop drumming," said Maggie, cross at Mrs. Butterfield's nonsense. "Just don't climb the tree again, understand?"

He nodded.

Mrs. Butterfield glanced at the kitchen clock.

"My bones is aching me something awful." As the other two took no notice, she added. "I'll just take myself up to my room."

Maggie glanced at her watch.

"Yes, it's time for one of your programs."

With another humph and head held high, Mrs. Butterfield trundled from the kitchen.

"Robin, have some biscuits." Maggie handed him a tin, but he waved it away. "Not hungry, really."

"Your mother must feed you well." Maggie was a little hurt that he didn't look forward to treats from her. She had always imagined her Sean would tease her for snacks. She wished she could mother Robin a little, could reach out to tousle his thick, Gypsy blue-black hair. But he would hate that. Instead, she sat down.

Robin threw his wand into the air and caught it.

"I saw you at the door of the church with your mask on." He gave her a wicked grin.

"Just one of many," she answered proudly. "How did you like Piety?"

"Looked like Remote to me." He twisted his gold necklace. "I've come to do a new trick."

"Another?" His magic frightened her. She wished he would forget about it.

"Yes. With Gypsy blood comes ancient knowledge."

Maggie thought how old and wise and menacing he sounded at moments such as this — his skin darker, his eyes flashing, his hand making strange patterns with his wand — as if truly some ancient wisdom resided in his genes.

"You'll need a scarf?" She started untying the flowered one she wore, but he didn't need that either, having put his tall silk hat aside.

"I'll need a larger audience."

"Mrs. Butterfield will never come down."

Robin bent and looked under the kitchen table, where

Felicity snoozed.

"Ah, just the audience I want." He pulled Felicity from her basket.

Felicity gave a howl.

Nervous, Maggie, took her from Robin and grasped her tightly. What if the trick went wrong?

Robin stepped closer, threatening the puppy with his wand. Maggie edged backwards in her chair.

"Perhaps you could do your trick another time?"

Ignoring her, Robin held his necklace with one hand and waved his wand over Felicity, intoning, "Abracadabra."

Maggie gasped as Felicity disappeared right off her lap. Even the weight of her vanished as if she had never been there. Mystified and horrified, Maggie looked about the room and under the table.

"Robin, what have you done? Bring her back!"

Robin rubbed the medallion of his necklace, and Felicity reappeared, growling fiercely, her whiskers twitching.

As Robin again raised his wand, Maggie put out a protective arm. "No, Robin, no!"

But the magician merely reached forward, held up one of Felicity's spaniel ears and drew out a large roundsteak bone. He bowed, laughing wickedly.

"For you, Felicity."

These tricks couldn't be happening, Maggie knew; yet here was the bone.

"Why do you question my magic, Mrs. Featherstone?"

He reads my mind, thought Maggie alarmed. I'm certain now that he reads my mind.

Just then, the puppy snatched the bone from Robin's hand, jumped off Maggie's lap, and scurried with the bone to the kitchen corner, where she commenced gnawing.

"You can't have it!" Robin dashed after her, fell onto his knees beside the puppy, seized one side of the bone, and pulled.

Surprisingly strong, Felicity pressed her front paws to the floor and tenaciously held on.

Robin let go of the bone and taunted her.

"You know what happens to dogs who defy my magic."

Felicity gave a scream, but she covered the bone with her paws, then snarled viciously at Robin.

"You must leave her alone. I'm terrified you'll hurt her. And she might bite you."

Robin looked up at Maggie, and Felicity saw her chance. The bone firmly between her teeth, she dashed out of the kitchen and into the hallway, Robin at her heels.

"Robin, come back."

A few moments later he returned, defeated.

"She's disappeared."

"We'll get your bone back soon. In the meantime, I insist you stop teasing her." And me, she thought.

"You don't understand. These props aren't mine."

"Whose are they?" What if Felicity bit Gerald? Maggie wondered.

"They belong to somebody you don't know. I've got to return them all."

"She'll tire of it shortly." I wonder if I should have a professional trainer.

"Shortly is too late. It has to go right back or I'm in trouble." Robin slumped into a chair opposite Maggie.

"Maybe just one prop missing won't be noticed."

"It'll be noticed all right." Robin rested his chin on his hands, looking like Felicity when she put her head in her paws, and pondered his loss.

"Don't Gypsies tell fortunes?" asked Maggie to cheer him up. "Suppose you tell my fortune." Of course, if he really can tell fortunes, mine will hardly raise his spirits, she thought bitterly.

Robin lifted his head and eyed her suspiciously. “I shouldn’t think you’d want that.”

“Whyever not?”

“Well… it’s just…”

“Come on, let’s see what my future holds.” She felt embarrassed at the hollow sound of her cheerfulness. “Do you use tea leaves?”

Robin gave her an exasperated look.

“I read palms.”

He reached for her hand, but she unconsciously drew it back.

“I have to have your hand.”

Slowly Maggie put out her right hand. He took it in his left and studied it solemnly, running a thumb over the deepest lines.

As he did so, Maggie studied his long lashes, his high cheek bones, his sensitive mouth. Could this handsome little boy truly be in tune with mysteries from a forbidden realm? she wondered.

He dropped her hand.

“I’d rather not.”

“Robin, what do you see? Tell me.” Yet even as she asked, she was terrified of knowing.

He took her hand back reluctantly.

“It’s an Irish hand.”

“You can see that?” She must stop now, before he told her any more. She tried to draw her hand away, but he held on to it.

“It may come out all right. But it’s not what you think, or what you think you want.” Robin sounded all-knowing.

“What will come out all right?” She looked into his striated green eyes which glowed at her intently.

"What should."

"Well... isn't it... I mean... a fortune can't be bad if things come out all right. Can it?" She wished he didn't look so gloomy. "I thought fortunes were supposed to reassure people."

"If you think so." He gave her one of his infuriating smiles.

So, he was teasing her.

"You're not supposed to be so vague, Robin. You're supposed to say things like, 'A handsome stranger is coming into your life'."

"He is."

"Is he? Well, that's exciting; and you left it out altogether. And then you say, 'You will go on a long journey', or something about travel."

"You will."

"Heavens no. I've just had a long journey. You must fit the fortune to the person."

"Do you have Gypsy blood, Mrs. Featherstone?"

"Not that I know of."

"Then I should leave the fortune telling to me."

"But you need to add these touches. They'll give your predictions a flare. Oh, and you're supposed to leave me with a word of hope or caution."

"All right, if I must. But I don't like to."

"Well?"

"Beware."

"Beware? Beware of what?" A feeling of panic washed over Maggie.

"That's it. Beware." Robin jumped up, pushing his chair back so suddenly it fell over and banged on the tile floor as he grabbed his hat and ran out the door.

CHAPTER VII

Maggie seldom went to the village store. When she did, no one was friendly. As she met some of the neighbours at Mass at the Priory, she found she didn't have much in common with them. The women talked about sewing and bee-keeping and growing better courgettes, while their husbands discussed sheep farming and grain prices and beef slaughtering — any number of country matters.

She felt cut off in the country. She longed to talk about the latest plays and the opera and art exhibitions. She got Gerald to nearby Brighton once or twice for a play, but mostly he declined, saying he was too tired after work. She suspected he saw plays in London, for he could discuss them at parties. But he claimed only to read reviews.

She had always spent so much time on Gerald's comfort, on their shared interests, but now he seemed not to need her.

Sometimes Maggie would buy a day return ticket and take the train into town for lunch and a play — but alone, for she had met no one in Sussex to share her pleasures.

Mostly she frequented the London art galleries. She knew every Turner at the Tate. She studied the artist's increased subtleties over the years and wondered if people actually changed that much within themselves or only grew in the understanding of their work. Had Turner been in search of his core as Maggie was of hers? Had his core ever got mixed up with someone else's, so that he couldn't extricate his being from another's?

She didn't tell Gerald about her adventures into town because he never wanted to hear about her days. And he didn't much like it if she asked about his.

As he penetrated the system, becoming more and more a part of some unseen superstructure, Maggie felt him shrink to a shadow figure in her life. Yet a shadow she could not disentangle from her own.

Then one day, as she walked not far from the British Museum, she saw them — Miss Always and Gerald. They strolled in a little park across the street from her and were munching on popcorn and laughing. That was not like Gerald at all, to munch on popcorn, and certainly not in a public place. He hated popcorn, said it stuck in his teeth.

Maggie supposed the two were on a lunch break, although Gerald's office was nowhere near here. On second thought, she was forced to admit they were probably on an outing, just as she.

At first she wanted to slip on Remote and hurry past, praying they wouldn't see her. She knew she'd feel humiliated being seen by them, but wasn't sure why.

She felt shocked, angry, betrayed.

"Just a simple stroll in the park," Gerald would cavil. And his accusing look would say, "You're overreacting."

Too angry for Remote and an escape, Maggie crossed the street toward them, hoping traffic would hide her. The two never looked up, so she edged closer and positioned herself behind a tree as they approached her.

Miss Always's hair flowed from her head like a madonna's, swirled down her shoulders, covered her tight black sweater, and gleamed gold in the oblique sunlight. Her red skirt was too short and her black patent heels too high.

Gerald looked so very Italian, so suave and charming and in command. His dark hair appeared thicker, and his face more composed. His brown eyes looked livelier and his lips fuller as he smiled, displaying the old dimples. His white, even teeth appeared larger and more masculine.

As they walked past her, she gasped. Gerald ate his popcorn mechanically, gazing into his secretary's eyes the same way he'd once looked at Maggie.

And Miss Always — did Maggie ever gawk at Gerald like that? Smitten?

God, Gerald and Miss Always! A woman with no Presence, no style, little intelligence!

Maggie tried to calm herself. It wasn't as if she hadn't guessed. But to have to witness it, to admit it as fact. Perspiration trickled down her back, and she shook all over. Her heart pounded fiercely.

She'd need a new mask immediately, and she knew exactly what it would be: Cloak and Dagger.

That very minute she designed it and slipped it on, and as she did so, wondered for a fleeting moment what Piety would do. But she didn't want to know. Piety be damned. She planned to fight.

Yet were her weapons — wit, talent, Presence — of any consequence against Miss Always's weapon — Youth?

If only Gerald didn't look so damned Italian. He even reached up to stroke a moustache long gone. Gerald, smiling at Miss Always in the sunlight. The dimpled smile he saved for Madeline! "My look!" She bit her lip to keep back tears.

The scene went on endlessly as if re-run by some crazed projectionist. She saw the sun directing his beneficent rays on this couple only, bathing them in a warm Sicilian glow, blessing their love with golden flecks of light.

Maggie, too, was in the film. She stood in the snow, alone, a dark cloud enveloping her.

The film began again. The sun showered its blissful light on the chosen pair. The couple smiled. Gerald stroked his non-existent moustache. Miss Always put her arm through his. He fed her a bite of popcorn. The sun beamed its benediction.

The two took yet another turn about the little park. Maggie must act, but she couldn't think what to do in the glaring sun. Would it shine half so brightly, she wondered, if her storm cloud didn't threaten?

As the couple finally started for the street, she made her decision. She'd follow them. And not just today. She'd see where they went each day. This definitely was war.

She had another moment's doubt as she reflected that spying was not an honourable thing. Yet the British were honourable, she reasoned, and they were very good at it. The world's experts, she supposed.

Outside the park, the couple walked at a faster clip, Miss Always's hand on Gerald's arm, Maggie behind at a discreet distance. They reached Oxford Street and turned right. Was this the way back to the office? Surely not. Miss Always stopped to look in a store window.

Maggie forgot to stop. Almost upon them, she flattened herself against a building. As she waited, she turned, and her eye caught the movements of a window dresser working on a display of remarkable hats. A disguise to wear with Cloak and Dagger!

She sidled to the entrance and rushed in, praying the two wouldn't get away, purchased the largest hat she could see — one with a veil — and rushed out.

She needn't have hurried. The two were just strolling off, still arm-in-arm.

Maggie adjusted her hat by peering in a shop window. Actually, it looked rather smart — black, as were her shoes and handbag, with soft black feathers on the brim. The veil covered her face admirably.

Gerald would never think she was under a hat, since she never wore them. She'd always loved hats, but felt women shouldn't have to cover their heads in church and blamed St. Paul for degrading women.

"He always looked down on us," she'd said to Gerald when the Second Ecumenical Council concluded. "Now that hats are no longer required, I vow I'll never wear one again."

And she never had until this moment.

Suddenly, Gerald rushed to the street, hailed a taxi and helped Miss Always in, jumping in behind her.

Maggie waved frantically for another. Just as one stopped, a man pushed her aside and entered, and the moment was lost. Spying was not going to be easy.

She caught the next taxi and went to Victoria Station.

Once there, she felt a little faint and realized she had missed lunch, so bought two chocolate chip cookies.

Raising the veil on her hat, she munched, not really tasting them, as she stared vacantly into station shops.

The cover of a romance caught her eye. A loving nineteenth century couple sat on grass in a park. His arm was about her and she held a fluffy white dog. She even had red hair and he appeared dark and handsome. The way Gerald and I should be, Maggie thought. Then she took in the title, *The Dandy's Deception,* and decided she'd better read how the hero deceived and what the heroine did about it.

She quickly purchased the book.

On her way to the train, people pushed past, some bumping her. It didn't matter. She felt as if she'd pulled a thread at her hemline and the entire hem was unravelling without her being able to stop it.

A boy carrying a large box of popcorn nudged her aside. The smell nauseated her.

Mother of God. Gerald and Miss Always!

Maggie's stomach felt queasy. She shouldn't have had the cookies.

What if they saw me? she wondered. What if that's why they jumped into the taxi? The thought nagged her during the trip home, and the movement of the train made her feel worse. The wheels on the track now repeated, "They recognized you. They recognized you."

When Maggie finally arrived, Felicity greeted her, jumping up, snagging her stockings, then sticking her whiskers into Maggie's leg.

"Sit, Felicity, sit." Oh, dear. She wasn't supposed to say that to a show dog. Heaven forbid Felicity should now sit down in the middle of a show. What would Gerald say?

She didn't want to admit that Gerald would probably not even notice as he gazed into Miss Always's eyes.

Maggie made a cup of tea with a tea bag in one of her blue and white striped cups and sat at the kitchen table. She hadn't let the water come to a boil, and the tepid tea had no flavour, but the warmth comforted her.

Had they seen her? Just in case, she'd buy a different hat tomorrow. She liked her disguise. Never totally out of fashion, hats graced the heads of women who wished to be thought of as chic and maybe a little bit gutsy, even eccentric, but were certainly not seeking perfect concealment.

Oh, she meant to follow them again.

"I'll learn what those two are up to, Felicity. Just you watch. They think they've hidden their secret as carefully as you have Robin's bone. But I'll ferret out exactly what has been going on, exactly what I'm to expect in the future."

Strange, Gerald had always wanted a wife who was there when he got home, who cooked for him, nursed him, decorated his house tastefully, played the attractive hostess, cheered him on as he marched to the fray each morning. And Maggie had accomplished all these things. Now Miss Always, who appeared to Maggie incapable of decorating or cooking or nurturing, was a kind of beloved office pal, a woman who shared his work. Had his needs changed so very much?

Maggie felt a stab in her breast as she remembered that she and Gerald had once been pals.

That night Gerald came home late.

"Exhausting day," he claimed, but he did not look as exhausted as he did relaxed. Maggie noticed a kind of brightness in his expression she hadn't seen in a long time, and his lips looked a bit swollen.

The next morning at the breakfast table Maggie sat in her robe and accepted Gerald's perfunctory goodbye kiss.

The minute he was out the door, she flung off the robe. Underneath she wore a trim black outfit. Today she'd buy a smart white and black summer hat. She'd definitely have to retire yesterday's black straw.

She phoned for a taxi and waited outside. When it screeched to a halt near the station, she stuffed the fare into the driver's hand, jumped out and rushed past the guard, calling, "I'll pay on the train." She entered the nearest carriage. A guard gave the signal. The 8:23a.m. fast train pulled out of Hassocks and sped to Victoria Station. She'd arrive with plenty of time to get to the stores and shop for her hat, then position herself near noon to follow the — she didn't want to think "lovers" — the couple.

At a hat shop in Knightsbridge she found just the hat she'd envisioned: black with a wide brim that turned up to show white round her face. Simple. Smart. And, with a black veil that covered Cloak and Dagger admirably.

By 12:30 she was travelling up one of Lloyd's outside lifts to the gallery above the main ground floor. She didn't watch the view but concentrated on her plan to spy on Gerald where he worked at his marine syndicate's box.

At 12:45, she exited onto grey composite flooring, like

the grey of the building, like the grey of her mood. She edged to the front of the gallery.

Looking down, she could see the stands and desks where high risk business was transacted. And then she saw Gerald. Miss Always stood beside his desk. He rose, took her elbow. Her elbow! In public! Where he was known! Where everyone could see!

As Maggie stared, immobile, the two walked towards an exit. Then Maggie gave a start. What if she lost them?

She dashed out of the gallery and onto the moving staircase, then froze as the stairs plummeted her downward. Oh, Mother of God, there they stand at the bottom. Maggie tried to walk back up, but was prevented by those behind her. I'll be propelled right into them.

As she reached the ground floor, almost on top of them, the couple headed outside. Maggie hung back, then followed them into Lime Street, where Gerald hailed a taxi.

While Maggie signaled for another, she prepared herself. When a bushy-haired man tried to elbow his way inside, she acted. One kick with her high heels, and the man went off limping.

Maggie couldn't believe it when Gerald's taxi stopped at Simpson's on the Strand. Why a tourist attraction? Why not some discreet, quiet, quaint spot for his lady love?

Then it dawned on her that no one Gerald knew would be at a tourist attraction. How clever of him. But how very boring for Miss Always, who must have seen every place he took her numerous times before.

And how very stupid of Gerald to suppose Maggie had taken no notice of his interest in Miss Always. If I were going to commit adultery, I'd make sure I wasn't found out, she thought. Then she had the terrible feeling that Gerald just didn't care if she found out.

At 1:10, Maggie paid her driver and followed the

couple inside, past the Victorian foyer, which appeared crowded and noisy. She hid behind another couple going upstairs, then sidled to the West Room entrance and waited for Gerald and Miss Always to follow the maitre d'hotel. The grey-blue of the walls and grey-brown of the carpet calmed her.

Once they were seated, she stepped up to the head waiter and pointed to a table close to their booth.

Under the shadow of her new hat, its veil raised to cover only her eyes, Maggie dared to peek at the couple.

"Does madam wish a cocktail?"

"Oh, my no. Not while I'm working."

The waiter raised his eyebrows.

Intimidated, she stammered, "A glass of white wine."

"Very good."

She shifted her chair so she could see Gerald even better. What she hoped to accomplish by watching the two she wasn't sure. Whether she wanted to work out some pattern to their movements or to see how intense they felt about each other, she hadn't decided.

The wine arrived. She took a sip and stared at her subjects. While she could watch them, she still had some measure of control. Thirty years of her life sat only a few yards away, and she wasn't going to lose sight of it yet.

Why did Gerald, at Miss Always's side, look so young? Rather like the old pictures in their album. He'd had a wonderful sense of humor then, Maggie recalled.

Now he never laughed with her, just with Miss Always.

And the two sat in a booth. Gerald tucked his glasses into his coat pocket; Miss Always fingered a teaspoon. Then Gerald covered her right hand with his left and slipped both under the table. Miss Always giggled. Gerald pressed his forehead to hers. Miss Always looked up and kissed him on the nose. To Maggie, a booth implied just such intimacy. Anybody could sit with anyone else at a table. But a booth gave a Do Not Disturb suggestion.

Yet Maggie remembered feeling very romantic at tables in small restaurants in Brittany. She and Gerald would stop for lunch and share a table with the local patrons. They'd sip bubbling hard cider and watch women, with starched white lace headdresses at least two feet tall, stretch dough paper thin and throw it onto hot metal over charcoal fires. They could hear the crêpes sizzle.

They ordered ham and egg crêpes, seafood crêpes, brown sugar crêpes, strawberry crêpes. Gerald put his hand on Maggie's and smiled at her in that special way he had — teasing and loving at the same moment. "And you'll end with a chocolate crêpe, right?"

"Yes, madam?"

"Chocolate," said Maggie.

"We take the dessert order later, madam." said the waiter, who did not seem to notice Maggie's startled expression. "But we do have a tempting selection: spotted dick, that's a tasty suet steamed pudding, cream caramel, treacle roll, bread and butter pudding…"

The last choice brought Maggie out of her daydream with a jolt. She remembered all the bread and butter puddings she'd choked down as a child.

"Will it be the prime rib for the main course, madam?" the waiter asked.

She looked up at him and noticed that his two front teeth were bucked and pointed outwards in opposite directions, so that as he spoke, he looked as if he were spitting teeth.

"Or today's special, steak and kidney pudding? The chef says the kidneys are really lovely."

The waiter spoke so loudly Maggie was sure he would cause Gerald to look her way. She automatically put a finger to her lips.

"The rare prime rib?"

"I'd like the ribs please."

"The ribs!"

Maggie put up a hand to guard herself from the teeth.

"Surely I did not hear correctly? Madam said the ribs?"

The man at the next table turned to stare.

"Shhh. Yes," Maggie whispered.

As if to compensate for Maggie's whispers, the waiter's voice became louder still. "Cannot be done, madam."

"Why not?" She was angry now. Others were turning to look. "I thought that was your specialty."

"Speciality," he carefully added an extra syllable. "Prime rib of beef. But not the *ribs,* madam. Not the ribs."

He looked across at the man wheeling round the carving trolley with the rarest of beef inside. "Robert," her waiter called to him, "we never serve ribs, correct?"

Robert looked suitably shocked and mouthed, "Never."

There were titters at nearby tables.

"But my dog would love the ribs."

"You're considering a 'doggie bag', madam? A 'doggie bag'!" This last he said so loudly that only true love could have kept Gerald concentrating on Miss Always.

Maggie slumped in her seat, pulled down her veil and waved him away.

"Another one," she pointed to her glass of wine.

"But madam has not yet drunk her wine."

"Another," Maggie whispered.

"Will someone be joining you?"

Maggie sighed in relief and nodded yes.

"Of course, madam. I did not realize." Running a long tongue over his bucked teeth as if checking to see they hadn't flown out, the waiter departed.

Maggie watched as Robert wheeled his trolley to

Gerald's table and cut thick slices of beef for him and Miss Always. Beef that they didn't eat as they gazed into each other's eyes, held each other's hands.

Had Maggie imagined Brittany? Had she and Gerald ever truly sat like that? Ever gazed at each other, seeing no one round them? Suddenly, she couldn't recall. Frantically, she groped for memories and none came.

After toying with his Yorkshire pudding for some moments, Gerald took a small box from his pocket. Maggie felt ill. Not jewelry, Gerald, not jewelry, she thought.

He never gave Maggie gifts any more, hadn't for years.

Miss Always opened the box and drew out a thin gold chain and locket. She held it up, letting it catch the light. Then she turned and lifted her long tinted golden hair as Gerald leaned over and fastened the chain. He kissed Miss Always's neck, kissed it on the same spot where Maggie loved him to kiss her.

Maggie's mind suddenly spun into action. She remembered such kisses. She recalled intimate looks. A terrible pain in her gut caused her to bend over.

Gerald rose to go and helped Miss Always to her feet. No one helped Maggie, who got up unsteadily, her two glasses of lukewarm wine barely touched. She left enough money on the table to cover her own unordered lunch and followed the couple down the steps and outside.

They took a taxi. Maggie's cab followed along Gracechurch Street, then into Leadenhall Street, then paused. She watched the two enter the oilrig-like building that housed Lloyd's.

For a minute she gazed at the mass of exposed pipes. Finally, she asked her driver to take her to Victoria Station.

If I could stop them, she thought, no harm has been done.

In her heart she knew she could as soon stop a gusher as cap the unleashed emotions of Gerald and Miss Always.

CHAPTER VIII

Maggie browsed in Liberty's crystal department. She still had time before pursuing Gerald and Miss Always during their lunch hour. She felt depressed and gazed intently at each object in the hope one would cheer her.

The crystal head of a smooth fox terrier caught her eye. Its nose was pointed, one perky ear flopped at the tip, the other raised as if it were listening.

"Foxtrot," she murmured in relief and joy.

"One of a kind," an anaemic young male clerk, his face covered with acne, told her. "A designer piece. And doesn't it seem to have spirit? Why, I wouldn't be surprised if it barked." He kept fingering a sore on his chin.

The crystal sported a designer's price, but Maggie felt reckless. Finer than any piece in her collection, it had Foxtrot's pert personality. She held it up and watched the light create a snazzy pattern of sunbows.

"It's signed," said the young man. "Right here." He pointed to the base.

Maggie decided she'd place her crystal Foxtrot in the window where the sun would play upon it. It cheered her more than anything had in a long time. "Foxtrot, you always bring me hope," she thought.

"Wrap it carefully, please," she said to the salesman.

Hope, Maggie remembered, was one of the seven gifts of the Holy Ghost. And Patience. She wasn't strong on that either. She had better have some spiritual direction, or at any rate, a spiritual friend. She decided to ask Father Humphrey from the Priory to tea.

Madame Tussauds? Maggie sat in her taxi in the frantic

traffic of Marylebone Road, stuck behind giant exhaust-belching, noise-spewing tourist buses, and watched Gerald walk beside Miss Always towards the entrance to the waxworks. He appeared debonair, young, energetic — his Italian best.

The couple had settled on Tuesdays and Thursdays for their outings. Last week they'd taken a boat trip to Greenwich on Tuesday and a tour of Westminster Abbey on Thursday. This past Tuesday they had chosen the Tower of London.

Maggie was not pleased with the stops they usually picked for lunch — health food places like Oodles. She decided Miss Always deserved Oodles.

Ironically, Miss Always wasn't seeing the English Gerald. She would be bitterly disappointed when she did. Maggie smiled wickedly beneath Cloak and Dagger. Miss Always deserved the English Gerald.

Maggie — dressed in a purple wrap dress, a Paloma Picasso fringed shawl over one shoulder, and a jaunty purple hat — hurried to the entrance of the Victorian building. She briefly glanced at a brown cameo of Madame Tussaud which stood out against the cream of the exterior. Inside, she looked up at the staircases which circled to both sides. She couldn't see Gerald or Miss Always.

What if she went up one side as they climbed the other, and they met?

No. She'd be careful. She ran up the stairway to her right. The box office at the top had a line. Still no Gerald and Miss Always.

Just as her turn to buy a ticket came, the little boy in front of Maggie dropped his gum on the toe of her shoe. Balancing on one foot as she struggled to remove the gum with a Kleenex, Maggie dropped her change. Would she ever catch up with Gerald now?

At the lift, a group of young school children tried to play tag round her. When the lift arrived, they swarmed into it, shoving Maggie with them. Its occupants screaming, the lift made its way to the top floor, where Maggie was spewed out the door and into the Tableau Room.

She peered about. Where on earth had they got to? If they were hidden behind some tourist group, she might never see them.

It dawned on her that, with limited time, Gerald would head for the greatest tourist attraction in the museum, the Chamber of Horrors. That was in the basement, and she'd have to go through the entire exhibition to reach it.

Eyes only for Gerald, heedless of kings and queens and presidents, she elbowed her way past groups gaping at lifeless figures, down a flight of stairs and through the Grand Hall.

She ran down another stairway to ground level, then turned right and took the narrow, slightly curving, stairway to the Chamber.

An exhibition guide guarded the entrance. Maggie stood still to catch her breath, hoping he wouldn't notice she was panting. Just as she started to walk sedately inside, the Newgate bell to her right resounded with a mighty bong.

She shrieked and jumped inside a dark alcove.

Sensing someone behind her, she turned to stare into the death mask of King Louie XVI, his head sitting on a pike next to that of Marie Antoinette.

Bong. The Newgate bell tolled again as she backed away from the gruesome heads.

Then Maggie saw Gerald and Miss Always. They stood on the cobblestones of a Victorian street in Whitechapel. A wax drunkard, collapsed, gripped his flagon outside the

Ten Bells pub as Gerald and Miss Always gazed down at a disemboweled victim of Jack the Ripper.

Bong. The prison bell rang out.

Maggie stood immobile. She hated waxworks. Yellow figures not alive, yet not altogether lifeless. Dead bodies, carefully embalmed and dressed. Hair waved just so, but never quite the way the person had worn it. Nails painted. Bodies balanced in lifelike poses by a mad mortician.

As a child she'd been brought here by cousin Magnus, whose life ambition was to be an undertaker. He'd revelled in the Chamber of Horrors, and Maggie had run out, screaming. For weeks after she'd had nightmares about the waxy bodies executed by electric chair or firing squad.

She couldn't remember what had happened to Magnus, whether or not he'd achieved his ambition. She did recall that when he visited, they all had to save the fat from their meat for him

"Magnus is coming next week," her aunt would say. "I've been saving coupons for a nice, fatty joint of beef for dinner." Maggie would watch in horror as he swallowed great globs, grease running down his chin.

Over the years, in Maggie's mind the fat and waxworks had congealed into one experience. She was not so fortunate as Proust, going back in time with *petites madeleines* soaked in tea. Yellow fat on a roast took her back to the Chamber of Horrors at Madame Tussaud's.

And now Gerald brought her here.

Bong, sounded the Newgate bell.

The couple moved on, and Maggie crept after. With eyes only for each other, they never noticed.

They joined a group crowded round a tableau of a young naked woman, a look of abject terror on her face, held in a bath by a tall man, hair parted in the middle, a smug grin on his face, and shirtsleeves rolled up to get a job done. She'd grasped the sides of the old cast-iron enameled tub in a struggle to pull herself out but to no avail. Bubbles actually came from her mouth as she attempted to get air.

Maggie gasped with her.

Bong, the bell resounded.

Gerald and Miss Always strolled away, pulling Maggie with them. As she left, she noticed the details: brass taps on the tub, a mirror on the bathroom wall. Then, to her dismay, she saw herself in that mirror.

She was shivering as she caught up with the two, standing like wax figures: Gerald, his arm round Miss Always's shoulder in a protective gesture, and she, head against his shoulder.

Melting, Miss Always looked up at Gerald as his hand slid down her back, then circled round until it fell on one of her bra-less breasts. And there it stayed, fingers fondling, as the two stared, unseeing, at a tableau.

Maggie could not endure watching Gerald's atrocity She edged back in horror.

Bong.

She groped her way to the stairs and started to climb blindly, leaning against the brass railing for support and gasping for air as if she were drowning. The deathly reverberations of the bell throbbed in her ears.

Outside, she stood in front of the building, gulping in huge draughts of exhaust-filled air. Finally, she felt able to hail a cab.

She knew the two would leave here, go to Oodles for lunch, and devour sandwiches laden with alfalfa sprouts. Gerald hated alfalfa.

Maggie wondered if she herself could ever eat again.

CHAPTER IX

Maggie, *The Reluctant Duke* in her lap, sat on the terrace, letting her eyes wander past the white chestnut blossoms, down the slope of the lawn to the flower beds, then up the slope of the knoll to the South Downs beyond. She felt she had to sit outside because Gerald and Miss Always worked inside on Saturdays. Since discovering romance novels at Victoria Station, Maggie had been reading them. In a romance, the heroine invariably caught and kept the hero.

Such heroines had spunk. Maggie compared herself and came up wanting. Not much spunk.

Maggie did have Sticktoitiveness. Her Aunt Maude had put that next to Presence and capitalized it as well.

Of course, heroines, in their eagerness "to put the past behind them, to get on with their lives," showed almost too much spunk. Maggie would have liked to know that they experienced pain and guilt and hatred.

Even so, the heroines were fighters. Miss Always, Maggie had to admit, would make a good romance heroine. She knew what she wanted and went after it. Maggie just dug in her heels and wouldn't let go, rather like Felicity with Robin's bone. Nothing romantic in that stance, Maggie had to admit.

She rose, put her book on the wicker table, and picked up her large green garden hat. Then she took up her gloves and trowel and walked barefoot across the soft green grass, still damp from dew, down to the ring of multi-coloured flowers near the birdbath. The rich red, pink and white rhododendrons would soon give way to lavender campanula, mauve Canterbury bells, and vivid blue delphiniums. She knelt to weed.

She loved all her flowers but in particular the roses. She had already added a section of old roses, varieties that had graced English gardens centuries before. These were not as showy as modern hybrids, more like little pink cabbages, but Maggie was a purist, preferring authenticity.

One patch of flowers, next to the red rhododendrons, clashed with the others — Miss Always's patch of yellow pansies.

Maggie felt that the garden, except for the one discordant blemish, affirmed her. She spent as much time in it as she could, escaping from the house that expressed her enemy.

She sat on her heels and looked back at the house, where Gerald and Miss Always worked. In a kind of weird flash, Maggie realized what she should have known. Miss Always had bought this house for herself and Gerald. Maggie was the interloper. Mother of God, what a strange feeling that thought gave her.

She kept weeding, her trowel sinking easily into the soft earth. How strange, she thought, when we look from a different angle. Suddenly things we took for granted are not so at all. And we see hidden meanings everywhere.

Gerald had had no right to displace Maggie from her house in Hollywood. She ought to have fought him on her home ground. She'd acted weakly. Not with the spunk of romance heroines. But she hadn't then known what she was fighting.

Surely she and Gerald had long since become warp and woof of the same cloth, their pasts too intricately woven to be separated without destroying the entire piece. The fabric might have weakened a little, but it was still good.

Gerald no longer took marriage as seriously as Maggie. He'd implied recently that it was not a spiritual bonding but just a habit. Perhaps he was right. But giving up a habit of thirty years would tear Maggie apart. Even heroin addicts got methodone. What could she take that would help her over the hellish nights and days of withdrawal? Who would mercifully administer the antidote?

She didn't know what love was any more, but she could understand addiction.

Now she also had a suspicion, from comments by Miss Always, that the two were up to some strange manipulations at Lloyd's. Lord Wizzell and Mr. Normington seemed to figure in them and had been invited to lunch next Saturday. She hoped she was wrong, but Lloyd's structure offered a temptation to underwriters to tamper with funds.

Maggie sat up, took off her sun hat and gloves, wiped her brow with the back of her hand, and looked about her. From where she worked, the lawn stretched back to the house. Across the lawn came Miss Always, golden hair streaming about her face. Maggie shuddered as if seeing a worm on one of her roses.

Miss Always wobbled on stiletto heels, which punctured the perfect green surface of the lawn. Her short leather skirt was so tight she took tiny steps, making twice as many perforations as necessary. She walks on my lawn as if it is hers already, thought Maggie.

Miss Always waved at Maggie, and Maggie waved back.

Felicity romped at Miss Always's side. This made Maggie furious. She had left the puppy with Mrs. Butterfield, since Felicity dug up flowers as tenaciously as Maggie did weeds. What right did Miss Always have to bring Felicity with her? Did she plan on confiscating her spaniel as well as her husband and house and garden?

"Good morning, Maggie," Miss Always sang. She appeared always cheerful, always smiling. But her happiness never struck Maggie as genuine.

"Good morning, Miss Always," Maggie responded

after quickly slipping on Acceptance. She'd wait this out and hope Gerald would tire of Miss Always.

"I hope you don't mind my calling you Maggie? Gerald said I should." While Felicity dug up a rhododendron, Miss Always plucked at a deep red petal.

Her little-girl manner of speaking sounded ludicrous in the honey-rich voice. Maggie still expected her to squeak.

"Maggie, you can call me..."

"How can I help you, Miss Always?" Maggie cut her off and snatched up Felicity. She didn't want to know Miss Always's first name. Gerald didn't dare use it. If it was never uttered, if Miss Always possessed a surname only, Maggie had a fighting chance.

Miss Always looked at Maggie questioningly. Maggie realized Acceptance was not very cordial. She held Felicity in one arm and shielded her eyes from the sun with the other. What was Robin's spell? Arbadacarba?

"Gerald wanted me to tell you that he'll be going into town this afternoon." She added breathlessness to the honeyed tones. A nervous laugh bubbled to the surface.

"What a shame, when you came all the way to the country to work with him."

"Oh, yes. But we'll go back to London about five." Another bubble of laughter. "There's a shitty evening meeting."

"I see," said Acceptance. "I know all about evening meetings, especially on Saturday."

"Oh?" Miss Always clearly didn't know how to take Acceptance. But she finally said, "Good."

Discretion, that's what the two think they're practicing, Maggie decided. They think I don't know, and what I don't know can't hurt me. But Miss Always is taking Gerald's time. And she's taking Gerald's energy. I have only the empty shell that comes home tired from late night meetings.

When Miss Always did not leave, Maggie, still holding Felicity in one arm, edged on her knees to the pansy patch and with great pleasure uprooted each plant, one by one.

Mesmerized, Miss Always let her breath out with a faint, "Bloody hell." When every plant was dislodged, she stepped across the lawn — a little less cheerily, Maggie thought, than when she had come — making fresh tracks, like an animal. Halfway, she turned and said, "Well, goodbye then."

Thinking of the time reminded Maggie to collect Mr. Beveridge for his weekly visit. Father Humphrey, the priory priest, had given her the name of this shut-in who had a Tartar of a wife and needed occasionally to escape. Maggie had found him such an interesting character — a one-time vaudeville song and dance man — that she looked forward to bringing him to her garden.

Robin had said he'd come today to entertain Mr. Beveridge, and Maggie felt uneasy. She worried about Robin. Should she let him keep visiting, keep practicing his magic? Was she becoming too fond of him?

As she hurried upstairs, she noticed her Steuben crystal lion on the entrance hall table. She'd put it in the drawing room only last week. Why did Mrs. Butterfield constantly move pieces in the crystal collection? Maggie had asked her not even to dust them. And where had the pieces got to?

Maggie loved the purity of crystal. People often thought that crystal with colour was to be prized, but it was just the opposite. The pieces with the least colour created the most interesting patterns with natural light.

Come to think, she hadn't seen her panther or her swan lately.

She changed into comfortable trousers and was soon

driving the Mercedes down country lanes, lined with thorn hedge, to the appalling house of Mr. Beveridge's daughter and son-in-law.

They never took the old man outside, said he didn't like to go out. Said in their back lawn he'd see only weeds.

Maggie pulled up to the depressing brick council flat. The doorbell was broken, so Maggie knocked. Mrs. Beveridge grudgingly opened the door a crack as she wiped her hands on a dirty flowered housedress.

"It's surprising you'd come here to the likes of this house." She opened the door a little wider and peered with sharp eyes through wisps of brownish-red hair, white roots showing. "And in that big car."

She always said that. Then she opened the door wider still, a frown on her face. "Is it nice enough out to be taking Da?" She always said that, too.

She turned toward the room, "Here, Harry, that woman's here again. Go git Da."

Harry, in his undershirt, lay propped on a worn brown couch in front of the telly. He got up slowly and scratched his stomach.

"So you're takin' the old man, are you?"

He always said this as his wife, all spindly and beige and lifeless, stood silently in the kitchen door.

Maggie helped by carrying the collapsible wheelchair to the car and putting it into the trunk. Then Harry came, bearing Mr. Beveridge, frail, with an unhealthy pallor, withered skin hanging on his face and arms. Maggie couldn't imagine those feet tapping, those arms swinging. And today she couldn't imagine what had happened to his hair, which had turned a shocking pink. Since no one acted as if anything were out of the ordinary, Maggie decided she had better wait to ask.

Not too soon for Maggie, she and Mr. Beveridge were

driving back to the Hall. She didn't try to converse on the journey because he was hard of hearing. She imagined he liked to enjoy the countryside in private.

Once home, a glum Mrs. Butterfield helped Maggie get the wheelchair set up and Mr. Beveridge into it.

"That Gypsy boy's been in the tree again," she grumbled.

"Oh, dear," said Maggie. "I hope you told him to come down."

"Ain't my business. My, no. If he wants to live up there, that's his concern. And those crystal pieces you always say I move or take? Well, I think he's the one who does it. Make no mistake, Gypsies is thieves."

"Thieves?" shouted Mr. Beveridge. "A body's not safe anywhere these days."

Maggie wrapped the car rug round his legs so he wouldn't get a chill. Then she pushed the wheelchair to the back garden and down the slight slope towards the flowerbeds.

"Are you enjoying today, Mr. Beveridge?" She yelled, sounding as cheery as Miss Always as she pushed him across the lawn and towards the rhododendrons.

"Yes, yes."

"What have you done to your hair, Mr. Beveridge?"

"What?"

"Your hair!"

"Wife tried a new dye."

Maggie faced him, carefully mouthing her words.

"Surely this isn't a dye on the market?"

"Mixed two or three, I think. Maybe more. Knows not to put it on her now."

"I should think so."

"Really? You like it? Think she should try it, do you?"

"Well, perhaps not." Maggie looked down at peaks of

orangey-pink, quite as colourful as her rhododendrons.

She pushed past the birdbath and, using all her strength, she struggled up the knoll, where they had a lovely view of the downs. Then she sat on the ground beside his chair.

"The colour can be changed," she assured him.

"Oh, no. They'll be this colour all summer."

"I mean your hair."

"Oh, that. Don't matter. Wife always tries things out on me first."

"Don't you mind?" He looked so very frail, as if he should mind.

"Well, I used to when I was younger. Then I got to thinking. What the hell's the difference? I thought. And since I couldn't see the difference, I gave up bothering myself about it."

"That's very philosophical."

"Hell, it's plain horse sense. Life's a sight more peaceful now."

Maggie liked watching Mr. Beveridge as he enjoyed her garden. Gerald called the old man "Maggie's stray." He called Robin that as well. "I see you're wasting your time again on your strays," he'd said only last night.

What was a waste of time and what was not? Maggie wondered. Did Gerald's lying between Miss Always's white thighs, listening to her honey-rich laughter, gain him points in the Hereafter for worthwhile usage of time?

Robin's call interrupted her musing. He ran across the lawn, Felicity after him, his golden chain catching glints of sunlight.

"I learned a new trick," he called as he threw a stick for Felicity to catch.

"What's that he says?" asked Mr. Beveridge.

"Trick," Maggie told him, wishing Robin wouldn't

show them.

"Boys shouldn't play tricks."

"This is magic."

"Don't believe in magic."

Maggie sighed. They would both get magic whether Mr. Beveridge believed in it or not.

Wearing his tall silk hat, Robin stared down at Maggie. The icy green of his eyes in the warm light made the striations pronounced. Then he smiled knowingly.

"You will want to see, won't you?"

"This is Mr. Beveridge."

Robin shook the old man's hand.

"Don't believe in magic, boy. And I hate magicians. There used to be a magician in the last vaudeville show I was in. I was the real entertainer. I danced. I sang. Made folks laugh, made them cry, made them applaud. Then one day that damned magician forgot to cage his rabbit after his act. It hopped onto the stage while I was dancing. I didn't see it, tripped, and fell off the stage. Hurt something in my back, I did. Ain't never danced again." He paused, caught in another time.

Coming back to the moment and focusing on Robin, he reiterated, "Don't believe in magic."

Robin eyed him cynically and unsympathetically said, "That's all right. You can watch anyway." He took off his hat and placed it on the ground, then called to Felicity.

"Oh, no you don't!" said Maggie in alarm.

"You do believe, don't you?"

"Can a person fit in that hat?" Beveridge asked.

Robin laughed.

"Depends on the person."

"Could you get me into it and wave me off somewhere where I wouldn't need this damned contraption?"

Robin stared at him and thought for a moment.

"Where there are others with pink hair?"

"Can't do it, can you?" Beveridge shook a fist at him. "Think you're clever. Can't do real magic when it's called for."

Robin took no notice.

"About my trick..." he said to Maggie.

"Perhaps another time?" She felt nervous.

Robin, taking no notice, drew his wand from his back pocket.

"You won't pull anything from the hat that will spoil my lawn or flowerbeds?"

Robin glanced back at the yellow pansies strewn on the lawn, then turned and grinned at her.

"I think somebody's already done that. Scarf please."

Maggie reluctantly untied the navy one at her neck.

He grabbed it, threw it over the hat and chanted his magic while waving the wand.

Finally, Robin raised an arm triumphantly into the air.

As he laughed and danced round the hat, Felicity barking and gamboling with him, the scarf moved, first slowly, then fitfully.

Maggie stared, biting her thumb.

Beveridge, through some magic of his own, had mentally left for a different setting taking no notice of them.

At last Robin whisked off the scarf, and Maggie could see... nothing. She crept a little closer to peer in, but she saw only the hat's lining.

"What's... what's in there?"

Robin chuckled, picked up the hat, held it upside down.

"What was under the scarf?"

"Why did something have to be under it?"

"It moved."

"That was the magic."

"Oh, I see." Maggie sat back, not seeing at all. "I don't think I like that trick."

"It's not easy to do." Robin collapsed on the ground

beside her and pulled Felicity onto his lap.

"Then why do it?" Maggie felt let down and cross. Her scarf dancing about on its own. Nonsense.

"It's an advanced trick, harder than any of the others."

Maggie could hear the hurt in his voice.

"Well, I suppose it was very good," she consoled him.

"It's just that I'm getting tired of the easy tricks like this one." He jumped up, reached into his hat, raised his arm, and out came a violin.

"But Robin, how can this be? A violin can't fit…" Her voice trailed off as she remembered Felicity in that hat.

Tucking the violin under his arm, he pulled out the bow. As Felicity cocked her ears and growled, Robin adjusted the instrument under his chin and began to play what sounded like a mournful Gypsy air, as if he had caught Maggie's mood. The music sang of purple and brown hills — dark, mysterious, beckoning — only far, far away. Passages swelled with overwhelming desire and dipped with inexpressible loss as they told of love as distant as the hills.

Playing the final note with a flourish, Robin slipped the bow into his tall silk hat and followed it with the instrument. Then he plunked next to Maggie again.

"Remarkable, Robin."

"In magic, things are never what they seem."

Maggie thought of Miss Always and Gerald.

"They rarely are in life either," she said bitterly. She took Mr. Beveridge's wrist and felt his pulse to be sure he was still with them. He did go off like this every so often. But she supposed anyone would do the same, given a Tartar of a wife who dyed one's hair shocking pink.

Still, nothing was ever one-sided. Maggie wondered what she herself did that sent Gerald to the unsuitable world of Miss Always.

CHAPTER X

July arrived, and Maggie's buying of hats continued, with Gerald none the wiser, for he never entered the mask room. If he had, in only a few weeks he would have found twelve hats, the most expensive money could buy, all arranged under labels denoting mood. The saleswomen loved Maggie, for nothing struck her as too extreme or too expensive. She looked only for what became her and what could hide her mask when necessary. She also thought in terms of what suited her masks. A wonderful broadbrimmed blue straw became Remote remarkably. And a saucy little pale green thing with wisps of veil and flowers was adorable on Interested and Entertained. She even looked forward to an autumn and winter collection of hats.

In the garden, raspberries prickled on their stems. Mornings when she wasn't playing sleuth, Maggie, a large basket beside her, would kneel at the back of the garden with Mrs. Butterfield, plucking them.

"Lor, ma'am, this is hard on my rheumatism."

"I'm sure it is, Mrs. Butterfield. I'd suggest some other activity but everything you do, even sitting at the table for your numerous cups of tea, is hard on it, wouldn't you say?"

"Indeed, that's the truth of it. Some were meant to suffer."

And some were meant to chatter about suffering whether they did it or not, thought Maggie. Mrs. Butterfield had the constitution of a horse. The post each day saw her, agile as a young girl in her hurry to fetch it. Not that she received letters, but she loved to look at the postmarks of the letters for Maggie and Gerald. Maggie supposed that mail from foreign places was a topic of much importance to Mrs. Butterfield's cronies.

"That Gypsy boy's been in the tree again."

"I wish you would tell me when that happens, Mrs. Butterfield. And do try to get him down."

"Ain't none of my concern."

"Well, you always tell me after the fact."

"If you want a thief about, it's one thing. But to blame me for that missing crystal is another."

"I have never blamed you, Mrs. Butterfield."

"Not in so many words. But in your heart you do. Starts up my rheumatism something awful."

The garden buzzed with insects. A large bumblebee flew past Maggie's head. Felicity yapped and swatted at it.

Sitting back on her heels, Maggie breathed in the splash of colours and lush fecundity of her garden. So much green, after the brown hills of Hollywood, amazed her.

Outside, she watched the flowers and fruit and baby birds grow. Inside she watched the relationship between Gerald and Miss Always blossom. Maggie herself seemed at a standstill.

Saturday usually meant that she spread delectables on the luncheon table while, with stealthy glances and nods, Gerald and Miss Always put aside their shared facts and figures.

Today Maggie had decided on a spinach quiche and tossed salad. She would serve Gerald's favourite rolls with raspberry jam, and a jello fruit mould with sour cream for dessert. Fruits and vegetables from her garden, prepared in her kitchen. The only two spots that did not belong to Miss Always.

Maggie hated serving her bounty to her enemy. But she had time. She'd wait this out. Wouldn't notice anything. Sometimes she felt it was better that she and Gerald had moved to England, where Maggie didn't have well-meaning neighbours to tell her of Gerald's affair. "Persistence pays," her aunt used to say, and Maggie kept her heels dug in, making sure no one knew what she saw.

As Maggie mused, Felicity scooted about the garden after birds. Catching nothing, she rushed up, flung herself at Maggie, then jumped into the basket of berries, tipping the basket and sending those berries she hadn't squashed, rolling on the ground.

Mrs. Butterfield took immediate affront at this, as if Felicity had deliberately planned to give her rheumatoid joints more work. She glared at the redstained Felicity. "And me with the rising damp in Mr. Featherstone's study to worry about."

"Don't fret, Mrs. Butterfield. I'll clean her up."

"But the berries. And we was to make more jam this morning." She wiped her eyes with the back of her hand, then blew her nose on her checkered apron.

While Mrs. Butterfield, with total lack of alacrity, returned to picking the remaining berries, Maggie scooped up Felicity and took her to the conservatory, where she kept a tub to wash the puppy.

"Stay there," she commanded as she ran to the kitchen for boiling water to add to that from the garden hose. But Felicity trailed Maggie like a shadow and was soon rubbing raspberry juice against kitchen chairs, while Maggie heated the electric kettle.

"Come along then." Giving up hope of a stain-free smock, Maggie put Felicity under her left arm, picked up the kettle in her right hand, and marched to the conservatory.

Maggie wet Felicity thoroughly and squeezed out baby shampoo, briskly rubbing it into the puppy's coat. Felicity squirmed, then turned and yapped loudly.

Maggie looked up, startled to see two men watching

her. One, short and dapper, had grey hair, a grey moustache, and a grey complexion. His well-worn grey suit with vest looked like something out of the Edwardian period, and he carried a grey bowler hat. His companion, a large black man with a moustache and beard, wore ragged blue jeans and a colourful red flowered shirt and red bandana.

"Goodbye," said the black man, pleasantly.

The little grey man stepped forward and, with a flourish of his bowler, made a slight bow.

"He means 'hello'. He says where he comes from, the two greetings are reversed. I think perhaps he sees things in reverse."

"Oh?" said Maggie, bewildered.

"We're here to do odd jobs, madam," continued the little grey man. "Have you any work for us?"

Maggie hesitated as Felicity's wiggling sent suds flying into her face. "Well..." They didn't seem to be up to any mischief.

"Work's hard to find, madam," said the little grey man, his partner standing mute. "We can do about anything."

"We planned to paint the garden fences," said Maggie, knowing Gerald would be furious. "Would that be something you could handle?" She rinsed Felicity. "Paint and workclothes are in the tool shed." She supposed they were wearing their only clothes.

"Yes, madam," said the grey man with a broad smile.

His friend mumbled something, then pulled a drawing from his knapsack and held it up for Maggie's inspection, while Felicity splashed. Maggie, her hands occupied, bent sideways and studied it, not sure which way was up. He had drawn any number of lines and created amazing but disturbing patterns. She looked at him for some explanation.

"The world," said the grey man. "This is the way he sees the world — all confusion."

"Does he?" said Maggie. "It's much the same way I see it."

With a cracked pitcher, she poured clear water over Felicity. Then she tried to keep the puppy from squirming out of her arms as she wrapped her in a towel and held her.

"World quarreled on us," said the black man in a baritone as he studied his drawing.

The world had certainly seemed to quarrel on him, Maggie thought.

"How do you two happen to be together?"

The grey man cleared his throat.

"We met on the road. My friend escaped an institution of sorts, said he'd had shock treatment, though he appears very alert to me. At any rate, no one claims him, and he does need some looking after."

The black man smiled.

"I look after friend." He put his arm round the older man's shoulders.

"He certainly does, madam. I'm very fortunate."

"And your names?"

"I'm Mr. Dunkley," said the grey man with another little bow. A peer of the realm could not have introduced himself with more self-possession.

"Your Christian name?"

"Oh, madam, never seek to know it. My lips are sealed on that point." He quickly turned to his companion. "This is Mongoose."

"Mongoose?" Maggie asked, alarmed at the idea of an animal that stole.

"I'm no t'ief." The black man looked worried.

"Let me explain," said Mr. Dunkley, whose self-important manner fascinated Maggie. "Mongoose got his nickname on the Caribbean island he once called home, though we don't know which island. He sings one song. It seems to be all he knows — a song about the mongoose. So apparently someone started calling him that, and the name, shall we say, stuck."

"Mongoose." The black man smiled and nodded.

"Yes... well, it's a little early, but I expect you'll want sandwiches and coffee before starting on heavy work."

"That would be appreciated, madam," Mr. Dunkley answered.

His cheerfulness made Maggie feel a little guilty.

"Mrs. Butterfield," she called. "We have two for... brunch."

As a grumbling Mrs. Butterfield led them to the kitchen, Mr. Dunkley strutted at Mongoose's side. The black man strode with a graceful rhythm and sang:

Sly Mongoose, dog know your ways.
Sly Mongoose, dog know your tricks.
Mongoose went in t'e farmer's kitchen,
T'ief out one of t'e fattest chickens,
Put him into his waistcoat pocket.
Sly Mongoose.

The song did not allay Maggie's apprehension.

"Felicity," she finished towel-drying the puppy, "you'd better keep an eye on them."

While Mrs. Butterfield put the finishing touches to lunch, Maggie rushed to her mask shelf. What should she wear? She picked up Anticipation, then put it aside. She had only last week fashioned Non-committal. Perhaps that would do, though she felt more like Non-compliant.

Adjusting her mask, she hurried back to the dining room just as the couple was entering. Maggie sat at one end of the table, careful to avoid the griffins, and Gerald at the other with Miss Always, as always, between them. Maggie noticed that Miss Always's golden hair seemed especially bouncy today and tumbled onto her yellow sweater, accenting rather than concealing the torpedo tits that did not seem to need a bra, perhaps had never experienced one.

Soon, very soon, Gerald would wake up, and Miss Always — her golden hair swirling about her — would blow from the house in a cyclone-like, sickly yellow swirl, never to be seen again.

Gerald looked particularly Italian today in his dark blue sweater and white slacks. The colours suited his thick, dark hair with bits of grey at the temples. His brown eyes, smiling and soft in contrast to the lines around them, made his face look very alive, very lived in. He sat sipping white Bordeau with complete insouciance, smoothing his onetime moustache, reminding Maggie of the photographs taken in Siena. As Maggie gazed at him, she herself felt Italian in her scarlet trouser outfit with long flowing scarf.

Suddenly, Gerald leaned down, his head almost hitting the table, peered out the window and became quite English.

"Who's that painting the fence?"

Felicity growled.

"You said it needed painting," said Maggie. "You even bought the paint." She checked to see that Non-committal was in place.

"They look like odd workers. Who recommended them?"

"Their references seemed impeccable." She turned and looked to see her workmen in coveralls, one wearing a grey bowler, the other a wide-brimmed straw hat with a red band and a matching red bandana at his neck.

"I could have sent a painting firm," chirruped Miss Always. "It's best to hire a firm, then someone is responsible for the fucking idiots."

Gerald laughed and looked at her as if she'd said something adorable.

He'd throw a fit if I talked like that, thought Maggie. She felt hurt that he had obviously set limits regarding what he'd accept from her, that he refused to think what she said was endearing.

"Precisely," said Gerald. "A firm would have been the answer. Darling, if you would just let Miss Always handle such things." He smiled at his secretary. As he turned that smile on Maggie, his Italian teeth shrank to English teeth and his large brown eyes narrowed and stopped shining. "Just where did you find them, my angel?"

"I think they're quite good. Eager. Willing."

Colourful, she thought.

Mrs. Butterfield brought in bowls of a clear broth and harumphed at Maggie.

Gerald took a mouthful of soup, then put down his spoon.

"They're not more of your strays?"

"I don't know what you're talking about."

"They're tramps, aren't they?"

"I don't think of them that way at all." Maggie twirled her scarf nonchalantly. How Non-committal remained in place under the circumstance she could not tell. "I think of them as free spirits, travelling about the countryside seeking work."

"If they were good workers, they wouldn't need to travel about the countryside."

Gerald sounded awfully prissy at times, Maggie

thought. "Gerald, you know how many worthy people are out of work these days, and not just in this country."

"I don't agree. Industrious people with the right attitudes get jobs." Gerald put his spoon down and pushed his soup aside.

"Oh, yes." Miss Always popped a ripe olive into her mouth and chewed it daintily while they waited for her contribution. She added nothing more.

"By the way, exactly what do you think I'm doing," Gerald snapped, "when I write our rather large check to charity each month? Larger than necessary because of you." He looked at Maggie condescendingly. The effect was spoiled somewhat by her knowledge that his anger had upset his stomach.

"I think we're salving our consciences."

"Nonsense," he grumbled as Mrs. Butterfield plunked down the salad and quiche and started to clear away the soup bowls.

"That's all right then." Miss Always handed Mrs. Butterfield her empty soup bowl, obviously glad that a serious conversation had come to an end.

"We ought to aid individuals," insisted Maggie as she passed the quiche. She noticed that Gerald took almost nothing. He would never mention his indigestion in front of Miss Always.

"That's not our job," he countered. "Organizations exist to handle these things."

"How does our check assist those two out there?"

"That's academic."

"It's somebody's job to help those two, and no one has done it."

"So you take them on. More strays." Gerald shook his head helplessly. "And Mrs. Butterfield tells me that Robin fellow is here most days with his magic tricks, when you could be making valuable friends for us." He rubbed his forehead as if the thought gave him a headache. "And she said he steals. I thought you valued your crystal collection more than that. I just hope one of your strays doesn't murder us in our beds."

That might be a job for them at that, thought Maggie maliciously. Miss Always strangled with her own dyed golden locks, while Gerald watches.

"You're not listening. I say, Maggie!"

"What?" Oh, Mother of God! Non-committal had slipped. She surreptitiously slid it into place.

"I said, you're not listening. And you're not eating."

He shoved his own plate aside. "Somebody's got to enjoy this quiche."

He looked at Maggie, his eyes saying, "I certainly can't." She'd known he'd have to find a way to blame her for his indigestion.

"I'm enjoying mine." Miss Always reached for another roll.

"Maggie," Gerald shifted in his chair as he shifted thoughts, "Miss Always has been regaling me with little stories about her childhood, how she used to poke hedgehogs with a stick to see them curl into a ball."

Miss Always nodded and smiled.

Maggie felt queasy. Mother of God, he's treating her as if she's a child, as if she's demented. Maggie stared hard at Miss Always. Leave it to Gerald to be fooled by hair dye in his search for youth. It would be a pity if some of Mrs. Beveridge's pink concoction found its way into Miss Always's bottle.

"Darling, you've left us again."

How sweet Gerald sounded now. She looked up but had to wonder how Gerald was going to find her in Miss Always's eyes. She felt sick.

"I think I shall actually have to leave you," Maggie got up, her napkin over her mouth. She rushed from the room, flinging off Non-committal as she ran. That mask was totally inadequate.

After bathing her face in cold water, she headed shakily towards the garden, but stopped in surprise upon seeing Gerald near the patio with Mongoose. Gerald seemed furious.

Maggie started over, then decided to wait a moment and listen.

"Goodbye," said Mongoose pleasantly.

"Good, you understand you're to go!" Gerald spoke slowly and loudly.

Mongoose nodded happily.

"Yes."

"Right away," said Gerald.

"Yes," said Mongoose, smiling.

"I don't think you understand," said Gerald, exasperated. "Is your friend here? Maybe he can understand."

"No," said Mongoose.

"Where is he?"

"Here," said Mongoose.

Maggie smiled at Gerald's consternation. To her, Mongoose made sense. They had just been watching Mr. Dunkley in the side garden, and he was here at Raven Hall.

"God," said Gerald, putting his head in his hands.

"Paint fence now." Mongoose smiled, tipped his hat, and sauntered away, his long limbs moving rhythmically.

"No, not paint fence, you dunce."

Mongoose didn't turn back.

Maggie approached Gerald. "Please leave it, Gerald. I didn't fire Mrs. Butterfield, whom Miss Always hired. I don't expect you to fire people I hire. This is my concern."

"I won't have strange people like that in my house."

And I don't like the strange person you invite to my house, Maggie thought.

She stood looking out at her garden, listening to the bleat of sheep in distant fields, and the titlarks and robins in her own trees. Summer meant fecundity, light, warmth. Yet her own summer at Raven Hall seemed to foreshadow winter with its desolation and despair.

In mid-afternoon, Gerald took Miss Always to the Hassocks station, a trip that lasted a couple of hours; whereas Maggie could do the run in twenty minutes. Of course, he listed the necessary stops on the journey there and back.

"The Mercedes gave out on me again," he would say. "Wouldn't you know I'd get a lemon." Didn't he realize that Maggie knew the mechanic was closed Saturday afternoons?

Maggie hurried out to her new workers. She wanted to reach them before Gerald got home.

She found that they'd completed a sizeable amount of painting and had done a splendid job.

"You're very good," she said.

"Yes, madam," said Mr. Dunkley. "We work hard. I hope you want us back tomorrow?"

"Where will you stay tonight?"

"Well… we thought… in the village… You see, we have sleeping bags."

"You don't have a place?"

"No, madam, we do not. However, we are enterprising and will come up with something. And if not, the stars overhead make a fine canopy on a summer's night."

"But a chilly one. You could stay here, you know, in that

room next to the conservatory. I've been storing some boxes... if you wouldn't mind moving them to the garage?"

Mr. Dunkley beamed, his grey face taking on some colour in the late afternoon light.

"Thank you kindly. Your thoughtfulness is much appreciated."

Maggie thought he sounded rather like a talking business letter and wondered what he had once done for a living.

"It's just that... well, you see my..." Maggie hesitated.

"Your husband, madam?"

"Precisely."

"Have no fear. We shall stay well out of the way. He'll never notice we're about."

"Good. I thought you might take over the gardener's duties as well." She'd get rid of one of Miss Always's finds. "Now about wages." She handed Mr. Dunkley several pounds. "I expect you'll need this now. Then we'll work out the appropriate wage."

"Admirable, madam. Admirable."

"Good. Mrs. Butterfield will give you supper in the kitchen when you're ready."

"World quarreled on us," intoned Mongoose, shaking his head.

"No," said Mr. Dunkley, "the world is smiling on us now."

As she walked back to the house, Maggie could hear the Carribbean song:

Sly Mongoose, dog know your ways.
Sly Mongoose, dog know your tricks.

CHAPTER XI

Lord Wizzell arrived first in his Jaguar. As he parked in the front drive, a taxi drove up with Mr. Normington. Maggie, watching from the drawing room window, decided both men appeared as gloomy and tense as Gerald. Even so, she couldn't help smiling at how odd they looked walking next to each other: Lord Wizzell, immense in an ill-fitting, wrinkled grey suit, his bushy red and white mustachio concealing his mouth and nostrils, and Mr. Normington, small, pale, nattily dressed in navy blue, his dark hair smoothed down with too much hair cream.

Watching their troubled faces, Maggie recalled that Miss Always had also seemed upset when she'd arrived. And yet Maggie had been told nothing. They had a secret, an ominous insurance syndicate secret, a syndicate that Gerald headed as active underwriter; and Maggie felt real danger for herself and him.

As Mrs. Butterfield, looking as glum as the two men, led them into the drawing room, Gerald and Miss Always entered.

"Ah, George," Gerald extended his hand to Lord Wizzell. "And Harold. Good of you both to come. Hate to have you give up a Saturday."

"Let's all have a sherry," said Miss Always, who wore a ruffled pale blue dress, a matching ribbon in her hair. "Maggie, shall I pour?"

Maggie decided her enemy, blonde hair streaming, looked as if she were trying to be Alice in Wonderland. Instead of answering, she walked over to the men, who warmed themselves by the fire. While Miss Always busied herself with drinks from the portable bar in one corner, Maggie attempted to greet her guests.

"We're in this together, Gerald," said Lord Wizzell,

twirling his red and white moustachio with his left hand and giving Maggie his right. "Damned exciting, I say."

"Difficult to pull off, but a great opportunity," Gerald replied, clearly enthusiastic about Lord Wizzell's backing.

"Yes, yes, difficult," agreed Mr. Normington meekly, extending a limp hand for someone to shake, presumably Maggie.

"I say..." Maggie tried to break in, but realized she wore Invisible. In a group of men discussing business, every woman wears it, she decided.

"All for one and one for all, what?" added Mr. Normington, though he didn't look happy about it. Maggie recalled his large, commanding wife with blue-white hair carefully waved, and decided he was often forced to agree.

Invisible or not, she could hold off no longer. "Gentlemen," she shouted as she would to Mr. Beveridge, deciding that if she couldn't be seen, she must make herself heard, "what is this about?"

Abruptly, the men stopped talking and turned startled faces to her. "You can't imagine how difficult it is to get Gerald to tell me his business secrets," she laughed.

"Maggie," Miss Always put a hand on her shoulder as she handed her a sherry, "you don't want to know. All hush, hush. Wouldn't do for someone outside the syndicate to hear."

"But I already know you're up to something. And I'm automatically involved with the syndicate through Gerald."

"Maggie," Gerald said sternly.

Mr. Normington, looking uncomfortable, sidled across the room to the window and gazed out.

"I say," he said, "that fellow I saw when I arrived, the one out there trimming the hedge? Where did you find him?"

Gerald choked on his swallow of Tio Pepe.

"What does he look like?"

He thinks Mr. Normington has seen Mongoose in his strange attire, thought Maggie. In the business world, everyone is supposed to look like everyone else. Even the gardeners must be a certain type. The only ones who can look different, and even decidedly scruffy, are the Lord Wizzells of the world, who can get away with spots on their suits, since they have Blood with a capital "B."

"Don't you know who I mean?" Mr. Normington appeared confused as if he might be seeing an apparition. "He's shorter than I am…"

Certainly not, thought Maggie.

"Yes, dreadfully short… grey hair, grey moustache."

"Oh, him. One of the gardeners," said Gerald.

"That can't be." Mr. Normington peered out to catch another glimpse. "He was a solicitor, don't you see."

"Impossible." Gerald laughed.

"I never forget a face. He practiced divorce law some years ago. My wife and I were separated. Oh, it's no secret. You see, I love to tango." His pointed nose twitched, his eyes gazed heavenward and his cupid mouth curled into a smile. "And very good I am, too." He put his arms out, stood on his toes like a toreador and performed gliding tango steps. Bumping into Gerald, he stopped, smoothed down his already smooth hair and cleared his throat. "But Mrs. Normington won't dance. I can tell you the strain on me was severe. I had thought, don't you know, that one could tango through life with one's partner." He cleared his throat again, making a small, high, raspy sound. "At any rate, that fellow out there was the solicitor. I couldn't forget a thing like that."

"Was he any good?" Miss Always asked.

"Well, no. That is, I think if you pay someone to do a thing, they ought to do it." Mr. Normington gave a little sigh. "Naturally, Mrs. Normington and I are devoted to each other." He ran a finger under his collar as if it hurt his neck. "Nevertheless, he didn't do his job right. Not right at all. I hope he doesn't ruin your hedge."

As they stood sipping their second glasses of sherry, Maggie realized they had divided into two groups: Gerald and Miss Always by the fire; Maggie, Wizzell, and Normington by the window. Normington was stroking her arm, running his fingers from her wrist to her elbow in a gentle caress. She shivered.

"Maggie," said Lord Wizzell, "One of the things I admired about you was that you weren't one of those modern women who poke their noses into men's business. Or so Gerald told us."

Maggie snatched her arm away from Mr. Normington and turned to Lord Wizzell.

"As you see, I'm very modern."

"But you don't... what was it those American women did, burn bras? You didn't do that, surely?"

Maggie was certainly not going to tell him that she felt more comfortable in a bra so wouldn't burn one. Mr. Normington was at her arm again, causing sensations she didn't want to feel. Whatever was she to do?

"Mr. Normington?" she turned to him.

He quickly pulled his hand away.

"Is your wife liberated?"

"Oh, yes."

As Maggie spoke to Mr. Normington, she felt Lord Wizzell blow into her ear.

Maggie whirled round, and when her back was turned, Mr. Normington moved his hip against hers.

Maggie swung back to him, just as Lord Wizzell gave

her derriere a pat and said softly, "I'm certainly one to give a woman her way. You'll find in England, my dear, you ladies have always been liberated."

Maggie turned round to face Lord Wizzell and received a little pinch on her arm from Mr. Normington.

"An example, Lord Wizzell?" What was she to do and still remain a good hostess?

"Look at... at..." he searched for a name, "...at those Bronte sisters. Yes, look at them for example." He chuckled low, and brushed a strand of hair from her cheek.

That these men felt they had the right to flirt, that Gerald wouldn't care, depressed and infuriated Maggie. Unable openly to insult Gerald's guests, she did the only thing possible, prove them wrong.

"Aren't you aware," she sputtered, "that the Brontes first published under men's names?"

"Oh, I say!" said Mr. Normington.

Maggie watched Lord Wizzell's face. That had done it. He turned a dark purple.

"You don't tango, do you?" whispered Normington.

"Yes, I do!" Maggie grabbed him and led the dance to where Gerald and Miss Always stood. How dare they put her in this situation? "Perhaps we should take up the tango, Gerald, darling. Mr. Normington can show us how it's done."

"Oh," said Mr. Normington, stepping back, edging two fingers into his collar, and rubbing his neck. He looked round the room, bewildered.

"Shit," said Miss Always, coming out of Wonderland.

"I see what you mean," said Maggie, looking at her pointedly. "There's so much furniture, we'd not be able to move. What a pity."

"My angel," Gerald's voice quaked with anger, "isn't lunch about ready?"

"Right. I must just see to things. You will excuse me?"

On her way to the kitchen, Maggie wondered if she'd prepared enough food. She'd forgot what a huge man George Wizzell was. On the other hand, Mr. Normington, small and thin, no doubt ate like a tit. But how dreadful of them to flirt so shamelessly.

Mrs. Butterfield summoned the guests and Maggie seated them, Lord Wizzell on Gerald's right, Miss Always on his left, since all three men couldn't be huddled together at one end of the table. That put Mr. Normington next to Miss Always and on Maggie's right.

The luncheon started smoothly. Mrs. Butterfield refrained from blowing her nose on her apron and actually served from the correct side. The vichyssoise tasted suitably chilled and the molded chicken salad kept its shape. Gerald acted charming as only Gerald could.

"I think," he said, "that we'll turn to Switzerland for the nominee."

"And the client will be?" asked Lord Wizzell.

"My name, of course," Gerald answered.

"Don't know that I agree with that," said Normington.

"It's all right," said Lord Wizzell. "It's Gerald's syndicate, after all. We're lucky to be a part of this."

"The re-insurance policies will be placed with the Jamaican company?" Mr. Normington sounded uneasy.

Lord Wizzell chuckled.

"Smart move that."

Gerald laughed as well.

"Especially as the holding company is in Denmark."

"You've created an admirable chain," said Wizzell.

"It sounds too mysterious," said Maggie.

"Nothing to interest you," Miss Always added quickly.

Lord Wizzell took a gulp of chardonnay. "We'll have to watch closely. If policies are called up too soon…"

"I don't like that," said Normington, his nose twitching.

"I have it under control." Gerald smiled confidently.

While Maggie watched Gerald, she wondered if indeed he had become taken in by his own charm. Lord Wizzell and Mr. Normington sat rapt in attention, clearly following his lead. And Miss Always was literally transported by Gerald's magic, an almost beatific smile on her face.

The men ignored Maggie, and again she felt invisible. They seemed to be creating a kind of black magic that frightened her.

As they finished berry sorbet and sipped on the last of the wine, Maggie gradually became aware that Miss Always's chair had moved towards Gerald's, and that Lord Wizzell's and Mr. Normington's had surreptitiously slid to Maggie's end of the table. She glanced to her right, and Normington smiled knowingly. To her left, Lord Wizzell twirled his moustachio and leered.

"It's so pleasant here." Lord Wizzell put a large hand over her own.

At the same time, under one griffin's giant thigh, Mr. Normington slid a small, stockinged foot, ready for play.

Maggie couldn't get her mind off the fact that she and Gerald had once tangoed through life but had not done so in a very long time. The old record shattered, the new rhythm quickened. Gerald now performed tricky steps, and Maggie could not comprehend their pattern.

"Let's go into the drawing room for coffee," she said.

"Just when we're becoming better acquainted?" Lord Wizzell's large foot struck at her from under a griffin's leg.

"Coffee." Maggie pushed her chair back.

She saw Lord Wizzell make a face and mouth "frigid" to Mr. Normington, who nodded his assent.

The conceit of men, she thought. They easily think if you haven't responded to them, you can't respond at all.

CHAPTER XII

Disgusted as they sometimes made her, Maggie continued her Cloak and Dagger trips to London. She felt she was saving Gerald. He didn't know it, but somehow her unseen presence was reminding him of their union. Of his real needs, his home.

And the trips fascinated her in a morbid sort of way. Is that how I once appeared with him, she wondered.

Today she stood in the entrance porch of the old Lloyd's building, across the street from the new structure. Gerald seemed always to use the Lime Street entrance. She'd see him from here. And she was hidden by the masses of people passing by.

She wore her Burberry raincoat, black boots, and a smart black rain hat pulled over one eye. Waiting for the two to appear, she shivered more from apprehension than from cold.

She didn't want to admit that by keeping Gerald in sight she kept some vestige of security. Oh, not monetary security. A hold on the past, on the future.

In her worst nightmares now she stood on a deck of a cruise ship. Suddenly on the deck of a passing liner, she saw Gerald. She called to him, reached out to him, but he stood gazing out to sea, apparently not seeing or hearing her. Frantically she looked at the faces of Gerald's fellow passengers. All blank. Only Gerald had a face, but he wouldn't turn it directly to her as he sailed into the distance amid streams of yellow confetti. She screamed, but the wind blew her cry back at her. A piece of confetti struck her eye, and she awoke crying.

She pulled her raincoat tighter about her neck and checked her watch: one-thirty. The couple was later than usual coming out. Several times Maggie was forced to open her newspaper and appear to be searching for some information, so no one would wonder why she stood in one place so long.

As her anticipation waned and her disappointment rose, she felt even colder. Should she leave? She had been so sure today would bring some revelation to Gerald that Miss Always was not for him.

Gerald's voice broke into her thoughts and she looked up from her paper to see him calling a taxi. One stopped. The two entered. Maggie quickly followed, hoping they'd pick some nice lunch spot for a change. She was starving.

Rain hit at Maggie's taxi, slowly progressing through heavy traffic. As the rain gradually increased, the driver turned on windshield wipers. They made a steady, almost musical beat to Maggie's pursuit of Gerald to Mayfair, through Carlos Place, to the Connaught Hotel.

Excellent, thought Maggie. I've been longing to visit the Grill Room.

She sat in her own taxi while the two rushed onto the porch, laughing and waving aside the doorman, then spun through the revolving door.

Maggie quickly paid her driver and hurried after them.

Inside, she found herself in a small, cream-coloured reception hall.

Then, as she brushed the rain from her coat, she saw the two directly before her… at the reception desk. She stared blankly as her mind took a minute to focus on this fact.

The only thought she had was that Miss Always's five-inch heels must have sunk into the lush, pale burgundy carpet, but they hadn't left tracks in the close pile as they had in her garden.

The desk clerk rang a bell and a valet, dressed in black, rushed up. Maggie stood immobile as he took a key and led the two toward an elevator.

Mother of God. They're not having lunch. Whatever shall I do?

It wasn't supposed to come to this. Today was Gerald's day for discovery, not hers.

Cloak and Dagger crashed to the floor and was kicked aside by a hotel guest, walking briskly to the exit. Maggie stumbled to one of the large cushioned chairs in an alcove and sank into it.

She stared down at the upholstery beneath her hands. She studied its varied reddish shades, like splashes of blood, she thought. Someone has yanked out my entrails.

In the cavity she felt an excruciating pain. She hugged her arms round her, but that didn't help.

She arose, shakily, and staggered to the revolving door, but could barely push her way out. Blindly, she floundered off the porch and into the rain, not seeing the doorman, who hailed her a taxi.

She headed home. But how long would home remain home?

As her taxi from the station rounded the drive, Maggie saw Father Humphrey's black Renault in front of the house. Mother of God, I invited him to tea. How could I have completely forgotten? How can I manage it?

Maggie rushed inside, shedding her raincoat and hat in the hallway.

"Father."

He rose from Miss Always's yellow chintz sofa and shook Maggie's hand. She led him to a rather uncomfortable hardbacked chair closer to the fireplace and lit the fire. She could not bear Miss Always's colours at the moment.

What was in the cupboard for tea, she wondered, and

could only remember a sorry piece of sponge cake with crumbling chocolate icing. Hopefully, Mrs. Butterfield would come up with something.

A movement outside caught her eye. Robin, hanging upside down from the tree, watched them. She ran to the window. "Go away. Shoo."

He disappeared in the leaves, but Maggie didn't see him climb down. "I don't know what to do about that neighbour boy. He may get hurt."

"I think he'll be all right. Just being a boy."

"But if he falls."

"You look upset about something else, my child."

"Oh, no, Father. Just a little rushed today." She sat beside him by the fire. Mother of God, she thought, Gerald and Miss Always in bed together at the Connaught.

"That's splendid," he said cheerily with a slight lisp.

He had a round face on a round body and reminded Maggie of a story she had read as a child about a potato who laughed and grew fat. The potato had not had very nice skin, and neither did Father Humphrey.

Maggie had heard gossip that Father Humphrey experienced an occasional moment of mysticism, somewhat like the poet Donne, she supposed. He didn't look at all mystical to her, though each time she saw him, she found herself secretly checking his hands for a stigmata. Of course, then his palms would be wrapped and smell horridly of camphor or some such medication and people would come from every country to see him pray and levitate and whatever else he did to show he possessed God's special blessing. She couldn't quite imagine his lumpy body levitating. No, she decided, Father Humphrey was quite ordinary.

"Mrs. Featherstone?"

"What? Oh, yes?"

"Mr. Beveridge tells me he enjoys his outings here."

"I'm so glad, Father. I enjoy having him."

Maggie was relieved when Mrs. Butterfield entered with tea. She had risen to the occasion, adding bread and butter sandwiches and hot scones to the sponge cake with chocolate icing. Father Humphrey piled the scones high with clotted cream, and raspberry jam. Mrs. Butterfield mumbled something about no hope for more raspberries this season, but Father Humphrey, having missed Felicity's antics in the berry basket, did not quite catch Mrs. Butterfield's drift.

"Did your woman mention something about more raspberries?" He lisped wonderfully on 'raspberries'. "Truly this is sufficient. I could not possibly do justice to more." He shook his head and a crumb wavered on his round upper lip, then fell to his cassock as he spooned out more cream. He reached for the sponge cake.

He has too hearty an appetite for a mystic. Maggie hadn't really thought much about mystics before, but supposed they laboured under gigantic spiritual crosses as they trudged through their Dark Nights. At least they should. Surely a mystic didn't finish off the preserves and the cake, leaving a smudge of chocolate on his round nose, like a bump on a baking potato.

"Mrs. Featherstone, you're not having any of this wonderful tea."

How could she tell him that her husband had visited the Connaught with his mistress? Was sleeping at the Connaught as they talked. That she was panting and clawing under the weight of her own cross, in anguish greater than she could describe.

"Not hungry, I guess."

"Too much pudding at lunch?" He laughed and actually did look a trifle fatter, just as did the potato in the children's story. "I've come, by the bye, to bless Raven Hall and rid it of any undesirable spirits." His sibilants for the undesirable were nothing short of magnificent.

"Oh?" Would a blessing rid the hall of Miss Always? Maggie wanted to ask. She had to hope that it would.

"What a fine idea, Father. Let's begin at once." This was action. This would take her mind off her pain.

He wiped his palms with his napkin and threw it onto the tea table. Then he stood and went to the couch, where he unrolled his stole and surplice which he'd bunched into a ball. He struggled into the surplice, put the stole about his neck, and reached into his pocket for a small plastic bottle. Unscrewing its lid, he screwed on a sprinkler cap.

"I've brought a little holy water for the blessing."

Like a sugar shaker, thought Maggie. She hoped the house was in order. She mentally checked each room.

Felicity had pulled any number of papers and books and pillows out of place. She had also distressed the wood on Miss Always's furniture to a greater degree than had the antique makers. But for the most part the house stood inspection; and Felicity, yipping excitedly and parading on her hind legs from time to time, accompanied the tour.

Father Humphrey sprinkled holy water and made the sign of the Cross, blessing each room in the name of the Father and of the Son and of the Holy Ghost. He caught himself on this last one, changing Ghost to Spirit, as the Third Person of the Trinity was now known. Maggie blessed herself with each sprinkle of the holy water and prayed that this powerful Trinity would keep out a certain undesirable worldly influence.

It was only when they came back down to the door of the mask room that Maggie hesitated and Felicity growled.

Father Humphrey looked at Maggie apprehensively, then tapped on one of the heavy oak panels.

"I sense bad vibrations."

She couldn't quarrel with him there, but vibrations did not seem the point at the moment. That he did not discover all her hats mattered more. The masks, of course, he couldn't see; nevertheless, he might wonder why numerous labels marked empty shelves.

"I... a... I think we won't go in there, father."

"My child, it would seem this room is in definite need."

"Another time." Maggie smiled and took his arm, attempting to lead him away. "Or why not bless it from this side of the door?"

"Certainly not." He gave a chortle. "I think it essential that I attend to it now."

Maggie laughed, dropped his arm, and stepped a little forward, barring the door.

"There are certainly no evil spirits in this little room, father, but there is a mad jumble of things. You really will embarrass me if you go in now."

"My child," he smiled as patronizingly as one could with a chocolate smear on one's nose, "priests share your most intimate secrets. I won't mind your 'mad jumble'."

Maggie looked at him suspiciously. What secrets did he know other than those rather harmless ones she told at confession, secrets which were not so very secret with Mrs. Butterfield in the house. She wondered if her thought of Mongoose strangling Miss Always was a sin. It did meet some of the conditions. It was a grievous matter. But had she given it sufficient reflection? It had all happened rather rapidly. She faltered a bit on sufficient reflection. And then there was full consent of the will. Had she consented? Really consented? She feared she might have. At the moment she would certainly consent. She would have to rely, as she usually did, on sufficient reflection to save her.

The hall clock chimed, echoed by a cuckoo.

Father Humphrey looked at his wristwatch.

"Ah, I'm afraid I have another appointment. But splendid tea, splendid tea."

Splendid lisp, Maggie thought as she walked him to the drawing room to get his case and then to the entrance way. At the door she handed him his hat and umbrella.

"Don't get wet, Father."

He opened the door and peered out. "It looks a little clearer now." He took Maggie's hand. "I'll pray for you."

She didn't say anything. She couldn't.

She heard him start up his car, and went to the window to watch him drive away, then she looked down to inspect her crystal Foxtrot. Light creating sunbows in the little animal always soothed her, gave her hope.

He was gone. Foxtrot was gone. She rushed through the drawing room, throwing magazines aside, moving objects. She searched the dining room. Mystified, she sought Mrs. Butterfield in the kitchen.

"My Foxtrot crystal has disappeared? You didn't by chance move it to another room?"

Mrs. Butterfield turned from the sink, where she was peeling vegetables for dinner, and sniffed.

"He gave it away then, didn't he just."

"Who?"

"I told them you wouldn't like it none."

"Who gave it away?"

"But he said you'd have no objections."

"You mean Gerald? Gerald gave my Foxtrot away?"

"To that Always woman that's always here, always underfoot. She said she liked it. He said you had lots more crystal, said you wouldn't mind."

"But he knows that's a special piece. My favourite. It has memories. It can't be replaced. It's my Foxtrot."

She felt unbearably sad. Unbearably betrayed.

CHAPTER XIII

"Gerald?"

Maggie had deposited Felicity in her basket in the kitchen and now approached Gerald in the drawing room to confront him. She'd been depressed all day after seeing him with Miss Always at the Connaught Hotel. Now she felt furious. How dare he skulk about town, betraying her? If he wanted their marriage to end, why didn't he say so?

"Yes, my angel?" He didn't look up from the newspaper.

Maggie sat beside him on the couch. She could still feel his back to her as he stood at the Connaught's reception desk.

"I want to talk."

"Sounds serious, darling. I'm not up to anything serious tonight."

"It is serious, Gerald. We must talk. Now. There never seems to be a good time."

Reluctantly he put the paper aside and faced her, his eyes, no longer Italian, narrowed in secretiveness.

"Gerald, we've spent thirty years together. Thirty. We've had some hard times, some terrible times, but we've always got through them."

"I can't see that we're having a hard time now."

"The worst time ever." She could see the pale burgundy carpet that held no tracks.

"Nonsense." His eyes closed to slits.

Her heart felt sore. How could she put this so he'd understand, so he'd respond?

"Gerald, we need to do things together. You and Miss Always work Saturdays, Sundays. You and I could be using our weekends to explore England, to play tennis on our court, to travel to France, to do so much. I fear I'm losing you, darling, because we're never with each other."

"Maggie, I'm in a new job. I need to give it all I've got. You have no idea of the demands."

"I have every idea," she snapped, releasing her anger. "Don't you speak to me of demands!"

"There's your Irish temper getting the better of you."

"I'd rather have an Irish temper than a cold, unfeeling English one."

"Really, darling. I suppose next you'll be suggesting counselling."

"Gerald, I need to be with you at weekends. I need an end to these dismal Saturdays. I need you to show that you care about our marriage, that you care about me."

"If you don't know that after thirty years, God help you." Gerald rose in a huff and walked out of the room.

"Gerald," Maggie screamed, "I need you to show me."

But he either could not hear or would not.

The next evening Maggie arrived home with a fresh rawhide bone, which she threw to Felicity. She never had found Robin's bone. And she had a new hat — a white creation, covered with cherries and with a long pale green veil — for herself.

As she unwrapped her hat, she noticed what looked like red spots on the kitchen's pale oak floor. Her heart flew to her throat. What had happened to Felicity? A coyote? Not in England. Tuberculosis? Bleeding ulcers? Glass from the dustbin?

The puppy sat in her basket, seemingly content as she chewed on the rawhide. Maggie rushed over and picked her up. She felt something warm and sticky on her left hand. Drawing it away, she saw blood.

This wasn't supposed to happen yet. Felicity was barely

eight months old. Maggie wasn't ready for Felicity in heat.

She ran to the kitchen bookshelf and found her bible, a little book about King Charles spaniels. Racing through it she discovered that indeed eight months was possible.

Shit! she thought. Then she realized that was what Miss Always would say — her pink cupid lips mouthing obscenities, her rich honeyed voice panting them, and her hair swirling in a tinted halo. Miss Always rendered such incantations harmless, provocative even.

"Shit, Felicity!" Maggie repeated.

What did one do with a bitch in heat? Maggie had no idea. And it was after hours for the vet, who would also be closed tomorrow.

She always felt somewhat unprepared for emergencies. In California, she had dutifully got her earthquake shelf ready, with extra water, food, flashlight, transistor radio, and a wrench to shut off the gas main. But she had forgotten to get the tablets to purify the water, and their gas main had some pipes around it so that the wrench she'd bought didn't fit. Then one by one the cans of food went bad. She replaced a few, but it seemed such a waste to keep buying food and throwing it away.

She could think of only one thing to do about Felicity's condition, but it would have to wait until tomorrow. Until then, Felicity could remain in the kitchen, which already looked as if the Canterville ghost had visited and resurrected a bloody stain from centuries past.

Gerald came home late after a dinner meeting. Always late. Pleading exhaustion, he went straight to bed.

The next morning, as soon as Gerald left, Maggie rushed into the mask room and chose Vague. She mustn't look too remote or she might not get what she was going for. She decided she had created Vague for just this moment. With it she wore a navy suit and polka dot scarf.

Her hat was a broad-brimmed navy straw with matching polka dot band. The veil was long enough to tie under her chin and not so sheer as to allow Vague's features to be seen easily. She deemed a veil essential this morning.

Maggie took the train into London. When she arrived, she hurried to the taxi stand and went immediately to Harrods, which she knew had everything.

Inside, she made sure the veil covered her face, then discreetly asked directions and hurried to the appropriate department. Once there, she looked about timidly for a saleswoman. Instead, the only assistant on the floor was an elegant young man. This wouldn't do.

Just as she gained courage to approach him, a tall, dignified man, looking embarrassed, walked up to the clerk.

Maggie crept a little closer and waited.

As she watched him, she gave a start. Lusty hair! The kind of hair she had dreamed about these many years. The kind of hair the man she wanted to make love to would have. When she was in her teens, girls sat around describing the perfect man for themselves. Maggie wanted an imposing sort of man, like the army officers she saw. One who would command in battle. And he would have thick, thick hair and perhaps a moustache. She had thought, once, that Gerald had lusty hair. But that was in his Italian period. His English hair didn't seem lusty at all.

She sidled round to see the stranger's face. Handsome, the lines only adding to his dignity. Eyebrows flecked with grey, matching the thick charcoal hair. She couldn't see the eyes clearly, but imagined them a piercing blue, just the sort to go with lusty hair. The cheekbones were strong and the chin firm. He looked as if he had been a colonel in the army. To think! The man she had dreamed of, only to find him too late and in such odd circumstances.

She edged closer still. What was it he was saying? Sanitary towels for his dog? Mother of God, did his dog have the same problem?

"Bikini Days for Little Bitches," the elegant young man said in an actor's voice which could have carried to any gallery. He held out a small box. "Just the thing. A most comfortable sanitary belt for the little pooch."

"Whatever you think." The man with lusty hair waved his hand, looking as if he were trying to wave the salesman and the box of Bikini Days away, just as Robin might with his wand.

"But we must pick a colour for your little pooch." The salesman went right on. "We have quite a range: white, black, yellow... I'm not sure we could manage pink. Oh, and string. One of our customers, a white poodle, modelled for *Sportsdog Illustrated* in her string Bikini Days."

"I-I don't know," stammered the man, whose face had turned a not altogether appealing shade of red.

The salesman took a bikini from its box and held it out for all the world to see. Maggie glanced about, hoping no one else was looking. Nothing seemed to embarrass the young salesman. The young were so... so... but she could not think what they were other than a total embarrassment to those slightly older.

Maggie tightened her veil. The lusty-haired gentleman wiped his brow with a pocket handkerchief.

Maggie peered at the Bikini Days for Little Bitches. Rather small, actually, like a tiny black bikini. She wondered if Felicity should have white or black. The latter would blend with her black spots.

"And we have a broad range of sizes," the salesman said proudly. "A poodle did you say? I've been supposing a miniature, but of course, if you have one of the large bitches we can manage that as well."

"A Yorkshire terrier." The man with lusty hair waved his hand again, but neither the salesman nor the Bikini Days left the scene.

Instead, the young man draped the black model over his shoulder and opened another box to produce a white one, even smaller.

"A Yorkshire would require size 2 or 3. Is it a large or small Yorkshire?"

"Medium."

"I should say 3. They can be tightened, you know." He demonstrated as his customer looked about furtively.

"The 3. Wrap it up please."

"Is your dog more silvery or blue-black? Or perhaps tan predominates?"

"Anything. Anything at all. I really must leave."

"Certainly. I think the tan Bikini Days, sir. You've made a wise choice."

Mother of God, thought Maggie as her turn approached. She wouldn't mind having Miss Always's vocabulary at her command at the moment. The salesman annoyed her. He seemed so damnably delighted at his customer's confusion.

Concentrating on such thoughts, Maggie was not prepared for the hasty retreat of the man with lusty hair. He swung about, and she felt a terrific force that took her breath away and knocked her to the floor.

She sat for a moment, stunned. As she protested, the young salesman and the gentleman each grabbed an arm and helped her to her feet. While they asked about sprained ankles or broken bones, Maggie checked to be sure Vague was in place, but it seemed to be missing. She hurriedly adjusted her hat and retied the veil.

"I'm quite all right. Truly. Quite all right. Please don't

fuss."

"I can at least buy you a cup of tea to make up for this," the gentleman with lusty hair was saying.

"But you see, I must buy, that is..."

"Bikini Days for Little Bitches, ma'am?" The salesman's face lit up as he repeated loudly, "Bikini Days?"

"Shh," said Maggie, glancing at some others who had entered the department. "I mean, yes. A size 3, I think, in black."

"Not white? Not grey? Let me show you grey."

"Black, please. And I'm in a hurry."

"Of course. Just think. Two size 3 bikinis within fifteen minutes. Quite a coincidence that. Do you have a Yorkshire, too?"

"No." Maggie couldn't think what had happened to Vague when she fell.

The lusty-haired gentleman edged to the department entrance and stood waiting for her at a safe distance.

"She's a size 3, too," the salesman called to the gentleman. "Not a Yorkshire, though."

"Really, I must go," Maggie hissed.

"There you are. I hope your little pooch enjoys it. Should you want other colours... a wardrobe of colours might be nice."

"Thank you very much." Maggie put the small package into her handbag.

"The little towels. You're forgetting the little towels. Let me show you how they fit." He deftly opened a box, slid a minute pad into a grey bikini and held it up for those entering the department to see. "Total comfort. Total security."

Maggie, feeling totally uncomfortable and insecure, dropped the box into her handbag, handed him a note and waited restlessly for the change. Then she walked with as much poise as she could muster to where the gentleman, who was still rather red in the face, stood.

"What we won't do for our dogs," he said, giving a forced laugh. Awkwardly holding his parcel in one hand, he took Maggie's arm with the other and led her away from that detestable scene.

"Yes, anything for our dogs," she agreed. What was she doing having tea with a stranger? This reminded her of a movie she had once seen with, was it Richard Burton and Sophia Loren? She wasn't sure. Anyway, she rated it frightfully romantic, but nothing good came of the encounter.

Affairs weren't very successful, she decided. The characters in the film could fling caution aside and be passionate, but only for a short while. In real life, throwing care aside seemed an impossibility to Maggie. How Gerald managed it she couldn't think. But he'd find it didn't work, just as she was sure Richard Burton had in the film.

Maggie herself wasn't going to get involved with someone. She was a married woman.

What was she thinking? This was an invitation to tea to make up for having knocked her down. Tea with a nice gentleman. Harmless. A little spice on a bland day.

Yet he did have a distinguished face. And, yes, his eyes shone a piercing blue beneath his thick eyebrows and lusty hair.

She had thought they'd stop at one of Harrods's food bars, but no, he insisted on taking her in a taxi to Fortnum and Mason.

"The only place for tea. That chocolate cake, sort of fudgy," he mumbled by way of explanation. "Can't get it anywhere else that I know of."

Simple tea became complicated tea. Maggie's sense of caution increased.

"This way, Mr. Trueblood. Your favorite table is ready."

The waiter showed them to a table in the far room, almost as if they were hiding. As her host ordered, Maggie watched a small vase filled with a cluster of pink lilies similar to those called naked ladies in California.

Did Mr. Trueblood come here with other women? Maggie felt a little stab of jealousy.

Gradually she untied her veil and raised it onto her hat.

"Lovely," he intoned in his hearty, low voice.

Maggie found that if she looked at him, she could not keep her eyes off his thick charcoal hair. She had been right to dream of such a man.

With tea and the fudgy cake, Maggie felt more reckless. She had every right to this little tea party. Gradually, she began to relax.

"Mr. Trueblood..."

"Now, now, Adair. On the way here you promised to call me Adair. I really cannot take tea with a woman who calls me Mr. Trueblood. Tea is so, so... intimate."

Maggie gulped. She hadn't thought about tea itself as intimate. Now it became positively sinful... and with fudge cake. Devil's food. It probably was devil's food.

"Your dog, Little Pooh, is it? Tell me more about Little Pooh."

"Oh, such a charmer."

Maggie loved the way he smiled when he mentioned Little Pooh, the way his eyes sparkled.

"She's the cleverest puppy imaginable. Only nine months, mind, and she talks to me."

"Oh, come."

"Truly. Talks to me. I say, 'Is daddy's little girl happy'? and she goes, 'Urawr'. Just like that. 'Urawr'."

"How astonishing. Of course, Felicity doesn't talk, but she is awfully clever as well. When I say, 'Time for your bath, Felicity' she knows to hide under the bed."

"Remarkable. What would we do without the clever little beasts?"

Gerald would never think that. He never wanted to hear about how clever Felicity acted.

"I must thank Little Pooh for bringing us together." He moved his hand past the tray of tea cakes, past the vase of naked ladies, and covered her own that rested on the table.

Piercing. She had been right. The blue of his eyes pierced right through her suit, her blouse, right into her restive heart.

She looked at the creases round those eyes and at the rugged tilt of his chin. He appeared so very strong, but he was sentimental about his little dog. There were so many layers to him. Just like the fudgy cake, she started to think, but that didn't seem the appropriate simile. No, this was the sort of man who would swim the Hellespont.

She wondered how Mr. Trueblood, how Adair would react to Miss Always. He would know her type straightaway. He didn't appear to be seeking Youth but rather a woman with strata of complexity, one with his many interests.

Only then did Maggie remember that she had never located Vague — had no doubt left it amidst the packages of Bikini Days and little towels at Harrods — and now wore no mask at all. Yet with Adair that didn't seem to matter. She didn't need a mask. How relaxed that made her feel. How wanted.

"What is it you do, Adair?" She pictured him on the battlefield commanding men, or as a master spy, thwarting the KGB at every turn.

"Investment counsellor. Stocks and bonds, that sort of thing."

"I'm..." Maggie stirred her tea vigorously, "I'm

married."

"A lovely woman like you would be bound to married."

Maggie laughed in confusion.

"Do you really think so?" He doesn't know how little married I am, she thought. "And you?"

"Alas, dear lady, I have lost my wife. I go home only to Little Pooh."

"Did she die? Your wife, I mean?"

"Yes. Pneumonia."

Strange, thought Maggie. Not many people died of pneumonia these days.

"How sad they couldn't treat it."

"Quite."

All too soon tea time ran into train time. Maggie bade farewell to Mr. Trueblood, though not without his promise to call and set a time and place to meet just once more.

She felt decidedly wicked as she sat in the southbound slow train, having missed the fast, and had to wait at every stop. That didn't matter. She had promised to see Adair Trueblood again.

There was always a moment when one knew one was attracted. A person could walk away that second. With Maggie it had been in the pet department. Once she had drunk her tea and Adair's hand had rested on hers, she could not back out so readily.

How easily we are ensnared, she thought, by something as harmless yet as magical as a cup of tea.

She had a little more sympathy now for Gerald and Miss Always. That moment of escape came and went so fast. There seemed no chance for sufficient reflection.

She let her mind drift away from Gerald and Adair, let it float above the sound of the train on the track, let it drift away from who she was and where she was going.

CHAPTER XIV

Felicity lolled on her back on the Persian carpet in the drawing room, her head resting on a gold velvet cushion, one of many she had pulled from the couch. Now that she wore her black Bikini Days, she was fond of showing it off.

"Brazen hussy," Maggie groused.

Felicity made no response.

"Child of passion."

Felicity, remaining on her back, put her right front paw beside her head, while the left remained on her hip.

"What is the world coming to, when my dog lolls about in her sanitary belt as if she were Manet's Olympus?"

Felicity slowly crossed one hind paw over the other.

"You'll come to a bad end."

Maggie felt irritable, and the grey morning did nothing to improve her mood. Her mind kept racing over her meeting with Adair Trueblood. Of course, the meeting itself, mixed up with doggie sanitary towels, had been less than romantic. But everything that followed fitted her romantic ideal. Even his name clanged with the consonants of a hero and pulsed with the promise of a faithful man.

Nevertheless, actually to meet him again seemed unthinkable. Not that she had heard from him, but his piercing blue eyes had confirmed his promise to call. She never received those vibrations from Gerald any more, sensations that gave her the knowledge he desired her.

She must think what to say when Adair posed the question, for she felt panicky at the idea of losing him. She couldn't go back to the loneliness that Miss Always's presence with Gerald produced.

She consoled herself with the thought that Adair was a gentleman and as such might agree to a platonic relationship. Yet his eyes had said something quite unmistakable. Oh, dear. It was nice, it was heaven, to be desired. But to Maggie, desire and lust were two quite separate things.

As Maggie bent to pick up pillows, Felicity defiantly jutted out her square chin and gave a little warning growl; so Maggie left her to her exotic dreams and walked into the mask room.

She simultaneously snapped on the switch and shut the door. When the lights did not go on, she found herself almost in the dark. Though the curtains were open, the pale morning light remained pasted across the window, rather than filtering through the room.

As Maggie stood silently, her thoughts a cobweb of guilt and longing, a faint humming sound tore at the filaments.

The hum grew louder. Maggie glanced at the spinning wheel. It was turning in a lively fashion. Rather than feeling surprised, she felt it should have been turning so right along. Soon she heard a woman's high voice, like a young boy soprano's, singing the *Mass of the Sixth Tone* which Maggie knew from choir days.

The high voice became louder. Another childlike voice harmonized, then a third. While the voices sang, a grey light gradually illumined the room.

It didn't occur to Maggie to be frightened. The voices sounded lovely, and the Gregorian chant, solemn. *"Kyrie eleison. Christe eleison."* Lord have mercy. Christ have mercy. Maggie could not resist the urge to join in.

As her voice blended with the others in the *Gloria,* three figures gradually appeared. One was seated at the spinning wheel; the other two squatted on the three-legged stools. Though grey and transparent, they appeared to wear wimples and veils.

Maggie remembered about the former convent on this

property. Were these ghosts of earlier times? It seemed quite natural that she should sing with them.

Enjoying herself, she sang loudly, happily, then realized she was singing alone. The three nuns had stopped and had turned to her. As they stared she nodded, embarrassed.

Now they became more intense in colour and shape until they no longer appeared diaphanous, and the wimples shone white against the grey.

"Do you live here?" asked Maggie. She felt huge as she towered over the tiny spirits.

"Yes," said the nun at the spinning wheel in a surprisingly sour fashion. She had a sharp, thin face, pointed nose, pointed chin, tight lips.

"We have lived here," said the little nun closest to Maggie, "for six hundred years." Her face was round and soft and sad.

"But that's impossible," objected Maggie.

"I mean on this site, dear. Our convent chapel once stood here."

The third nun raised her eyes heavenward.

"I can't see why we haven't been accepted after all this time."

She had beautiful features, Maggie thought, but a spoiled turn to the nose.

"I, for one, feel quite bitter about it," said the nun at the spinning wheel.

"That's probably why we're still here," said the beautiful nun.

"I'm not happy about it at all," said the round little nun. "I've suffered and suffered, and still I'm unacceptable."

"That's too bad," said Maggie. "I wish I could do something to help."

"Oh, you've cheered us immeasurably," said the round

nun. "We've been so lively since you came."

"We love your hats," said the sharp nun at the spinning wheel.

"And your crystal," admitted the beautiful nun, glancing towards the shelves.

Maggie spun round. Glistening in the eerie grey light, her crystal madonna, crystal statue of St. Anthony, and nearly her entire animal collection, even the Lalique panther and the Steuben lion, rested on a top shelf near the window.

"But I haven't seen my collection here when I've come for my hats."

"We did not mean you to," said the nun spinning.

"We like pretty things," said the beautiful nun. She jumped up and ran to the hat shelf. There she chose a royal blue hat with a long red feather and put it on over her veil. Then she picked up Maggie's Baccarat crystal vase and, in the strange grey luminescence of the room, gazed at her elongated reflection. "We look quite fine in these head coverings," she said.

The other two hurried over, tossed hats about, then both grabbed for a green hat with loops of dark green grosgrain and feathers on the crown.

"Please, don't break the crystal," wailed Maggie.

"I wanted that one," said the round nun, sadly.

"It looks better on me," retorted the sharp nun, running her fingers over the grosgrain and feathers.

The round nun tore the hat away and waltzed about the room with it held high, feathers flying.

"Really, sisters," said Maggie. "You must not."

"I'm Mother Magdalene," said the sharp-faced nun, stopping her chase. "I'm supposed to be in charge."

The round nun giggled as she plopped the hat, lopsided, onto her head. "I'm Sister Aloysius. My father left me in this convent. I never wanted to be a nun, and I have been one for six hundred years." Tears came to her eyes.

"And I am Sister Orelia," said the beautiful nun, with a touch of haughtiness. "My affianced was a nobleman who got me with child, then left me here because of the scandal."

"I myself," said Mother Magdalene, "was from a noble family with too many daughters."

"And too little money for her dowry," chimed in Sister Aloysius. "Only the church would have her."

"That does not concern her," remarked Mother Magdalene, with a look in Maggie's direction.

"But it does," said Maggie as the nuns threw the hats back and took their places on the three-legged stools once more. "You've all been treated very badly."

"You pity us," said Mother Magdalene. "But we pity you, too. We noticed men have not improved much."

Heavens, if they looked to Gerald as a modern example, well... Maggie didn't know how to refute that charge.

"I will admit," Mother Magdalene went on, "we all feel cheated. We wanted life, and we never had it. We wanted pretty things, and we were denied them..."

"And now we want to rest," interrupted Sister Aloysius, "but that is barred from us as well."

"I'd still prefer pretty things," said Sister Orelia.

Before Maggie could respond, they began chanting the Credo.

"Really, sisters, we should discuss this."

But they looked straight ahead and continued singing. Ever so gradually, chanting the *Mass of the Sixth Tone* in high voices, they disappeared.

Maggie stood alone in the dark, narrow room, baffled. Had she truly experienced the nuns or had she imagined them? Had Robin and his magic played a part? How much did her own loneliness influence the moment?

She tried the electric light again, and it came on. Glancing at the hat shelves, she found them awry, the hats now higgledy piggledy. And there stood her crystal collection.

Whatever had caused the vision and whatever it meant, it had definitely occurred.

A small bouquet of flowers arrived from Adair with a note signed 'From friendly neighbours, the Truebloods', to hide his identity. Maggie felt like a girl receiving her first orchid, though these were yellow roses, an unfortunate choice.

"Stocks and bonds? We must have them over sometime," was all Gerald said.

Then Adair called. He had worked out a code to send her messages. If, for instance, he mentioned he saw a certain play last Wednesday at the matinée, that was an invitation to go the next Wednesday. Very clever of him. Maggie felt the excitement of a child.

Gossamers of guilt now floated to obscure corners of her mind. How 'every day' her friendship with Adair was. How comfortable. How normal and platonic. Yet how very magical.

Maggie wore her lovely hats to meet Adair. She needed no masks. Those she reserved for Gerald and Miss Always. A couple of times she even stayed in town for dinner. Though she couldn't claim late night meetings, she could claim missing trains and even staying in town for a play on her own. She felt reckless, happy, young.

Now it was weekends she hated. She imagined Adair at home with only Little Pooh. Life seemed unfair.

On this particular Saturday Felicity, no longer in need of her Bikini Days, sulked in the kitchen. Maggie, missing Adair, sulked at the luncheon table with Gerald and Miss Always. Gerald did not look so bright today. In fact, he looked drawn and tired.

He'd soon weary of his inamorata and be back to normal, Maggie consoled herself. Of course, by then she might not want him back. She did have to admit, though, that all honourable men made mistakes at one time or another. And, despite Miss Always, Gerald was an honourable man. Oh, he took risks in business, but he respected that world, lived by its rules. He was just now in a kind of limbo.

Maggie glanced at Miss Always, but that woman appeared indomitable, showing up to work with Gerald every Saturday, rain or shine. Saturday luncheon with them both had got past the tense stage for Maggie and now caused her merely boredom.

"We really must get rid of those two tramps," Gerald tapped his spoon on the table.

"Mongoose and Mr. Dunkley work hard," Maggie sighed. "I can't see why you fuss so."

"It looks to me as if they're never moving, even when they work." Gerald laughed. He seemed so very English, so very pale and lackluster, having used up his Italian charm on Miss Always. "You obviously see something I don't."

"I think we need to be appreciated for our worst selves, not our best," Maggie said softly.

"Oh, I don't think Gerald believes in 'worst selves'," said Miss Always. "He expects all of us at work to be our very best." She smiled at him like a schoolgirl and patted the honey pot on her left breast.

"You will say exaggerated things like that, Maggie. It

simply makes me uncomfortable to have your strays underfoot." Gerald speared a bite of lasagne as if it might get away at any moment, and bit into it with his English teeth.

"In other words, it's because I hired them." Maggie twisted and untwisted her fuschia scarf. Lasagne had been a bad choice for today. Too heavy.

"I find Gerald likes to leave those things to me," piped up Miss Always, fingering the gold locket that hung on her full breasts. "And, Maggie, you should leave things to me as well. After all, I'm here to relieve you of any burdens."

Relieve me indeed, Maggie wanted to say aloud. Never have I had such a burden as your cheery golden self.

Gerald soaked up the last of the lasagne sauce with a piece of French bread. He didn't take butter these days. Keeping fit for Miss Always, Maggie supposed. She noticed little squint lines appearing, since he'd taken to going without his glasses when Miss Always was around.

"For the hundredth time, Maggie, you can't leave yourself open to strangers. They'll take advantage of you every time."

"Yes." Miss Always nodded agreeably. "The assholes always try to get away with something."

"But no one has so far." Not those you call 'strays' at any rate, Maggie thought.

Gerald's supercilious look said, that's beside the point.

"I wonder," said Maggie, poking with her fork at her tossed salad, "if the world isn't in a kind of Sodom and Gomorrha phase."

"What on earth!" Geraid rolled his eyes heavenward.

"Don't you remember," Maggie went on, "when Abraham said, 'Wilt thou destroy the just with the wicked'? or something very like that, and God answered if there were fifty just men, for their sake he'd save the city of

Sodom?"

"I thought it was forty just men."

"Well, Abraham got Him down to ten." She'd always liked Abraham for that. "If ten just men could be found, the city would be saved."

"What are you trying to tell us, Maggie? That we're doomed?" He started to push his glasses higher on the bridge of his nose, remembered they weren't there, and twisted his non-existent moustache instead.

She hated the facetious expression on his face.

"Maybe only ten just men are saving the world. Maybe for the sake of those ten, we haven't been destroyed. Don't you ever think of that?"

"Shit, I never do," said Miss Always with a smile.

"Nor I," said Gerald without a smile, though he glanced in appreciation at Miss Always.

"Oh, I do," said Maggie. "The thing is, don't you see, that none of us knows who the just men might be."

"Oh, my," said Miss Always, putting down her napkin and gazing into space. "Do we have to guess where they work, too? Like that game *Cluedo* — the butler did it in the pantry with a rope?"

"It's not meant to be funny," said Maggie.

"Oh, *Cluedo* isn't funny at all. Could there be a woman as well, like Mrs. Peacock?"

"We just don't know if there's a woman," Maggie replied.

"Well," said Miss Always, "it's hard to play if you're not clear about the rules. I guess the Archbishop of Canterbury. He must be just, or they wouldn't have made him an Archbishop, would they? Gerald, you take a turn."

"I think Maggie means... You've thought up a nice party game, Maggie." Gerald looked fierce. "But enough is enough."

"So cynical, Gerald? My point is that if God is saving the world, it's for a handful of truly good people — people we'd never recognize as such. They're not making a stir. They're not seeking converts. They're simply leading quite ordinary lives in communion with Him."

"But," said Miss Always, "if nobody knows about them, I can't see that they're doing much good."

"Precisely," said Gerald.

"Oh, but they are," countered Maggie. "They're quietly saving the world for the rest of us. One of them could be Mongoose. One could be Mr. Dunkley. We simply don't know."

"Maggie, this is too much!" Gerald tossed down his napkin and pushed his chair back. "Do you mean to tell me that you think a handful of people could be saving the earth? People who might not even be successful?"

Maggie laughed.

"Might not even work at Lloyd's!" Or wear honey pots, she thought, glancing at Miss Always's bosom.

Gerald's left eye was twitching, Maggie noticed. That meant he was not only very tired but under strain. She knew her arguments added to the strain, but she deeply resented Miss Always for exhausting Gerald.

He rose and strode out of the dining room.

"I'll have Mrs. Butterfield take you a bowl of fruit," Maggie called after him.

Miss Always stopped to peer out the window at Mr. Dunkley and Mongoose as the two furiously clipped hedges. Mongoose's deep baritone floated faintly across the garden.

"My goodness!" She stood, perplexed. "Maggie, I think Gerald could be one of those good people who are saving the earth. What do you think?"

"I think you could easily convince him of it."

Miss Always stared at Maggie, thought for a moment, then said, "Oh," and followed Gerald to the study.

Maggie headed for the garden and set out six new purple-rose Canterbury bells to replace the yellow pansies she had pulled out.

"Madam, if I could have a word?"

Maggie sat back on her heels and looked up to see Mr. Dunkley, dressed in his grey suit and vest. "Shouldn't you be taking the afternoon off?"

"Yes, madam, but a little matter has been niggling me."

"Something I can help you with?" Maggie removed her gardening gloves.

"It may be, madam, something I can help you with." He gave a little cough. "The matter is... delicate."

"I'm sure, Mr. Dunkley, that you'll present it tactfully." Maggie stood up.

"Thank you for that confidence, madam." He rubbed his hands together. "How to begin is the thing. You see, I go to the village from time to time — to Mrs. Hazlehurst's, to be precise — to natter a bit with the locals. And I hear things."

"Not about anyone at Raven Hall, I hope?"

"There you've hit upon it, madam. Oh, not about you or the servants. About Mr. Featherstone."

He paused, and Maggie remained silent. Was he going to tell her now that her husband was unfaithful? She didn't want to hear it.

"I really think I'd rather not..."

"Raven Hall is not your house. That's what they're saying. I'm pained to be the one to tell you that all is not ticketyboo."

Maggie laughed in relief.

"Mrs. Hazlehurst told me that when I first arrived. She thinks a noble family should still reside here. Gerald and I will never be accepted."

"She doesn't mean that, madam. She means the property is not in your name. It belongs to your husband only."

"Why, that's nonsense. We've always held everything as community property."

"I thought I should just mention it in case you were unaware."

"She's telling tales."

"You see, I was once a solicitor, a member of my father's firm along with my eldest brother. He practiced probate law, and I handled divorce cases. Abhorring my work, I too tried probate law, only to find that just as unsatisfying."

"Why does that woman gossip so?"

"After several years of practice, I saw the light, as they say. I'm happiest in a garden and in open spaces. The law firm was too confining. The machinery of the system was grinding me down."

"I suppose everyone in the village believes her." Maggie twisted the fingers of her garden gloves.

"Anyway, I couldn't bear discord. My attitude doesn't suit the law."

"What makes Mrs. Hazlehurst think she knows how our property is held?"

Mr. Dunkley pulled a white silk handkerchief from his pocket and mopped his brow.

"Through council tax letters from the local authority in your husband's name only. I believe in America you use the term 'property tax' instead of council tax. In any case, your name would appear as well, if you were a joint owner."

"Gerald wouldn't do something like that."

"I know it's distressing news, madam. But we solicitors have a nose for what's courtworthy, so to speak. Things look dark," he glanced meaningfully towards the house, "very dark."

"You have it all wrong, Mr. Dunkley." Could Mr. Normington be right? Could Mr. Dunkley actually have been a solicitor?

"If ever you should need the services of a former member of Dunkley, Dunkley, & Dunkley, I should be happy to serve." He reached into his vest pocket, pulled out an engraved business card, and handed it to her.

Maggie absently put the card into her skirt pocket as she watched Mr. Dunkley, with his jaunty, bandy-legged walk, disappear behind the house. What had he been saying? Council tax? Joint ownership?

She stooped, put on her gloves, and slowly turned over the soft earth, preparing it for her new plants. She felt numb. She, too, had been transplanted and needed all the care possible to survive, not schemes about her house.

She decided to put it from her mind. Gerald would have a logical explanation. For now, Adair was offering her the care she craved, and she would bask in his promise.

Beyond her the downs glistened in patches of pale green and greenish brown, and beyond the farmland lay the dark, sunflecked sea. She determined to feel peaceful here in her domain.

Digging six holes in the rich, moist earth, she placed the first plant into one, sat back, and surveyed her work. In the far corner of the garden, Felicity's yapping drew her attention. The puppy ran towards her across the lawn, something black wrapped round her, a portion dragging on the ground.

"Come, Felicity. Let me see what you've got."

Felicity bounded up to Maggie.

"Mother of God, a black lace bra. I'd never buy a skimpy, cheap thing like that."

Maggie slipped off her garden gloves and reached out to remove the bra from Felicity. The puppy backed just out of reach and jutted her chin out.

"Felicity, it would appear our enemy wears a bra after all."

Then the full impact of Felicity's finding the bra struck Maggie, and she felt ill.

In a hotel is one thing.

But in my house.

And after eating my luncheon. And in broad daylight!

"How dare they, Felicity." Maggie had never felt so left out, so alone. To be on the sidelines — and in her own home — was unthinkable.

Maggie reached for the puppy again. "Here, let me take that."

Felicity ran a few feet away.

"You could get hurt on the strap."

Felicity sat down to scratch.

"It could catch on something."

The puppy paraded again, just out of reach.

"You'll be strangled." How ignominious, Maggie thought, to be choked by Miss Always's bra strap.

"Felicity!" Maggie stretched to grasp her. Losing her balance, Maggie fell flat onto her stomach. But she'd caught an end of the bra.

Felicity tugged.

Maggie pulled harder.

The sound of material ripping broke the silence.

Felicity, surprised, stopped pulling, and Maggie grabbed her.

Sitting up cross-legged on the lawn, Maggie untangled the squirming puppy then held up the bra. "Pathetic, Felicity. Like something from Frederick's of Hollywood. You should be ashamed to be seen in anything so vulgar.

Miss Always ought to, too." But as Maggie looked at the cheap lace, now torn, and at the supposedly daring design, she almost felt a little sorry for Miss Always.

"Felicity, how shall we get this back to its owner?"

Suddenly Maggie felt inspired — a revelation of what to do. Something akin to the spiritual.

She put the puppy down, then knelt and ceremoniously slipped on her garden gloves. She folded the bra and carefully placed it into one of the holes she had dug. Slowly, she released the second Canterbury bell plant from its container, held it aloft, deep mauve blossoms newly opened, then formally placed it on top of the bra. She settled it in place, pressed it down, filled in the hole, and patted the earth flat.

No longer functional, if indeed it ever had been, the bra became the mythic symbol, Maggie wasn't sure of what, but it seemed to have a life of its own now. It had played seductress, temptress, sort of like Mary Magdalene. Now it must be the victim. As such, it must suffer the burial, the transformation. Maggie felt perhaps she ought to intone a few words of Latin.

She sat back on her heels, brushing dirt from her gloves and feeling a deep surge of almost spiritual satisfaction.

Felicity sniffed all round the plant, then dug about in the dirt. Finally, she sat beside the purplish buds, raised one paw, and commenced her dread whimpering.

Maggie looked back at the house and could see the curtains were drawn shut in the study.

Shaking, Maggie put her arms round the puppy, hugging her, as Felicity, head raised to the sky, rent the heavens with her primal scream.

CHAPTER XV

It seemed odd to Maggie to travel into London with Mr. Dunkley. But after visiting the Land Registry Office with him to find that her house's title was indeed only in Gerald's name, here she was in a taxi on the way to chambers where one Dunkley brother practiced as a barrister.

"See this view of the Law Courts. Most imposing."

Maggie gazed up at the giant brick back of the Royal Courts of Justice.

"Think of the number of financial cases tried here!"

"I think of the Old Bailey as the main court."

"The money is here," said Mr. Dunkley. "There's not so much money in saving lives as in saving fortunes."

The taxi turned on Chancery Lane, crossed Holborn, and stopped at an impressive Georgian building near Gray's Inn. Mr. Dunkley helped Maggie out and insisted on paying the driver.

Soon a pretty, blonde, efficient-looking secretary was ringing through to announce them.

Maggie and Mr. Dunkley sank into leather chairs.

"Here I am," boomed a voice fit for the London stage.

Maggie jumped in astonishment. Mr. Dunkley rose also.

A dapper little man, his black hair white at the temples, came toward them, juggling four small silver balls. As he walked, he didn't miss a beat in the rhythm. He juggled with a dramatic flair, and the room crackled with the energy of his presence.

"Mrs. Featherstone," said Mr. Dunkley, "I want you to meet my brother Basilio. He went to the bar, instead of working for our family firm of solicitors."

"Hello," said Maggie, and thought better of offering Basilio her hand.

"Charmed," said Basilio, seeming to look at Maggie and

the balls at one time. "Do be seated." He perched on the arm of a chair as Maggie, mesmerized by the silver balls, sank down, and Mr. Dunkley sat opposite her.

Basilio caught the balls, holding them tightly as if they were clients. Then he began rolling two in each hand. "Good for the nervous system," he explained. "Hits all the acupressure points."

"You juggle to calm the nerves?" asked Maggie.

"Good heavens, no," he objected in a resounding voice that Maggie felt sure would cause any juror to sit up and listen. "I'm rehearsing a court case."

Confused, she wrinkled her brow.

"Basilio and Figaro, my eldest brother," explained Mr. Dunkley, "believe the job of a first rate barrister or solicitor is to juggle, so they exercise with silver and gold balls."

"Oh," said Maggie.

"It's an advanced concept," Basilio's deep voice gave added importance to his comments. "With practice such as this, my mind is always centered on the essence of a case."

"I'm sure that gives the client confidence," said Maggie.

Basilio stared at Maggie in surprise.

"I'm not the least concerned with the client. Of what interest is he to me? A great nuisance, I should say. It's making the law work for your case, whether it was meant to or not. It's juggling so rapidly, so deftly, that the opposing counsel becomes confused." He laughed. "I'm rather good at this, am I not, Cherubino?"

Mr. Dunkley winced, whether at the sound of his Christian name or the question, Maggie wasn't sure.

"The best," he agreed.

"Ah, here's Figaro, here with a new case. His firm is right across the way. Most convenient, that."

In the outer doorway stood a thin old man, also short, with tanned, wrinkled skin, a bush of white hair, and a long beaked nose. He juggled four small golden balls. The balls clicked together as he caught them, walked over and shook Maggie's hand, and sat down next to Cherubino.

Basilio spoke up.

"I was about to tell Mrs. Featherstone that I specialize in juggling meanings, while you, Figaro, as solicitor, specialize in juggling people. You can't imagine the number of clients he brings in to this firm. Wherever possible he encourages court action, so I profit handsomely."

"I sit on Sundays with the elderly in nursing homes," Figaro asserted in a crisp, raspy voice.

Maggie waited for him to continue. When he said no more, she encouraged him.

"Nursing homes?"

"Didn't you tell her he handles probate cases?"

Basilio turned on Cherubino. "It is bad enough that you left the firm. Now you don't explain about it properly."

"He did tell me," said Maggie. "I just didn't understand the reference to nursing homes."

"Ah," said Basilio, "you juggled too fast for her, Figaro."

Basilio put a hand on Maggie's arm. "He's so very bright, he easily gets upset if others can't keep up. You see, he befriends the dying, and they have him make out their wills. Once they die, the families are too grief-stricken to change solicitors, and he makes a substantial profit. Do you understand now?"

"Oh, yes." Maggie saw the vulture-like Figaro, claws circling the iron bedframes of those whose circulation was waning. Waiting for death. She shivered.

"And," continued Basilio proudly, "the nursing homes appreciate Figaro, since he is so kind to their most hopeless cases. They always call him when a new one joins them."

"I think we had better be going," said Mr. Dunkley. "I just wanted Mrs. Featherstone to meet you."

"Cherubino, come join the firm again at any time," Figaro rasped. "We do need you." He turned to Maggie. "Cherubino specialized in heirs. Discord among heirs leads to lengthy and profitable litigation."

"I could have profited handsomely from his work as well," added Basilio, "but he refused to juggle," his deep voice sounded ominous, "and that's our speciality."

"I know," said Mr. Dunkley apologetically.

Basilio emitted a sound something like a loud "Ha!" Then he ruffled his younger brother's hair.

"Cherubino had them all agreeing in no time. I was never in court. I was losing money."

"It seemed rather pleasant when the heirs acted congenially." Mr. Dunkley looked sheepish.

Basilio shook his head.

"You were a good deal of trouble. But…" he slapped his younger brother on the shoulder, "… I should be happy to see you back in your firm."

"Thank you."

The older brothers shook hands with Maggie and before she and Mr. Dunkley reached the door, both brothers were juggling their gold and silver balls.

"That's dedication for you," whispered Mr. Dunkley to Maggie, shutting the office door behind them. "But how could I succeed in law with a name like Cherubino? I think it is our names that determine our fate."

Maggie laughed.

"Or perhaps your parents' love of Mozart."

As they walked down the stairway, Maggie realized that Gerald was becoming adept at juggling.

"You see why I prefer open spaces, gardens," Mr. Dunkley sighed. "I don't believe in juggling. It seems sad to me that our deaths are in the hands of jugglers."

"And our lives," said Maggie. "Don't forget our lives."

CHAPTER XVI

That night Maggie broached the subject of the house to Gerald. He was reading in the drawing room and had asked not to be disturbed.

"This interruption can't be helped, Gerald." Maggie sat on the overstuffed couch opposite his chair, her feet planted firmly on the floor so she could dig in her heels if necessary. "We've got to talk about the title to this house."

"The what?" He looked up astonished, automatically pushing his hornrimmed glasses higher on his nose.

"It's in your name only, when we've always held property in both our names."

"How on earth...?"

"That's not important. What's important is why?"

Gerald put the business journal down.

"Darling, you don't understand these things."

"I understand that you took the money from the home we owned together and now you own this alone. I want my name on the title."

"But that's impossible, my pet."

"It's imperative. It's my money, too."

"You don't understand. I've signed the house over to Lloyd's. To do that, the house had to be the sole property of one person. Surely you'll want the tremendous benefits we'll get from Lloyd's. We're so lucky to be investors."

"Lloyd's owns our house? Why would you do that?"

"No, of course Lloyd's doesn't own it. I obtained a bank guarantee against the security of the house and submitted it to Lloyd's as evidence of wealth. That allows me to underwrite business without involving our capital. Trust me, Maggie, I worked this all out carefully for our protection."

"In other words, not even our house is safe."

"I'm too careful for that."

"Gerald, don't treat me the way you treat Miss Always."

"Maggie, through my syndicate, we'll have more money than you ever thought possible." Gerald picked up *The Times,* rattled it, and tried to go back to reading.

All Maggie could think of was the gold and silver balls.

"And when Lloyd's syndicates take a loss? Doesn't everyone have to divvy up? You might as well go to Las Vegas and play the tables."

"We're protected, Maggie. I assure you."

Maggie got up.

"I'm horrified you want to gamble our home like this. I must say, I don't like the house, but I own it as well as you. I demand you correct the error. I refuse to let you sign it over." She walked out.

What could she do? What were her rights? She could certainly prove her right to half, but by that time, what would he have done?

She entered her room, followed by Felicity, who tumbled over, trying to jump onto the bed. Maggie picked her up and hugged her. "Felicity, I feel as if I've just been yanked from my soil and thrown aside on a heap."

Maggie's worst fear had come to pass. Amazed at herself, terrified, yet tingling and expectant, she had agreed to meet Adair for a day in the country — to go with him to an inn. She had agreed to commit a mortal sin. What would Father Humphrey say? For today had definitely been premeditated, gloriously premeditated.

She felt like a girl again. She felt somehow closer to her core. At least she was being honest with herself and taking [illegible] vanted to take. Gerald was no longer the only [illegible] h risk situation.

[illegible] uilty but only about her happiness. She thought

of Graham Greene's characters, who committed adultery so very glumly, almost as if it were a duty, an act to purify their souls from hypocrisy; whereas, Maggie felt joyous.

Why Adair, being single, didn't want her to go to his flat, she couldn't tell. Perhaps he thought that coming together in a quaint inn would be romantic. He could be so beautifully sentimental. So unlike Gerald's hardboiled business stance. She supposed men with lusty hair were more imaginative. Though to give Gerald credit, he had chosen the Connaught Hotel.

Wrapped in her terry robe after her bath, Maggie squirted herself with *L'air du Temps*. As she laid out peach silk lingerie, she could sense the presence of Miss Always's bra haunting her boudoir.

"Men prefer black lace," it said, "and a lower cut."

She should have gone on a buying spree. Well, next time. But would there be a next time? She'd been undesired for so very long, she didn't quite believe in Adair's passion.

She thought with a tinge of longing about the Connaught. The kind of understated, comfortable luxury she admired. But since Gerald went there, it would never do.

Adair was to pick her up at 11:00a.m. They'd drive to the inn, lunch, then... Oh, Mother of God, am I doing the right thing? But if not, why does it feel so very good?

Maggie agonized over what to wear. She wanted to create just the right effect. Finally, she decided on a new Emmanuel Ungaro Parallele outfit, the trousers in small black and white checks, the top in larger checks. The jacket nipped in at the waist and flared over the hips. It buttoned in a diagonal line with black buttons. A large, well-buckramed checked tie, knotted at the side of the neck and stood up on the left shoulder. The suit said "drama" but it also said "country", and Maggie felt satisfied.

In her ears she fastened giant gold earrings like miniature wreaths.

She slipped a sheer peach nightgown into her black lizard shoulder bag, put on her black lizard shoes and as a final touch, picked up red leather gloves. This was designer dressing, designer style. She no longer felt intimidated by the pathetic black bra.

Mrs. Butterfield had the day off. Felicity snoozed in the kitchen. Maggie felt free and playful for the first time since coming to England as she waited at the front window for Adair.

Promptly at 11:00, he drove up in a black Rolls. The car might seem garish with some other man at the wheel, but how elegant Adair looked. He, too, appreciated style.

She ran out, slamming the front door behind her. As she slid into the front seat next to Adair, she suddenly stopped.

"Mother of God, Little Pooh!"

Little Pooh, Yorkshire gold hair swept up in a pink barette and wearing a shocking pink mohair sweater, sat on the seat beside Adair.

"We could leave her here," Adair offered, looking disappointed at Maggie's reaction.

"The dogs might not get on — a terrier and a spaniel. Anyway…" She didn't like to say what he undoubtedly knew, that in the unlikely event that Gerald should come home early or Mrs. Butterfield should return, Maggie did not want to explain away Little Pooh. "It will be delightful to have her along."

As Adair leaned over to plant a quick kiss on Maggie's lips, Little Pooh snapped. Maggie jumped back to her side of the car.

Satisfied, Little Pooh settled herself between the lovers.

"Baby Snookums musn't be a meanie weenie," said Adair.

As Maggie started to laugh, she looked at Adair and realized he was quite serious. She coughed to hide her laughter. Perhaps she herself sounded just as silly with Felicity.

Maggie wondered how many of Adair's employees were lucky enough to understand this gentle side to the strong, commanding man. She supposed he had employees. He spoke reticently of high finance but never went into detail.

Adair drove several miles, then stopped in front of a dingy sort of inn. It sat right on the main highway with a gravel parking lot in front and neon signs in the windows, advertising beer.

It must be very colourful inside, Maggie supposed. She would have preferred a George and Dragon to the King's Head. After all, a decapitated head of Charles I did not presage good fortune for lovers.

Nor did Little Pooh. Maggie was both surprised and embarrassed when Adair brought not only his bitch but also a large box of Kleenex tissue inside. However, she soon understood that Little Pooh performed a certain pantomime.

The miniature bitch paraded into the bar with a tart-like wiggle. She circled the floor in this fashion until she had everyone's attention. Then she made her way to the center of the pub, gave three small turns and messed.

Maggie covered her nose with a handkerchief and wished she'd brought a mask. The few bar patrons clapped as Adair laughed, and Little Pooh did an encore of her wiggle and yapped as if she had done something terribly clever.

Maggie and Adair were finally seated at a small circular table ordinarily used for drinks, since a billiard table graced the section of the room that should have been for the luncheon crowd. Music, loud and wild, blared from the juke box, and several boys punctuated any brief silences with the click of billiard balls.

Maggie imagined the rooms themselves were charming as she choked down a limp salad in the smoke-filled room. Adair, pleased with his choice, ate a hearty meal of undercooked bacon and sausages and fried eggs.

"This gives you the full English flavour," said Adair, looking round, pleased, his blue eyes glowing.

Maggie hadn't told him about living in England as a child and hating it. She tried to strike a happy note by mentioning the little dog. Obviously he doted on praise of her.

"They didn't mind at all about Little Poop."

"Little *Pooh,"* he articulated. *"Pooh."*

"Yes, of course."

"No, they never mind. They love her here. You must have noticed."

"My, yes." So that was why he'd chosen this spot. Maggie felt angry. Her affair had been planned around Little Poop!

Mixed with her anger was the guilt she felt about the little bitch. She liked most dogs, but she didn't like this one, with its long swirling hair and vulgar sweater, sitting in a chair between Adair and Maggie. Just like Miss Always, she thought.

"Do tell me about your work, darling." She tried to shut out any thought of Little Poop. "You know how little I know about it."

He cleared his throat and turned a little red. Such humility, she thought.

"I make it a rule never to talk business. But in this case… I'm an investment counsellor."

"But I'm not sure what that entails on a day to day

basis. You said something about stocks. Do you advise people which stocks to buy? Could I buy stocks through you?"

"Oh, no." He covered her hand with his and smiled lovingly. "I advise only large corporations. And of course," he gave a deep chuckle, "I do a bit of buying and selling myself. You've heard of IBM?"

Maggie nodded, pleased he was finally warming to this subject.

"Only last week, I bought a small branch in America that specializes in the newest computers."

"You? All by yourself?"

He nodded, apparently inordinately pleased with himself, but she could understand why.

"I'm glad you explained. It's easier to picture you at work." So he held a high risk position as well. But surely he made few mistakes. He had the air of a truly successful man.

Adair took her hand in both his own. He looked so debonair today in a deep blue turtleneck sweater and tweed jacket.

Maggie's pulse quickened. She smiled warmly.

Little Pooh growled and snapped.

Adair laughed and withdrew his hands. "She will be jealous, the little darling." He sighed. "Do people ever love as deeply as dogs?"

Maggie thought she did but decided not to say so.

As Adair paid the luncheon bill at the cash register and chatted pleasantly with the bartender, Maggie waited impatiently at their table. She stared at the rows of hammered copper plates, at the old clock that didn't work but was set, so a card said, 'at the hour when Charles's head was severed from his body', at the pictures of famous people who supposedly dined and drank here — pictures apparently snipped from movie magazines and tabloid newspapers.

What kept Adair? She could hear his laughter. Didn't he know she was nervous, excited? She'd been left with Little Poop, as Gerald so often left her with Miss Always.

Adair returned, took Maggie's arm, scooped up the terrier with the other hand, and led Maggie to the stairs.

"Perhaps," said Maggie, "they could watch Little Poop down here?"

"Pooh! Little Pooh! Oh, they'd mean well. But someone could be careless. I couldn't stand worrying about her."

"No, of course not."

Maggie glided up the staircase to her tryst. She ignored the peeling mottled paper on the walls and the holes in the old brown rug. She and Adair were coming together in this humble spot to share the magnitude of their love.

The room had windows that looked out over the pub's entrance. The faded yellow wallpaper and the chenille spread reminded Maggie she was not at the Connaught. But what were superficialities when love reigned? Young again, she was ready to put up with hardships. The contrast between the decor and what she felt for Adair would make their adventure that much more splendid.

She smiled at Adair. He smiled at her and walked slowly towards her. Her hands could already feel the silkiness of his lusty hair.

He took her in his arms, and she could smell the faint scent of the Caribbean lime aftershave she'd given him. Reading romances had convinced her that pleasure points existed in the unlikeliest places, and Adair was sure to find them, busy as he was with his lips, his hands. He quite

[illegible] away.

[illegible] e here, she'd imagined that at the right

[illegible] go into the bathroom and change into the

[illegible] nothing she'd brought. But over lunch

she'd decided that they would slowly, seductively, remove each other's clothing.

Neither scenario was taking place.

Too quickly, Adair became explosively passionate. He flung down the zipper of his trousers and let escape — Oh, Mother of God — an unusually large rosy-purplish penis. The colour of my Canterbury bells!

The creature seemed to have a life quite its own.

She wasn't ready for this. Not ready at all. She looked about frantically. But Adair grabbed her.

Desperately he tried to undo her trousers' zipper, while pulling her onto the bed.

Only seconds before, Little Pooh had chosen the very same spot on the bed, and was not ready for this intrusion. Not ready at all. Snapping wildly in fear and confusion, she grabbed the fat, moist, snake-like object in her mouth. It writhed wickedly. Little Pooh pulled in the opposite direction, flinging her body about the bed.

"Ahhhh!" screamed Adair in agony.

"Yyyyy!" screamed Maggie in consternation.

"Grrrr!" threatened Little Pooh, holding on to her catch.

In seconds Little Pooh squirmed on the floor, yapping. Adair, bent over in pain, daubed at scratches on the now pathetically dwindled apparatus.

Maggie lay back, aghast. She dared not laugh.

A knock sounded and a woman's voice asked, "Is everything all right, then?"

"Fine!" Maggie called. She got up, feeling a bit shaky, and gathered her handbag and shoes.

She looked down at Little Poop in admiration. She didn't look back at Adair.

As she waited downstairs for a taxi, she knew what Father Humphrey would quote to her: "Vanity of vanities, and all is vanity."

CHAPTER XVII

"Bless me father, for I have sinned." Maggie knelt in the confessional in the old way, kneeling to one side of the priest, a curtain between them. It was difficult enough to tell her sins. She couldn't look at Father Humphrey as she did so. He would appear so confused and so humble she might laugh.

"You see..." she started. She could smell the incense from the afternoon's Benediction.

"Yes, my child, I do see," he lisped.

"But I haven't yet told you."

"I know your tryst was not all you had hoped for. But as it says in Ecclesiasticus, 'Gold and silver are tried in the fire, but acceptable men in the furnace of humiliation'."

"But how could you know?"

"Shhh, child. Don't speak out. People are still in church."

"Does everyone know?"

"Shhh. No." He chuckled. "I sometimes see... what would you call them...? Not visions... I just see things, know things."

"The rumours are true! You are a mystic!"

"Good heavens, child, I'm not sure I know what a mystic is."

"Do you have the stigmata?"

"My goodness, no. How appalling. I just have pleasant chats with God. I'm not very good at pain. I might fail, you see, so I have to be careful. We humans are so much better than God at giving ourselves more than we can handle. But my child, are you sorry for your sin?"

Maggie sighed. "I suppose you know the answer to that, too." She did appreciate Father Humphrey's calling her "my child", as if she hadn't actually attained the use of reason and could be expected to commit any number of transgressions. But the burden of this sin was heavy.

"You're sorry that Mr. Trueblood humiliated you."

"Yes." He even knows the name, Maggie thought, chagrined.

"And nothing more?"

"I guess I'm sorry for the whole thing, father. In fact," she shifted on the lumpy kneeler, "I know I am."

"Good girl. And try not to be too upset about your husband. Remember, 'Charity is patient, is kind... is not provoked to anger, thinketh no evil'."

"Even about..."

"Miss Always? Even about her. God loves her."

And Gerald loves her, thought Maggie bitterly.

" 'Charity beareth all things, believeth all things, hopeth all things, endureth all things'."

"I think I'm better at faith and hope."

" 'But the greatest of these is charity'. Now make a good act of contrition as I give you absolution."

"Oh, my God, I am heartily sorry..." Maggie had a strange realization that perhaps she had been asking Gerald to be someone he no longer was. That she had been forcing Gerald back into the old mould when he was, for good or bad, in the process of creating a new Gerald. "...and I detest all my sins..." She had always hated it that Gerald decided how she should act and react and then expected her to fulfill that role. "...my God, Who art all good and worthy of all my love..." Was she doing the very same thing to Gerald? "...I firmly resolve..." She shuddered. If that were the case, she no longer knew Gerald. "... and avoid the near occasions of sin."

"God bless you," Father Humphrey lisped. "I'll pray for you. And you must say a little prayer for me."

Maggie rose to leave as if in a dream. Father Humphrey,

with his admonitions of charity, was asking too much of her. God was asking too much.

Maggie sat on the lawn next to Mr. Beveridge's wheelchair. Robin lay on his back, waving his wand at the sky.

"Whatever are you doing, Robin?" Maggie asked.

"Moving the clouds."

"My, my," said Mr. Beveridge, "to think you've been moving them all these years."

"I'm moving them into shapes."

Maggie looked up and stared at a white fluffy camel. As she watched, it changed to a cat.

"I'll make a zebra, if you don't mind blue stripes," and a rather perfect zebra formed above them.

"Robin, you can't..." but Maggie didn't finish her sentence because he was apparently doing it. But though he frightened her with his powers, his magic seemed harmless enough.

"Pesty little dog," said Mr. Beveridge as Felicity ran to his wheelchair, stood on her hind legs and hit at him with one paw.

"Come now, Mr. Beveridge, she's very good with you."

"Don't like dogs," said Mr. Beveridge, whose pink hair had turned to purple under his wife's ministrations.

Robin sat up and stared at Mr. Beveridge.

"I liked you better with pink hair."

"What's that, young man? Speak up."

"You were nicer with pink hair," Robin shouted. "Purple has soured you."

Mr. Beveridge peered with watery eyes at Robin.

"You ain't so nice with black hair. And you've got funny eyes."

Maggie laughed.

"Come, Robin, what shall I do about Felicity?"

"I'll wager that dog's still got your bone." Mr. Beveridge pointed an arthritic finger at Robin and chuckled. "Had it for weeks now. Looks like you can't do a simple trick right."

Robin crossed his legs, tailor fashion.

"Training might teach Felicity to return things." He haughtily ignored Mr. Beveridge's attack.

"What good's your magic, anyhow, boy?" clucked Mr. Beveridge.

"My magic is very powerful."

"And it certainly cheers people up," Maggie added, though she didn't think "cheers" quite the right word. She wondered what more she should say to Gerald about the house.

"Never cheered me," said Mr. Beveridge.

Robin jumped up, got behind Mr. Beveridge's wheelchair, and pantomimed pushing him up and over the knoll. Felicity circled round them, barking.

"Robin, come back." Maggie made a face and shook her head.

He flopped down beside her.

"You're supposed to start showing dogs when they're still puppies, Mrs. Featherstone. You could get a dog trainer who's a handler in the shows."

Whining, Felicity ran to Maggie's side, lay down, and put her head in her paws.

"It will be good for you, Felicity," Maggie assured her. Maybe training Felicity would be the diversion that would take Maggie's mind off her worries about how the house was held and her humiliating experience with Adair.

"I know someone special," volunteered Robin.

Felicity snorted.

"Her mother breeds dogs, and she sometimes handles

dogs for other people. Amelia Letterby."

Felicity gave a yelp.

"But is she your age?"

"If she was his age, she'd be a dunce," said Mr. Beveridge. "I wouldn't take no suggestion of his."

Grimacing, Robin sprang up and waving his wand, danced about Mr. Beveridge. Felicity jumped beside him. "I'll turn your hair black."

"Don't you dare." With effort Mr. Beveridge put his gnarled hands over his hair. "I've kind of got to like purple, if that's anything to you. Purple's a royal colour."

"Then it's not for you," said Robin, stooping to pet Felicity.

"Robin, about Miss Letterby," said Maggie, and Felicity returned her head to her paws, growling.

"She's an old maid." Robin balanced on one foot.

"She's a girl of twenty," corrected Mr. Beveridge.

"Really, Robin, how can a young girl be an old maid?"

"That's what her mother says. 'That girl will never marry', her mother says. 'She's too bossy and too fat'."

"Oh, my. But you shouldn't gossip."

"What's wrong with a little gossip?" asked Mr. Beveridge as he gazed at the downs. "Sad thing is, almost none of it's true."

"I like Amelia Letterby," said Robin, throwing his wand into the air and catching it.

"That's good enough for me." Maggie smoothed back Felicity's ears.

"I'll go talk to her right now. Then maybe I'll get my bone back."

He ran off, almost bumping into Mrs. Butterfield, who brought out tea.

"Watch out there!" Mrs. Butterfield's frown lengthened her already long face.

"Save some for me," Robin yelled over Mr. Beveridge's cackles.

By the time Maggie and Mr. Beveridge were ready for their second cup of tea, and Felicity had eaten all the biscuits, Robin came running across the lawn, Miss Letterby in tow.

That she was an unusually tall girl, and large, could not be argued, but Maggie felt in awe of the grace with which she ran. She reminded Maggie of a Gaston Lachaise sculpture, tiny at the feet, huge in the body, yet seemingly weightless. Her pale blonde hair was gelled to stand straight up in several jagged peaks, making her look as if she'd just witnessed an act of brutality. The round red rouge spots on her face, the arched eyebrows and white powder, added to that effect.

Introductions took place, tea and cakes were consumed, and the lessons commenced.

Miss Letterby spoke in a high, breathless, shy voice, barely audible. Apparently Felicity could not hear it at all, for she ignored her summons.

Robin ran after the puppy, caught her, and held her writhing on the ground while Miss Letterby slipped a show lead over Felicity's neck.

Felicity squirmed.

Miss Letterby started to walk.

Felicity sat down.

Miss Letterby pulled.

Felicity drew back.

Miss Letterby yanked sharply, and Felicity fell, tangled between Miss Letterby's legs.

"My, hasn't she personality," said Miss Letterby in her shy sort of whisper.

"What's that?" yelled Mr. Beveridge.

"Make Felicity do something," said Robin.

"We can't force these toys. Oh no. If we used a choke chain," she explained to Maggie, who strained to hear, "it would hurt her little neck. We must be very gentle and coax her."

Felicity sat, ears cocked, and peered at Miss Letterby suspiciously.

Maggie felt a bit intimidated herself by this huge young woman who appeared so vague with people and so commanding with dogs.

"I shall keep trying," said Miss Letterby as she gave a hefty tug and Felicity, caught by surprise, went flying. "Head up proud, Felicity."

"Good," said Maggie. "You keep at it while I take Mr. Beveridge home." She started pushing his wheelchair across the lawn.

"Can't hear a word that one says," he called up at her.

"No need to push," Robin said, walking behind the wheelchair and causing it to go on its own. "Goodbye Felicity. Be good," he shouted.

By the time Maggie returned, Miss Letterby had worked a miracle. Felicity followed her on a lead.

As the sun set, Maggie watched a giant, gelled Miss Letterby, one arm raised as if answering a call from the heavens, the other held out in back, grasping the lead, trot round the garden, the tap, tap of her sandals against her heels the only sound. The dolman sleeves of her white blouse unfurled, she looked like a schooner in full sail, a miniscule and somewhat deflated black and white spotted dinghy in tow.

CHAPTER XVIII

After several weeks of training — Felicity with treats, Miss Letterby with tea cakes — Felicity and Miss Letterby were ready for the puppy's first dog show. Or so said Miss Letterby.

Amelia Letterby seemed to enjoy her work at Raven Hall. Instead of arranging for a class or two a week, she came every morning for coffee and biscuits, stayed for a hearty lunch, and never went home until after what she called "a proper tea", which often included eggs and sausage.

Robin usually accompanied her.

"In expectation of getting back my bone," he explained.

Mrs. Butterfield was displeased, and she looked displeased.

"Don't know how much longer I can work here," she complained. "What with feeding all these people. And I never was my best at lunchtime."

There was not a dry dishtowel in the kitchen.

"It won't be for long, Mrs. Butterfield. Just until Felicity is trained."

"Don't see that happening soon, if you'll pardon me. That Felicity's smarter than Amelia Letterby. Smarter than all of us, I'd say. I was never one to put a damper on things, but..."

"Thank you, Mrs. Butterfield. If you'll just start lunch."

And so it went most days. Each night Gerald asked how the training was coming. His expectations for Felicity ran high. At work he'd started talking about the upcoming dog show.

"She'd better do well, my angel. I've asked some people from work to her first show," he'd said only last night. Maggie had told him a hundred times that it was only a local dog show. "It's such an unimportant show. It doesn't really matter if Felicity wins or loses."

"Winning always matters." Gerald had looked at Maggie with disdain. Once that look would have perturbed her. Now she only thought how foolish Gerald acted.

On the day of the dog show Miss Letterby, wearing a giant plastic apron, came early to groom Felicity.

Crooning to the puppy in her shy voice, Miss Letterby washed Felicity, adding a bit of conditioner to give body to her long ears and a shine to her coat. When it came time to cut off Felicity's whiskers, the puppy twisted her head this way and that, so Miss Letterby, a placid expression on her face, held Felicity up by the scruff of the neck.

"Miss Letterby!" cried Maggie. "No! You might put Felicity's eyes out!"

But Miss Letterby's shears snipped gingerly round Felicity's nose, the puppy's eyes wide in terror. "You can't be timid with dogs," she said in her shy voice.

Maggie decided she herself was better off inside and went to join Gerald for breakfast. She hovered a moment in the doorway, watching him eat muesli. He looked his Italian best, even in English tweeds.

"Today's the big day." He gazed longingly at the bowl of sugar near the muesli box. "Miss Always should be here shortly, and we can leave for the show."

"It's only a practice event for Felicity."

"She practices at home. That's what the trainer's for. Felicity had better win. I'll bet half the office is coming to watch. If she makes a fool out of me, darling..."

"Gerald, I've never pretended to anything." She sat down and unfolded her napkin.

"She'll win. No dog of mine would dare lose." He laughed jovially.

Mrs. Butterfield brought in a tray of muffins, but Maggie decided on black coffee. Mother of God, she thought, what are we in for today? As Felicity gave a howl from the garden, Maggie wondered if Gerald would be laughing in a few hours.

Gazing at the butter dish, Gerald broke his dry muffin, then stopped to listen to Felicity's howling.

"What's she screaming about?"

"She's being groomed. I can't guess what Miss Letterby is doing to her, and I don't want to know." Maggie took a sip of coffee and made a face. It tasted more bitter than usual this morning. "Gerald, I want to talk to you about the house."

"Isn't she used to being groomed? Darling, I hope she doesn't do that at the show. What would my friends think?"

For the first time Maggie realized that Gerald lived his life around what people thought of him. Never, of course, what she thought. Now he expected her dog to please his friends. She hadn't realized before that Gerald was so insecure, so trapped in the opinions of his peers.

"The house," persisted Maggie. "I've given you plenty of time to put it in my name as well."

"I'm taking care of it. Nothing to worry about."

"But it should be handled by now. I should have papers to sign. Just how..."

"Hello." Suddenly Miss Always was standing by the dining table.

Right on cue, thought Maggie. Always Miss Always to keep us from having any kind of communication. That Gerald is taking care of the house scares me. I think it's time I consult with Mr. Dunkley again.

"What a cozy time breakfast is," said Miss Always, as she sat down and reached for a muffin.

Gerald slipped off his glasses, put them into his pocket and smiled his dimpled smile.

Maggie glared at her but not without noting that Miss Always's short greenish wool skirt and tan jumper made her look a bit dumpy. Maggie glanced down to see if Miss Always wore her five-inch heels for the dog show. She did.

"I came round the back way, and the kitchen door was open." She slathered butter and marmalade onto a muffin. "So this is the big day."

"No," said Maggie.

"Yes," said Gerald. "The Normingtons and Lord and Lady Wizzell and the Evanses... and I can't be sure who else is coming. This will be Felicity's first win."

Gerald's win, thought Maggie. She felt a little sorry for him, so badly needing to win.

"I just know she'll get first prize," gushed Miss Always.

"How do you know?" asked Maggie, dryly.

"Gerald said so." She dribbled honey onto a second muffin.

"Gerald, how do you know?"

"Because I'm paying for the handler. I don't shell out that kind of money without results."

Maggie shrugged.

"You might co-operate a little more with her training. Every time you go near Felicity you tell her how badly she's doing. And now you expect her to win." Maggie stood up, put down her empty coffee cup, then walked through the drawing room to the mask room.

She opened the door hesitantly and looked round the room for the little nuns, but no one came into view.

"Sisters?"

No answer.

Maggie went to the mask shelves, picked out her new dog show mask, Hearty, and tried it on. It called for a tweedy kind of cap to match her skirt. She pulled this down from the top shelf.

"Goodbye, sisters," she said, feeling foolish. She put the mask in place. With it and her hat, she felt better able to meet those coming to view Felicity's success.

Even though the show was nearby, Miss Letterby insisted that Maggie bring the water Felicity was used to from Raven Hall's taps. Maggie got the thermos ready and packed the cooked liver for Felicity's treats.

Miss Letterby put Felicity into her kennel, and they all piled into the trainer's van. Maggie didn't quite see how, but Miss Always ended up on Gerald's lap.

At the showgrounds, Miss Letterby loaded a grooming table, chair, grooming tools and the kennel onto a trolley and wheeled them near the proper ring.

Once set up, Amelia Letterby combed and clipped and thinned and smoothed down and fluffed out until Felicity looked lovelier than she ever had.

"I thought she was groomed already," remarked Gerald.

"I guess it all gets done again," said Maggie. "Miss Letterby is a real perfectionist."

"Good," said Gerald. "She does seem to know what she's doing."

Maggie made a face at Gerald, for, of course, Miss Letterby could hear him as he stood right beside her.

"Look at some of those other King Charles spaniels," he motioned to Maggie. "They're much prettier than Felicity."

"Shhh, Gerald, she's only a puppy. She hasn't got her full coat yet. You'll break her spirit saying mean things about her."

"It's just the truth," said Miss Always. "I think they're prettier, too."

"Shhh," pleaded Maggie. "Don't forget, personality

counts a good deal."

Gerald gave a snort.

"She's usually darned obnoxious. If I'd known she'd be judged on personality, I wouldn't have come."

"Gerald, she hears you. Look at her staring at you with those huge eyes."

Miss Letterby looked up from her combing.

"It's easy to spook a dog before a show," she said in her high, shy voice. "If you would like to stand away from Felicity, it would be a good idea. Come, Felicity, head up proud."

"Right," agreed Maggie.

"I'll stand anywhere I like," said Gerald. "Felicity, see all those beautiful dogs? You'll have to think positively to win against them."

"Gerald," Maggie sighed. "How is she going to think positively when you make her feel like... like... shit?"

"Maggie, let's not get vulgar."

"Did you bring a honey pot?" asked Miss Always. "You could stick one on her."

Gerald looked lovingly at his secretary.

"Come on." Maggie took both Gerald and Miss Always by their arms and led them to the ring, where the judge of toy dogs was still examining Pekingese. "You see, first she'll go against puppy bitches. If she wins Minor Puppy, she may go in against the winner of the Yearlings or Juniors. If she's the Best Bitch Puppy, she'll go against the older bitches for Best Bitch, then against the dogs for Best of Breed."

Gerald's face fell.

"You didn't tell me it was that complicated. How can she win against those beautiful older dogs?" He looked at the full-coated Blenheims and Tri-colours being groomed outside the ring.

"I don't know," said Maggie. "Maybe she can't. I'd love to see her win, though. She deserves a win, she's so spunky."

"Look!" Miss Always brightened. "There's Lord and Lady Wizzell."

"Sorry I asked them now," mumbled Gerald.

"Cooee!" Miss Always waved.

Maggie watched as the sanguine looking couple — he with red and white moustachio decidedly too bushy, she with odd little mousy bangs freshly pasted on — walked towards the ring. Maggie realized they lived in a world very different from her own, a world in which Gerald was now at home. And he'd brought that world to the dog show as if he were only comfortable in the heart of high risk, high power. She envisioned Gerald in his box at Lloyd's, underwriting risks that could turn from pure gold to fool's gold, his entire life based on juggling.

Maggie decided that Felicity's winning in her first dog show was far more chancey than the risks Lloyd's members took, say, insuring Elizabeth Taylor's nose. Or was it her eyes that had been insured by Lloyd's? Maggie wondered if Gerald had made bets on today's outcome.

A bustle of activity took place near the ring as handlers of English Toys, armbands in place, readied their entrants. Amelia Letterby came forward with Felicity and had no trouble elbowing her way to the ring's entrance.

A Blenheim puppy was called first and trotted smartly about the ring, its deep orange spots gleaming.

"Why are they showing orange and white puppies with the Tri-colours?" asked Gerald. "I think that one starting out is much nicer than Felicity."

"That's a dog," said Maggie, adjusting Hearty. "The bitches go next."

"The Blenheims are showier, though," insisted Gerald.

Hearty slipped, and Maggie pushed it back again.

Next came a Tri-colour puppy that toddled along unsteadily. Its owner, a willowy woman, took long, slow leaps so the puppy would appear to run well.

Another Blenheim entered and sat down. Its handler, a square, tweedy British woman, whose feet, in sensible brown oxfords, appeared bigger than the puppy, coaxed and pulled at the lead.

That such large people handled such tiny dogs fascinated Maggie, especially when she noticed the small owners leading Irish Wolfhounds and Scottish Deerhounds to their respective rings.

Yapping dogs in the adjoining ring caught her attention, and she looked over to see Yorkshire terriers. Mother of God, it's Adair with Little Poop.

Before she could look down, he raised his head and saw her. Both stared helplessly. Beneath Hearty Maggie could feel her cheeks burn.

"Here you are," said Miss Always. "I was just talking to... oh, there's someone I know." She waved at Adair. "My, doesn't he look red in the face?"

"Really," hissed Maggie, "I don't think you could know him."

"Cooee," Miss Always called as Maggie wanted to sink into the ground. How dare this woman know Adair?

Clutching Little Pooh to his breast, Adair Trueblood spun about and fled.

"Bloody hell," said Miss Always. "Did you see him just take off. He mustn't be the man I met."

Where had she met him? Maggie wondered. What was she up to?

Gerald nudged Maggie.

"It's our turn."

Maggie edged closer to the ring.

Amelia Letterby, Felicity in tow, prepared to enter. "Head up proud, Felicity," she said in her shy voice. She handed Felicity a nibble of liver and stuffed some, to be meted out to Felicity in the ring, into her own mouth. Maggie wondered how much would go to bait Felicity and how much would be swallowed to console Miss Letterby.

Miss Letterby stood still a moment, her head bent to one side as if listening to some other worldly command. At last, her arms went out — one up to the heavens, one down, holding the lead. Her white dolman sleeves caught the wind, and the schooner and dinghy were underway.

Though Maggie was familiar with such a sight on her huge lawn, she had never seen Miss Letterby at work in a small ring. She now felt so overwhelmed by the giant white apparition sailing before her, the slap, slap of sandals like waves hitting against wood, she forgot to notice poor Felicity.

When she did manage to look down, she knew the two were in deeper water than expected.

Felicity always ran round the garden with spirit, her head high. Now, though Miss Letterby kept reminding her, "Head up proud," and tempted her repeatedly, she did not reach up for the bits of liver straight from Miss Letterby's mouth. She did not jump up as she ran, the way she did at home.

Instead, she lowered her head, slunk to the ground, ignored Miss Letterby's tugs and squeals of encouragement, and moved as if treading water, while submissively following in Miss Letterby's wake.

"Where's her spunk?" whispered Gerald, as the Evanses and Normingtons from Lloyd's arrived. "She's always full of beans."

"Ah, Lord and Lady Wizzell. Our dearest friends," Edith Normington said so loudly several onlookers at ngside turned around.

But Maggie took no notice. She was only concerned with the fact that Gerald had indeed spooked Felicity. The puppy was lifted to the judge's table and stood passively, head down, while the judge, a small baldheaded man in a pink polyester jacket, frowned.

"He's looking her over again," said Gerald to Maggie. "What do you think he sees?" He turned to the Lloyd's group. "She looks good, doesn't she, standing there? Nice and quiet. A judge should like that."

"I think she's a little too quiet," murmured Maggie. How unfair. Felicity was so full of the joy of life. How easy it was for the cynical to crush the hopeful.

Felicity was placed on the ground and again performed her lackluster tread.

As suddenly as the show had begun, it ended as the judge handed a Blenheim's owner the red first place ribbon, a Tri-colour's handler the blue, Miss Letterby the yellow, and another Blenheim's handler the green.

"Is it over?" asked Gerald. "There's been no ceremony whatsoever."

"Third place!" cried Maggie. "How wonderful!"

"Third place!" Gerald was aghast. "That's worse than losing!"

"Nonsense, Gerald. It's quite good for her first show." Hearty pinched. Maggie slipped it off and tossed it into a nearby trashbin.

"What a pretty yellow ribbon," said Miss Always.

Felicity! Winning yellow! thought Maggie. What have you done?

Lord and Lady Wizzell and their small entourage crowded round Felicity.

"What happens next?" asked Lady Wizzell.

"I think that's it," said Maggie, taking Felicity from

Miss Letterby and cuddling the puppy, who looked as if she knew she'd let everyone down.

Lord Wizzell edged behind Maggie and pinched her derriere. Maggie moved closer to Gerald.

"Won't she be in other events?" asked Mrs. Normington as Mr. Normington, standing behind his wife, gave Maggie a conspiratorial smile and winked.

"Yes," Gerald turned to Maggie, "you said she would... the bitches... the dogs..."

"That's if she won first prize."

Gerald looked chagrined. The Lloyd's group laughed rather too loudly.

"Felicity looked so lovely," cooed Lady Wizzell.

"Yellow suits her," added mini-skirted Mrs. Evans, and Maggie looked at her sharply to see if she were being ironic.

Not one petted Felicity. Instead they backed away.

Maggie felt furious. It's as if they believe they can catch Third Place as one would catch the flu.

Though no one said it, the thought was in the air: they had come to see a loser.

As suddenly as the judging had ended, the Lloyd's group dispersed.

"Must get back to the City," said Mr. Normington.

"Jolly good show," young, bouncing Mr. Evans insisted. "See you at the office, Gerald."

Lord Wizzell twisted his moustache. "Good to have a day in the country."

"Goodbye. Goodbye..."

Gerald stood with Miss Always, dumbfounded. "Amelia..."

"I'm sure she prefers 'Miss Letterby'," Maggie whispered. "More professional."

"Amelia?"

"Yes?" Miss Letterby put down the kennel and looked at Gerald.

"I think you can guess how disappointed I am in you. I just can't have you working with Felicity any longer."

Miss Letterby's blue eyes became watery.

"Felicity has been very well trained, I can assure you."

"Come now..."

"You spooked Felicity. You criticized her and humiliated her — and she can understand every word you say. Now you want someone else to take the blame. Under the circumstances, she performed admirably."

"I agree with Miss Letterby," said Maggie. "She and Felicity did splendidly."

"But you lost," said Miss Always. "You were supposed to *win.*"

As they carted Felicity and her trappings to the van, Maggie whispered to Miss Letterby that she was to come to tea whenever she liked.

Maggie decided that her idea of who was a winner and who a loser, was so diametrically opposed to Gerald's it was no wonder they hadn't seen eye to eye in a very long while.

For the first time since she'd met Gerald, Maggie had the very strong conviction that *she* was right.

CHAPTER XIX

Maggie sat in the priory chapel, waiting for Father Humphrey to begin his sermon. She couldn't help thinking about Raven Hall. Mr. Dunkley had promised to investigate what on earth Gerald had done about the title.

But she was at Mass now and must concentrate on peaceful thoughts. She wondered if Gerald had peaceful thoughts. Why was Felicity winning first prize everything to him? Did he think that in Miss Always he had anything but a yellow ribbon winner?

Thank God Gerald hadn't ruined Felicity's spirit, and that Miss Letterby still enjoyed coming to tea. That's what counted. There'd be no more dog shows.

The uneasy feeling that she herself was in some kind of contest and was coming in third to Gerald's schemes and Miss Always's allure nagged at Maggie's mind.

Father Humphrey cleared his throat and began, as usual, in dramatic fashion. He flung his arms out and lisped, "We are made in the image of the Cross."

As Maggie thought about his statement, she realized he'd got it backwards.

But he went right on. "We could just as easily have been made in the image of..." he hesitated "... of hedgehogs." He looked satisfied with that.

Maggie was sick to death of Miss Always's hedgehogs, and now to have Father Humphrey throwing them up at her, and on a Sunday morning. It was just too much.

She had the disturbing mental picture of a round instrument of torture designed especially for hedgehogs. Then she could not chase the image of Christ as a hedgehog from her mind.

As Father Humphrey talked, Maggie got the vague impression that his sermon was actually about love and ering. He should be more responsible for his images so could follow the gist, especially since he was a mystic.

" 'If any man will come after me, let him deny himself and take up his cross and follow me'," quoted Father Humphrey.

Was it Thomas À Kempis or St. Matthew? He was fond of both. Maggie tried not to think of those in the congregation as small round hedgehogs, picking up their odd crosses. She sighed. She had not taken up her cross willingly, and she put it down more often than not, in fact, every chance she got.

" 'In the Cross is salvation, in the Cross is life, in the Cross is protection against our enemies, in the Cross is infusion of heavenly sweetness, in the Cross is strength of mind, in the Cross joy of spirit, in the Cross the height of virtue, in the Cross is the perfection of holiness. There is no salvation of the soul, nor hope of everlasting life, but in the Cross'."

Maggie began to feel he was speaking just to her but with slightly different words than those in his sermon. Yes, I am blissful, he seemed to say. But that bliss was long in coming, and it came from suffering. You cannot hide from suffering, my child — his eyes were looking right at her — you must embrace it. Only then can you transcend it.

And then the moment was over, and Father Humphrey lisped on, smiling sheepishly in a vague awareness that he had mixed his metaphors.

What did he mean? she wondered. Was she to somehow work it out with Gerald? Father Humphrey certainly hadn't been pleased she'd tried to find happiness with Adair. Or did he mean she was to embrace the single state and the loneliness that would result? Come to think of it, she couldn't be more lonely than with Gerald.

Why didn't Father Humphrey say exactly what he meant? One thing was sure, heavenly advice always seemed to come muddled up, in need of interpretation.

CHAPTER XX

One day, quite by accident, as if Fate wished to prove that after all it is a very small world, Maggie caught sight of Gerald and Miss Always in Brighton. What were the two doing so far from the office?

She'd decided to shop near home for a new dress for Gerald's next business party. Finding nothing she liked, Maggie had taken a walk to the pier, braving the wind on this cold late summer's day to watch the greenish water crashing underneath. Flags flying from the pier did nothing to add a festive note to the nearly deserted boardwalk and beach. What a strange day for Gerald to escort Miss Always.

Maggie was sure she hadn't been seen, but just in case, she pulled over her head the large scarf she wore with her Burberry coat. She crossed the street from the ocean side and followed them as they strolled past shops and majestic old hotels. They stopped outside one shop window, Miss Always pointing to something. Then they went inside.

Maggie walked closer. Oh, it couldn't be! Not one of those ghastly candy shops that sold hard Brighton rock candy in disgusting pink and white!

The pair came out. Miss Always, smiling like a child, carried a bag of candy. She offered the bag to Gerald and he pulled out a stick of rock candy.

Maggie wanted to call out. He would break his bridge on that. Miss Always shouldn't let him. But then she didn't know Gerald had terrible teeth, wore a bridge. We should inspect a lover's teeth the way we inspect his appearance, Maggie thought. And then she reddened a little, thinking of her own escapade with Adair and what she had had the privilege to inspect.

Just then Gerald bent his head and grabbed at his jaw.

He reached into his mouth and pulled something from it. His bridge, surely.

Miss Always looked concerned. She pointed in the direction of town, and the two hurried off.

Maggie didn't bother to follow. They would be up to little trouble this afternoon.

It seemed it wasn't Maggie's job any more to save Gerald from nuisance and pain. She supposed that's what striking out with someone else meant — more nuisance and pain with the shield of protection gone. But the hazards, she had learned to her disadvantage, were offset by the excitement of the new, the risk of the moment. Still, she had had enough of such adventures for the time being.

Gerald came home that night for dinner — broth and aspirin — mumbling something about a broken bridge and a trip to the dentist, and sore gums. Later, as he and Maggie sat before the fire in the drawing room, Maggie mentioned their next party as she leafed through a copy of *Country Life.*

"Will Miss Always be invited?" She looked up to catch his pained expression and imagined it was as much from her question as from his sore gums.

"Darling, Miss Always most definitely will be invited." He held an ice pack to his cheek.

"And any of the neighbours?"

"No, certainly not. This is a business affair."

Despite Father Humphrey's admonitions about charity, Maggie could not feel very eager or helpful about this soirée.

"The same guest list then?"

"Miss Always attends to those things."

"It is helpful if I know who's coming. And I must say, I don't like her caterers and don't intend to use them."

"If you insist." He put his head back and closed his

eyes.

Maggie stared into the fire and planned. She would serve a buffet — a ham, a turkey, perhaps a goose, and any number of breads and salads. Nothing to be cooked last minute. That way she'd have time for the guests. But she would need help, and whom could she trust?

If asked later where the idea came from, she would probably credit the fire. Suddenly in the flames, she saw Mongoose with his red bandana.

Why not? He'd be excellent help in the kitchen. Mr. Dunkley could mix drinks. He'd outcharm all the guests. But who would serve *hors d'oeuvres?*

A log slipped, sparks scattered, and Maggie saw Robin's sly Gypsy smile. If he would do it, he'd be perfect.

"You're very quiet, darling," Gerald said finally.

"Just making plans for the party."

"Well, you're an elegant hostess, Maggie. I know I can count on you."

"Yes, Gerald, you certainly can. I think this will be my finest party."

"By the way, you know those paintings you sold? You've never told me where you deposited the money?"

"Well," Maggie hadn't expected the question tonight. She decided to be direct. "I did what you asked."

"And where's the money?"

"I gave most of the paintings to the museum."

Gerald sat up, dropping his ice pack, and stared at her.

"I didn't ask that."

"Actually, you did. Years ago, we agreed we'd one day give them to the museum, so this was the perfect time."

"How could you do a thing like that without asking me?"

"It seems we've both done a good deal without checking with the other."

Gerald stared at her a moment. "You said 'most'."

"Most what?"

"You said you gave most to the museum. What about the others?"

"I stored my favourites. We'll be glad to go home to those."

"Home? Where have you stored them?"

"I... a... I forget exactly. I have it written down somewhere."

"You're sure? You can find it, can't you."

"Of course, but I'll have to rummage through my things. But we certainly don't need the name now."

"It's good that I should know. In case anything should happen."

"Gerald, you sound so ominous. Nothing's going to happen."

"Find it, will you, darling?" He held his head in his hands.

"I shall do magic?" Robin announced haughtily.

"No, Robin. I think not. There will be too many guests, and they'll all be talking business. I doubt they'll make a good audience." She really couldn't stand the strain of Robin's magic as well as that of the party. Who could guess what he'd think up?

He gave Maggie a curious smile as if to contradict her. "What mask will you wear?"

"Oh, I haven't thought yet. What would you suggest?"

"Charm?"

"No. I think it's a frightening kind of mask. Charm makes people let down their defences. They feel Charm really cares. But Charm cares only for..."

"...Charm." Robin laughed.

"What would you say to Tolerance?" Maggie was sure Father Humphrey would approve, though she disliked it.

Robin nodded, with that infuriating knowing look of his, so Maggie supposed Tolerance would be the choice.

Days of activity preceded the party. An early autumn chill in the air added to Maggie's mood of anticipation. She motored into town with Mr. Dunkley to fetch boxes of food.

Mrs. Butterfield, her large frame stooped over the kitchen sink, polished silver and pewter and washed the crystal goblets, breaking only six.

The day before the soirée, Maggie, with Mrs. Butterfield's help, baked chocolate cakes and macaroon jam tarts and readied the ingredients for lime chiffon, custard, and apple pies that would be popped into the oven at the last minute.

Mongoose melted chocolate and sifted flour and beat bowls of egg whites and ground almonds in a nut grinder, all the while singing in his deep baritone.

Mr. Dunkley polished the butler's pantry, got out all the bottles and mixes and glasses, and gave his approval to the pie fillings.

Robin pulled a bottle of nutmeg from his hat and urged Maggie to add it to all the dishes. He also licked the bowls and made measuring spoons and cups disappear, and Felicity pranced on her hind legs, begging treats.

"Robin, just don't do *anything* with my ham or turkey," Maggie cautioned as she prepared the honey and cherry glaze.

Delicious Christmas-type smells of sage and cloves and nutmeg filled the kitchen, putting its occupants into a party mood, all except Mrs. Butterfield.

"These men have no place in my kitchen," she whispered loudly to Maggie.

"But Mrs. Butterfield, you don't like to cook and said you wouldn't for a party of all things."

"Well, a body don't like to be left out, neither." She reached for the dishtowel tucked in at her waist and dabbed at her eyes.

"I think, Mrs. Butterfield, that your cleaning will be the key to the success of the party. I'm counting on you. And you'll be opening the door for all the guests."

"That don't make me feel better. I'm left out. That's what I am."

The night of the party arrived, and Gerald appeared relaxed, convinced by Maggie that all was in shipshape order. September had crept upon them. Summer ended that very night. The next day would be the first day of autumn. Maggie thought of tonight as a kind of farewell party, and she chose autumn colours for her flower decorations. As the dining room centerpiece she used two wicker cornucopias, their horns spewing grapes and apples and baby pumpkins and spider mums. And she smothered the drawing room with vases of creamy mums.

What she wore seemed particularly important to Maggie. She'd chosen a full length Chanel shirtdress in cream silk; a wide sash tied with a knot in front. As a jacket, she wore the matching ribbed cardigan that came almost to her knees. Her jewels consisted of eight long strands, four of gold, four of cultured pearls, with pearl bracelets at her wrists and pearl earrings, one large pearl each, surrounded by seed pearls. Her outfit looked dressy, but it also looked country. Elegant, casual. With Tolerance in place, she was ready for her guests.

In the kitchen to check her assembled staff, she was shocked to see that Robin no longer wore one of the white jackets she had ordered for him and Mr. Dunkley. Instead, he stood in a black swallow-tailed coat, looking, she had to admit, dashing.

Mr. Dunkley folded a napkin to wear over one arm.

"You're right out of a movie," Robin told him.

"And you as well. The mad magician." Mr. Dunkley's eyes twinkled.

Mongoose, in a white shirt, had already begun washing a few dishes left in the sink.

"A boy called Robin makes magic, makes magic..." he sang.

Robin's striated eyes, flashing as he listened to the song, made Maggie uncomfortable. As she turned to leave, she noticed his tall silk hat behind the cookbooks at the end of one counter.

Back upstairs, Maggie put aside *L'air du Temps* and instead daubed on *Anais Anais*.

Gerald knocked and entered.

"Will you do up my bow tie, darling?"

For just a moment, Maggie recalled parties of years past, parties at which Gerald would joke and tease.

Maggie watched his face as she knotted the tie. She was aware of how very English Gerald acted at the moment, how prim and shrunken from his expansive Italian self — eyes tired and lined, like eyes that expected to be covered by glasses, lips thinner and unsmiling — how very English he acted most of the time now when he was with her. Maggie wondered if he had exhibited this English side so many years ago or if she had simply refused to see it. How much do we pretend when love is at stake? she wondered. Then she had the awful thought that perhaps he no longer cared if she saw only this side of him.

Ready, the two descended the stairs together.

"I hope you found a good catering crew. I want everything to go off without a hitch tonight."

"An excellent crew." Maggie retied the sash at her

waist. She looked up to see Miss Always standing in the drawing room, awaiting them. "Ah, Miss Always, the first to arrive."

"I want to be sure everything is in order."

Mother of God, and in my home. We could light the house with her cheerfulness.

Maggie adjusted Tolerance.

"Everything is in splendid order, Miss Always." Father Humphrey is asking more than he knows, Maggie thought.

"I know what my job can be." Miss Always fluffed her golden locks. "I can greet the guests as they arrive, since I know them all."

"Good idea," said Gerald just as Maggie started to object.

How dare she play hostess? thought Maggie. She's like Goldilocks. Eating my porridge. Sleeping in my bed. If only the mamma or pappa bear, or even baby bear, would gobble her up.

Miss Always wore a long black taffeta dress. To Maggie, black was a sophisticated colour, but not on Miss Always, whose gown was strapless and very low on her very high breasts. The material hugged her body all the way to the knees, rounding startlingly at the hips, and flaring out at the knees in a huge ruffle to the floor. Frederick's of Hollywood again, Maggie thought, though obviously Gerald preferred that design to a Chanel.

Maggie would have to confess to Father Humphrey that she was inordinately pleased to see that black did nothing for Miss Always's complexion, that her enemy looked decidedly sallow tonight. Her blue eyelashes and eyelids, sparkled with glitter, and her bright pink, glossy lips stood out garishly against skin of a faint yellowish cast.

Maggie turned to Gerald and noticed what she should have known: that it was not the complexion or eyes or lips that he was studying.

The doorbell rang and Mrs. Butterfield, muttering to herself, opened the door and gathered wraps. As she showed the guests into the drawing room, Miss Always stepped up to greet them, so Maggie scurried into the kitchen for another last minute check.

"You'll remember to call me if there are problems?" she asked.

"Indeed, madam, we shall have no difficulty whatsoever. Attend your party with a relaxed mind." Mr. Dunkley gave a little bow, and stepped jauntily out the kitchen door with a tray of glasses.

Maggie hurried back to her guests in time to see Mr. Dunkley hand Miss Always a cocktail. Gerald started to cough violently. Maggie hit him on the back, but he pushed her away.

"That man," Gerald managed to stutter between coughs. "That man is handing out drinks."

"Mr. Dunkley? Yes, he is."

"Did someone not show up?" Gerald blew his nose and wiped his eyes.

"I don't know what you mean, dear." As she glided away, she noticed Mr. Normington rub his eyes and take a second look in Mr. Dunkley's direction.

Robin followed Mr. Dunkley. Balancing a tray of hot cheese puffs on one finger, "You've timed the cheese puffs to perfection," said Maggie. "I always manage to burn a few."

"I'm very careful," said Robin, grinning and twirling the tray as he passed it from one group to another.

Gerald came up to Maggie. "What's that boy doing here? And in tails?"

"Serving cheese puffs, darling."

"I can see that."

"Have you had one? They're delicious."

"*Where* is the catering staff?"

"You've seen two of them. Amazingly competent."

"Maggie, this is disgraceful. You could have let Miss Always handle this."

"Yes, and been in a muddle." Then she whispered, "I'll handle my own parties in my own house," and moved away to a group of guests.

Maggie nodded and smiled and shifted from group to group, hearing bits of conversation. Meaningless chatter. Small talk. She realized people talked *at* each other.

"Petroleum drilling is perfectly safe," said Mr. Brown to Miss Simpson, who responded, "As we waited in traffic outside the Haymarket that night, a car drove up, quite an ordinary car, and who should get out but Princess Di! I'm just certain it was. Looked cold, too, with no jacket and a strapless cocktail dress."

"Safety precautions with drilling now, don't you see?" continued Mr. Brown. "Blowouts are a thing of the past."

"I wonder if that was a bodyguard with her."

Maggie passed behind Miss Always.

"I poked at the hedgehog," Miss Always explained in her honey-rich voice to several elderly gentlemen.

"You must add brandy," Mrs. Evans insisted to Lady Wizzell.

"But I don't cook," Lady Wizzell protested.

"Brandy, not rum. Rum's so nice, of course, but not..."

"Our alarm system is such a nuisance," Mrs. Flemming, less charming than some, explained to Lord Wizzell, who leered at Maggie as she passed.

"We found *Sunset Boulevard* very clever," Gerald was telling Mr. Normington and Mr. Evans.

Maggie staggered and caught herself on the couch. Gerald was talking openly now about a musical he and

Miss Always must have seen. And the men seemed to know who "we" meant. He'd ceased to take precautions, ceased to protect Maggie.

Tolerance could not hide her humiliation. She had never before realized how much she felt validated by what Gerald thought of her.

Mrs. Butterfield mournfully hit a gong to summon guests to dinner.

After dinner, while Mr. Dunkley and Robin brought coffee and cognac, Maggie curled on the floor near the fire with some of the younger guests.

Then she noticed the oak door to the little narrow room slowly open. Maggie rose to her knees, but before she could stand, out came a diaphanous Mother Magdalene, wearing Maggie's green hat with the grosgrain and feathers.

Maggie meant to grab for the hat as it passed her but felt too stunned to move.

Sister Aloysius followed, Maggie's black straw tilted jauntily to one side of her head, the veil flying as if part of her wraith form.

A woman gave a little scream, and guests turned in the nuns' direction just as Sister Orelia, very grand in Maggie's newest creation with roses all about the brim, waltzed in a circle about the room.

"How can hats be floating?" said an amazed young man next to Maggie.

Thank God the guests can't see the nuns, she thought.

"Look! Hats in the air!" squealed Miss Always.

Maggie searched desperately round the room for help, and her eyes lit on Robin, who stood near the dining room, a superior grin curling his lips. He gave a nod and disappeared into the kitchen.

"Maggie!" Gerald's voice boomed across the room.

She stared at him, unable to rise from her knees.

Robin pranced back, wearing his tall silk hat and waving his magician's wand grandly.

"Magic, ladies and gentlemen. Magic. Observe the world's greatest magician, the one and only Robin."

He dashed in front of Mother Magdalene, and began to strut backwards round the drawing room, facing the nuns and waving his wand as if conducting an orchestra. The nuns seemed pleased to follow his lead, dipping this way and that and smiling at the guests, though only the hats could be seen.

Miss Always clapped.

"What wonderful magic."

In her relief, Maggie almost liked her.

"How I'd love to have one of those hats!" Miss Always gave her honey rich laugh. "That one with the roses."

Over my dead body, mumbled Maggie, now disliking her more intensely than ever.

Gerald rushed over to Maggie.

"I thought everything was going to go smoothly."

"What a show, Gerald," said Lord Wizzell. "That magician has got real talent. We could use him at Lloyd's."

They all laughed. Lady Wizzell applauded.

"You see, Gerald, they love it. A little magic lightens the mood." Despite her words, Maggie sank back onto the floor, one hand over her burning face, peeking out at the parade.

After the nuns had made three remarkable revolutions round the drawing room, they bowed. The guests clapped again as the hats dipped down, then up.

Finally, Robin gave a flourish with his wand and backed to the door of the narrow room. There he stood, waving the nuns inside, the hats bobbing and turning from back to front, as the nuns kept glancing back at the guests.

Once inside, Sister Orelia tried to rush back, but a

diaphanous hand grabbed her, pulled her into the room, and slammed the oak door shut.

Robin bowed to more clapping.

"Absolutely splendid party," said Mrs. Normington as Maggie rose. "We must dash... but entertainment! We didn't expect it. How clever of you."

"Loved it," said Mr. Normington. He bent toward Maggie and whispered, "Though I was rather hoping we could tango."

"What a lot of trouble you went to, Mrs. Featherstone. Gerald's a lucky man," said Mr. Brown.

"Grand food, grand company, grand magic," said Lord Wizzell, twirling his red and white moustachio.

Gerald, standing to one side of Maggie in the entrance hall, beamed through all the compliments as if he had done the magic himself; and Miss Always, who stood at his other side, beamed as well.

No doubt, thought Maggie, she's envisioning her own parties in my house and her own magic shows.

Mrs. Butterfield handed out wraps, then shut the door on the last guests.

"What a wonderful party!" Miss Always exclaimed, returning to the drawing room. She slipped off her shoes and curled into a chair in front of the fire as if she planned to spend the night.

Mrs. Butterfield snorted, then walked toward the kitchen stairs and her room.

"Miss Always is spending the night so we can drive into the office together in the morning," Gerald announced as if such an arrangement were natural. "I trust the guest rooms are in order?"

"I know just the room for her," said Maggie. Felicity used the one Maggie was thinking of as her romping area, strewing pillows and toys about. Efficient Miss Always could handle that. "I'll see to things in the kitchen."

Maggie felt more angry now than hurt. A subtle turning point had occurred tonight. Miss Always acted bolder, Gerald more obvious.

Oh, Maggie could order Miss Always from her house, but she would only seem unreasonable. Maggie had tried so hard to avoid a confrontation. She'd wanted Gerald to have all the time he needed. She couldn't believe he hadn't seen through Miss Always by now. Instead, he seemed as infatuated, *more* infatuated, than ever.

Maggie felt as if she were looking in the mirrors at a fun house: now I'm fat; now I'm thin. She had put on a splendid party and somehow fallen into a weaker position. The irony did not escape her. Forces were rushing her towards a new mirror — now I'm divorced. She did not know how grotesque she would look in that mirror. She did not know how she could identify with that unnatural image: all alone, without Gerald.

In the kitchen, indefatigable Mongoose had finished several loads of dishes. Mr. Dunkley gave a final polish to the butler's pantry ledge, and with his wand, Robin guided the last serving tray through the air to its rack.

"You are all amazing," said Maggie.

"Yes," said Mr. Dunkley. "We try to be. We enjoyed ourselves thoroughly, madam."

The huge black islander dried his hands and handed Maggie a piece of paper from the top of the fridge. "Mongoose has picture."

"Why, Mongoose, this is lovely." She stared at a crude picture of a house, with lots of green about it and brightly coloured flowers. Over all hung a bright orange sun.

"World not quarrel on Mongoose now."

Maggie smiled sadly. She couldn't tell him the world had quarrelled on them all tonight.

CHAPTER XXI

Maggie sighed. Even her most ordinary days s
trifle un-ordinary. She felt as if she were in Ca
waiting for aftershocks from an earthquake. She knew they would come, that the earth would continue to fault and fold, that her very foundation would be shaken, maybe even shattered forever. Yet she could do nothing but wait. She couldn't call for help. Couldn't scream out. Couldn't rush to a safer place. The shocks would come.

After several days or weeks of aftershocks, she would almost get used to them. That's the way Maggie felt today. The quake had occurred when she arrived in England and met Miss Always. Everything else had been an aftershock, some — like Gerald's putting the house in his name — almost as strong as the earthquake itself.

Maggie decided to have a day in London. This time there'd be no sleuthing. She wouldn't need a mask. She'd be anonymous, since she'd see no one she knew. She decided on Robin's favourite hat, the large black one with roses round the crown, the one Miss Always coveted. With this she wore a rose tunic dress and black and rose fringed silk shawl. She felt smart; she felt excited.

As the train lumbered past rows and rows of ugly brick houses, sporting sooty chimney pots, she decided she'd have a go at Harrods. Gerald's birthday was the next Saturday. She'd get him something, though she didn't want to. What would make no statement? A tie. Anyone could give a tie — an uncle, a child, a neighbour. Ties bore no real significance.

Liberty's of London was the perfect store for a tie, Adair had said, and he did have excellent taste.

"Not Harrods," he'd said. "Never buy a tie at Harrods." She had assumed he meant that Harrods's ties were inferior, but wished now she had asked him why. Never mind, that's just what she'd do, buy Gerald's tie at Harrods. She'd search for a perfectly ordinary tie. A rather unattractive tie. Gerald would never expect her to be so unimaginative and would be astounded.

Maggie found herself wondering what Miss Always might buy. A birthday lunch for the three of them, which she'd have to give since the date fell on a Saturday, would force Miss Always to produce her present. Gerald would know Maggie's tie was revenge, and he'd know Maggie would be laughing at Miss Always's present.

Maggie realized she'd made a decision. Too many points behind, she'd no longer compete to hold Gerald. She planned a respectable showing, a dignified exit. She planned to leave at *her* time in *her* way. And she planned to force Gerald to remember these last weeks forever.

She caught a taxi to Harrods and pushed past shoppers to Men's Ties. Entering the department, she stopped short. Above the crowd, she could see a head of lusty hair. Adair? Why would he be here after what he'd said about Harrods's ties? Maggie sidled closer to be sure if it were he.

Multi-patterned ties covered a counter and the man with lusty hair bent over them. He raised his head to address a young, rather smart woman. Yes. It was Adair. Maggie felt a twinge of jealousy.

Then she observed that he stood on one side of the counter, the woman on the other. He held out a tie for the woman's inspection, then knotted it round his fingers, showing her the effect. The woman shook her head, no, and he reached into the case for others.

He was selling ties! He was selling ties in Harrods! He worked as a salesman for Harrods!

Maggie quickly stepped back so she couldn't be seen, as a wave of pity engulfed her. Investment consultant! How very much he wanted to play at being important.

But, after all, isn't that what Gerald does? she thought. Play at being important.

And both are busy juggling.

Maggie stared as Adair joked with his customer. He took pictures from his wallet. Oh, no. Little Poop.

She felt bad, admitting to herself he was an imposter, a con artist. She recalled his sitting proudly in the Rolls and realized he'd rented it.

Maggie backed away from Men's Ties, from Adair Trueblood. Then she turned and pushed towards an exit.

She left Harrods, forgot the nice lunch she'd planned at some lovely place, and stopped at Liberty's for a tie for Gerald. She decided a less than attractive tie would prove too mean spirited.

Maggie no longer felt like seeing a play. She caught the next train to the country. As she sat back, downhearted, the train rumbled over and over, "Vanity of vanities, all is vanity."

Saturday arrived. Maggie had no choice but to bake a birthday cake. Gerald liked the yellow cake his mother used to make, with white icing on top and vanilla custard between the layers. A very bland sort of cake to Maggie's mind, but it was his birthday.

The front doorbell rang as Maggie opened the flour tin. Mrs. Butterfield, grumbling, went to answer it.

Felicity barked, and Maggie looked up to see Miss Always, laden with a briefcase and pot plant, toddle into the kitchen. She wore what was apparently her idea of birthday splendour — a yellow acrylic jumper with glitter patterned in large swirls over her breasts. In her ears sparkled rhinestone earrings. And round her neck hung

Gerald's gold locket.

"Don't you just love the glittery style?" she asked as Maggie took the briefcase from her and put it on a chair. Without waiting for a response, she handed Maggie the pot plant as well. "Isn't this manly? You can't very well bring a man flowers, can you? But a plant. And cacti are so masculine."

As Miss Always attempted to shoo Felicity away, Maggie stared at the bulbous growths, prickly with spines, and was not quite sure what Miss Always meant. Maggie did not, however, intend to ask. Nor did she intend to say that Gerald hated cacti ever since he'd had to dig them out of their garden in the Hollywood Hills.

"Ooh, a birthday cake. I just love birthday cakes. Can I lick the icing bowl when you've iced the cake?"

To Maggie there was something obscene in a woman's making love to your husband one minute and licking your icing bowl the next. Maggie intended to hold tightly to her icing bowl. Miss Always was not going to get that, too.

"Cooee?" Gerald's voice sounded from the back of the house.

"Oh, my, as usual Gerald is ready for work." She giggled.

Yes, work as usual, thought Maggie bitterly.

"I'd better go," said Miss Always, traipsing out.

Felicity snorted and curled in her basket for a snooze.

Maggie sifted flour furiously.

"Careful, ma'am. You'll have that all over the kitchen." Mrs. Butterfield coughed as she took plates from the dishwasher. "They say flour's as harmful to the lungs as polluted air."

"Yes, Mrs. Butterfield."

Maggie wondered if she should put bits of coloured candy on top of the icing. Gerald would call that childish.

Yet Miss Always would make a typical Miss Always comment, and he might wake up to how childish she acted. "Mrs. Butterfield, would you go to Mrs. Hazlehurst's and buy some of that coloured candy to sprinkle on the birthday cake?"

"Hundreds and thousands? Oh, I don't think Mr. Featherstone would like that."

"No, but Miss Always will."

"It ain't her birthday."

"Get the trimming, Mrs. Butterfield."

"Well, if he don't like it — and he won't — don't say I fetched it." She gave a dab to her eyes, took some coins from the broken sugar bowl, used as the kitchen's bank, and shoulders stooped, lumbered off.

"Mrs. Butterfield," Maggie ran to the kitchen door, "ask Mrs. Hazlehurst if she has some birthday poppers tucked away."

"Some what?"

"Poppers. Oh, sorry, birthday crackers."

"She won't. Only carries them Christmas."

"Ask anyway." Maggie went back to her baking, noticing for the first time how much flour she had spilled on the table and chairs, and floor. She finished her mixture and slid it into the oven.

As the cake baked, she set the dining room table. So, Miss Always wanted to lick my icing bowl! Maggie fetched the little earthenware pot of cacti — Gerald would hate it — and put it as centerpiece.

She returned to the kitchen and made the custard for filling.

The cake came out of the oven, cooled and was ready for icing before Mrs. Butterfield ambled back and placed her package on the kitchen table. "They had last year's Christmas crackers."

"I've given you quite a mess to clean up, Mrs. Butterfield." Maggie smeared icing on the cake and sprinkled on hundreds and thousands.

"Not likely. Got to rest now. My lungs hurt me something fierce, what with the flour and the walk."

"Surely you intend to help with lunch?"

"Not likely. I'll go rest now and see if I don't feel better."

Maggie sighed. As she put the icing bowl into the sink, Miss Always poked her head in the door.

"Icing ready yet?"

Quickly, Maggie turned on the tap.

"The bowl's just being rinsed."

"Shit," said Miss Always and minced back to the study.

Maggie cut up vegetables for *ratatouille provençale.* The recipe called for 3/4 cup thinly sliced onions. She'd add an extra cup. Onions gave Gerald wind. Her eyes burned as she chopped, but it was worth it.

Next she took up the garlic press. Two cloves of garlic, she read. She'd make it four. Gerald didn't like garlic. She put the press down. She'd chop the garlic.

She sautéed the onions and garlic as she sliced the courgettes and tomatoes. After adding a little salt and pepper, she added more pepper. Finally she sprinkled the mixture with olive oil and put it to simmer.

She'd serve it with a tossed salad, followed by a cheese course, and end with cake. She wondered how "afternoon work" would go after this lunch.

"Come on, Felicity. We'll wash you so you can attend the birthday party in style." Maggie grabbed an apron and towel and headed outside for the service room, Felicity at her heels.

Following the bath and blow drying, Maggie went to Mrs. Butterfield's room and bribed her with chocolates to forget her congested lungs and serve lunch.

By the time Maggie had freshened up and reached the drawing room, Gerald and Miss Always were having their pre-lunch sherry. Maggie, in green trousers, white blouse, and jade beads, felt underdressed next to Miss Always's glitter.

"Here, Maggie, we've poured a sherry for you." Miss Always jumped up and handed Maggie a glass.

"Thank you." She's playing hostess as usual. Maggie bit her tongue.

Miss Always raised her glass.

"To Gerald," she said.

Gerald smiled and took a gulp of sherry.

"Maggie, about those paintings you stored…"

"Not on your birthday, Gerald," said Miss Always, in such a proprietorial manner Maggie spilled some sherry.

What had Miss Always to do with the paintings? Maggie wondered.

They finished their drinks and moved into the dining room for lunch.

"Oh, crackers! How I love crackers! Can we pull them now?" asked Miss Always, breathlessly.

"Why not," said Maggie, pleased with the exaggerated reaction.

Standing together by the table, the three held crackers in their left hands, crossed arms and took the tab of the next cracker between their right fingers. "One, two, three," they intoned, then pulled the tabs with a bang.

Miss Always squealed in delight as she drew out a paper hat and a little pen. Maggie found a hat and a gold chain.

"That's bloody nice," said Miss Always, gazing wistfully at Maggie's chain.

"You must have it."

"Oh, may I?" She took it from Maggie and slipped it over her head, adding it to the locket Gerald had given her and seeming to enjoy both equally. "How does it look?"

"Very nice," said Gerald, no doubt admiring the way it hung between the swirls of glitter on Miss Always's chest.

"Aren't the surprises splendid?" Miss Always admired Gerald's key ring. "I do so love crackers. Put your hat on, Gerald. My, you look like a king."

Henry VIII, thought Maggie.

Miss Always had a pointed cap of pink. Maggie, one of yellow.

Maggie could tell Gerald hated the party, yet it didn't seem to dampen his admiration of Miss Always. He just seemed angry with Maggie, who found herself feeling grateful to Miss Always for breaking the gloom.

As they ate ratatouille, Maggie watched Gerald's expression. He hated it. Good.

"Maggie," enthused Miss Always, "this is the best ratatouille I've ever eaten. Isn't it Gerald?"

"Hmm," he grunted. With Miss Always present, he'd never say he couldn't eat onions and garlic.

Felicity jumped on Gerald and whined.

"Go away." He pushed her aside.

"She's had a bath in your honour, Gerald."

"It's a bit late to try to please me, Felicity. Third Place! I'm ashamed to own you."

"You don't own her. I do," said Maggie. "Anyway, it's time for the cake." Maggie rang for Mrs. Butterfield.

The cake, with coloured sprinkles and candles, was bourne in by a glum, stooped Mrs. Butterfield.

"Happy birthday to you," Miss Always and Maggie sang. Mrs. Butterfield sighed. Miss Always clapped.

"You cut it," groused Gerald to Maggie as Mrs. Butterfield handed him a knife. "And get that dog away from me."

"You needn't stay mad at Felicity. And on your

birthday."

"Look at the pretty hundreds and thousands!" gushed Miss Always. "Hurry, Gerald, you've got to blow out the candles."

Gerald reluctantly did as he was told. He missed one candle, and Miss Always hopped up, ran to his place, and gave a little puff to extinguish the flame.

"Now you'll have good luck." She glanced at him meaningfully as she took the knife and cut him the first piece of cake. Then she picked it up in her fingers and fed him a bite.

Like a wedding cake, Maggie thought with disgust.

Miss Always wiped her fingers and cut Maggie a slice, then sat down with her own. "Ummm. Maggie, this is the best cake I've ever eaten."

Maggie knew she should be furious, but instead she experienced a wave of decidedly inappropriate fondness for Miss Always. She felt a kind of sisterhood about the future. Miss Always was probably as frightened as Maggie. The world said, "You must walk two and two" and left you out if you didn't obey its dictum. Miss Always had never had anyone of her own to walk with.

She means no harm to me, Maggie thought. She probably likes me, maybe even better than she likes Gerald.

Maggie sighed. Miss Always simply fought for her own survival in a society which, even the little nuns agreed, still did not treat women very well.

"I do love this cake." Miss Always licked icing off her finger. "Homemade. May I have another little slice?"

Maggie laughed. "By all means. Why not take the rest home with you. Gerald is watching his waistline."

"That would be super. I don't bake myself, and a shop cake is not nearly so good."

"Time for your presents, Gerald. I hope you noticed the

lovely cactus plant Miss Always brought." Now Maggie hoped he would like it.

Gerald smiled lovingly at his secretary.

"I have another present as well." Miss Always toddled to her briefcase and pulled out a tie box just as Maggie rose and presented her own.

"I think I can guess what I'm getting," said Gerald, who liked to pick out his own ties.

Both women went back to their seats to watch.

He opened Maggie's first. "Ah, Liberty's of London," he said. She could tell he admired the subtle maroon paisley. Just the thing for his days at Lloyd's or his club.

"Harrods." He looked lovingly at Miss Always's box.

"The very best store," said Miss Always.

"Indeed." Gerald looked very British.

"The nicest man sold me this. Very distinguished. Said you would love it."

Gerald drew it out. Yellow, with little black dots.

Maggie looked down. He hated it. Maggie hated it. Yet now she didn't want Miss Always to see her disdain.

When Maggie looked up, Gerald was glaring at her, guessing at her disdain. Pulling off the tie he wore, he put on Miss Always's gift in what would have been a lovely gesture if it had been aimed at Miss Always, not at Maggie.

Maggie sipped coffee and watched the two.

"I'm so glad you like it. That nice man, Mr. Trueblood, was so helpful."

Maggie choked.

"Are you all right?" asked Gerald.

"Oh, my," said Miss Always. "You've spilled coffee on the tablecloth."

Gerald rose.

"Thanks for the party, Maggie."

"Yes, thanks." Miss Always rose and followed him.

Maggie sat at the table, finishing her coffee and feeling jealous of Miss Always and Adair Trueblood, though she couldn't think why.

Suddenly Miss Always was back.

"Maggie, have you seen my handbag? I can't find it anywhere."

"What a nuisance for you. I hope you didn't lose it coming here. It's terrible to have to replace a licence."

"Oh, I don't drive."

"Or keys."

"I have another house key under the mat. But I simply must find my bag."

"Well, let's search for it.

After half an hour, neither Maggie, Gerald, nor Miss Always had come up with anything vaguely resembling a handbag. Gerald was furious. Miss Always pouted.

"Why don't you get on with your work?" asked Maggie as the three stood in the drawing room. "Since it doesn't contain a licence and you have another key, you can get along until we find it. It's bound to turn up."

"It's just that, well, I had some medicine in it I need to take."

"Oh, I see." said Maggie. "Why not call the chemist?"

"Closed Saturday afternoons," groused Gerald. "I'd better take you back to London."

Maggie felt surprised.

"I thought you were spending the night so we could all go to the Normington's tomorrow."

"Yes," agreed Miss Always. "It really would be best if we stayed."

For the remainder of the day, Gerald and Miss Always sulked in the study, seeming to accomplish very little. Such a fuss over a handbag, thought Maggie. I suppose I shall never understand either one of them.

CHAPTER XXII

Maggie hurried upstairs and into her red tunic dress. She'd be late picking up Mr. Beveridge. After the old man's morning visit, she planned to go out. She had told Gerald she'd no longer be available for Saturday lunches with him and Miss Always.

Dissatisfied with her outfit, she took off the tunic dress and put on her glen plaid trouser suit. Perhaps after taking Mr. Beveridge home, she'd go into Brighton for some lunch or to watch the water from the pier. She wasn't very hungry these days.

She removed the glen plaid suit and donned her royal blue trouser suit with green and blue silk blouse. She couldn't seem to get moving. Perhaps it was the strange feeling she'd had since waking up — that things would not go right. She realized that was a ridiculous thought, since nothing had gone right since she'd reached England.

After collecting Mr. Beveridge and arriving back at Raven Hall, Maggie called for Mrs. Butterfield's help, but she'd already gone. Maggie now regretted giving Mr. Dunkley and Mongoose the day off as well.

"Just wait until I get the chair set up, Mr. Beveridge." She pulled the wheelchair from the boot and struggled with it. Then she wheeled it round to where he sat in the front seat of the Mercedes.

"I can swing in. Just watch me." To Maggie's dismay, Mr. Beveridge bent down, grabbed hold of the arms of the chair, and flung himself into the seat.

"You might have injured yourself. I could have lifted you."

"Tired of being lifted," he groused as Maggie wheeled him to his favourite spot on the knoll.

She still felt apprehensive. Maybe because the house

and grounds seemed empty.

And Gerald had acted odd. When she'd said goodbye on her way to collect Mr. Beveridge, he'd answered, "Enjoy the play." He must have thought she was going into London. She looked back at the house and noticed the study curtains were drawn, indicating he was not overly concerned about where she might be.

Before noon, the day grew damp. Maggie left Mr. Beveridge, who said he was quite happy with the weather, and ran inside for her Greek wool shawl, just as a car pulled into the front drive. The bell rang while she hurried down the stairs, almost bumping into Gerald as he answered the summons.

"Maggie, what are you doing here? I thought you left hours ago."

"Just to pick up Mr. Beveridge. We've been having a lovely chat in the garden, but it's getting cold."

Miss Always came from the study.

"Maggie! Oh, my. What a shock!"

"I do live here." Maggie looked from one to the other, wondering at the guilt in their expressions.

The doorbell rang again, and Gerald opened the door just a slit.

"Hello. Won't be a moment. I'll take you round to the garden." He stepped outside and shut the door behind him, before Maggie could see who had come.

"What's he up to?" Maggie asked.

"I think he promised to loan some garden tool or other."

"Gerald doesn't know a trowel from a spade. I'd better go see to it."

"Oh, no, Maggie!" Miss Always protested. "I need you to... to fix the zip on my skirt."

Maggie noticed Miss Always slip the zipper open.

Maggie stared at her a moment, then raced to the back

door and into the garden, just as Gerald and Lord and Lady Wizzell walked round to the front, Felicity in Lady Wizzell's arms.

Maggie recalled that the Wizzells had been to the dog show and hadn't even petted Felicity, nor had they asked for her at the party. Why would Lady Wizzell be holding Felicity now?

Maggie ran up to them, breathless with fear, but tried to appear nonchalant.

"How good of you to come. I see you're enjoying my little Felicity. But she'll get dog hairs on your lovely brown coat, Lady Wizzell. Let me take her."

Lady Wizzell held fast, almost smothering the puppy in her ample bosom.

Felicity whined.

"My little granddaughter is going to love her puppykins, and grandma will have to pretend she doesn't see all those dog hairs."

"What puppy is that, Lady Wizzell? Are you getting a puppy like Felicity?"

Lady Wizzell looked at Gerald, confused.

"Why, Felicity, of course. Gerald told us you wanted to get rid of her, and we jumped at the chance. Our granddaughter's first dog needn't be show quality."

Felicity snarled.

"Gerald was quite mistaken. I wouldn't part with Felicity for anything in the world." Maggie tried to take Felicity, but both Lord Wizzell and Gerald took her arms, preventing her.

"See here," said Lord Wizzell, his puffy face reddening "A bargain is a bargain."

"Maggie," hissed Gerald in her ear, "This is a business deal. I need Wizzell's help. Badly."

The Wizzells kept walking toward their car, Felicity

whimpering in her captor's arms. Maggie shoved Gerald aside, walked quickly beside them and again reached out for Felicity.

The puppy, unable to reach Maggie, commenced her primal scream.

"You don't understand!" Maggie, panting, had to yell over the screams. "There's been some terrible mistake. This is my little girl. I can't part with her."

"You'll have to work that out with your husband," shouted Lord Wizzell, hurrying on.

"Maggie!" Gerald grabbed her, pulling her back. "You're embarrassing me. This isn't like you."

"No, Gerald. It isn't." Maggie recalled the stranger trying to take her taxi. She stomped on Gerald's instep with her heel as hard as she could.

Lord Wizzell opened the door of their Jaguar for Lady Wizzell. When Maggie rushed up and tried to stop him, he pushed her aside. She took a deep breath, then grunted as she kicked him in the ankle.

Looking terrified, Lady Wizzell stood beside the open door, still hugging Felicity, who continued to wail.

Maggie tried to tug Felicity away. When the stout woman refused to budge, Maggie pulled at Lady Wizzell's mousy hair.

Just as Gerald limped up, Maggie threw her shawl over Lady Wizzell's head, and that woman added her howls to Felicity's.

Gerald stepped in, and both he and Maggie wrestled for the puppy as Lady Wizzle struggled with the scarf.

Maggie panicked. Everyone who could help her — Mr. Dunkley, Mongoose, Mrs. Butterfield — was gone. In a minute the Wizzells would drive off with Felicity.

With all her energy, she kicked Gerald again in the same spot. Ignoring his cry, she grabbed Felicity.

As Gerald reached for the puppy, Maggie thrust her knee into his groin with all the force she could command.

When Lord Wizzell, coming from behind, tried to take her left elbow, the arm that cradled Felicity, Maggie hit back with her right elbow, smashing into his rib cage. She spun towards the house and started to run with Felicity. She'd lock herself in her room and telephone for help.

As she neared the front door, out stepped Miss Always.

"Catch her!" screamed Lady Wizzell.

Maggie could feel the stout Wizzells bearing down upon her. She swerved round the house, heading for the garden. Maybe Mr. Dunkley and Mongoose were back, though she knew that wasn't likely.

In the garden sat Mr. Beveridge on the knoll overlooking the downs.

"Mr. Beveridge," Maggie cried, "they're kidnapping Felicity!"

The old man looked up, startled. Then manoeuvred his chair so it would roll down the slope and across the grass.

"Ayeee!" he shouted, waving his arms madly as the chair sped down the slope.

It came to a halt just as Maggie reached him, the group directly behind her.

"Give me the puppy." He yanked Felicity from Maggie's arms. "Don't like dogs, but they won't get this one." His usually ashen face held a glow, and he grinned.

Gerald rushed up and stood stymied for a moment. Then he reached out, putting his hands round Felicity.

"Wrestle with a cripple, would you?" yelled Mr. Beveridge. "You'll find I've got powerful arms from managing this contraption."

Gerald wouldn't let go, and Felicity growled fiercely. As he gave a tug to wrest her away, she bit down hard on his wrist. He jumped back with a cry of pain.

"Good Felicity!" Maggie felt jubilant.

"Get the jugular next!" cheered Mr. Beveridge.

"She bit me. Look, blood! Maggie, your dog bit me. Call a doctor." He pulled a handkerchief from his pocket.

"Oh, dear!" Miss Always fluttered about Gerald, ineptly bandaging his wrist with the handkerchief.

"Oh, my!" Lady Wizzell, a tip of Maggie's shawl still over one shoulder, the rest trailing behind her and onto the grass, tried to smooth back her hair. "We can't have a dog that bites. You didn't tell us she bites."

"You've certainly misled us, Gerald." Lord Wizzell put a hand to his rib cage where Maggie's elbow had hit. "I'm sure I have a broken rib. We'll talk more about this at the office on Monday. Come, dear."

"You'll be in pain for weeks," wailed Lady Wizzell as she led him toward the front drive.

Maggie stood glaring at Gerald and Miss Always.

"Just get away from me, you two. That was a despicable thing to do."

"My wrist. Look, it's bleeding. She must have rabies. She should be put to sleep immediately."

Maggie stepped forward.

"You touch her, Gerald, ever, and you're dead."

"Don't make idle threats to me."

Maggie raised her arm, brandishing an imaginary weapon.

"Blood will drip from my garden shears."

"Hee-hee," chortled Beveridge. "Justifiable homicide."

"The enraged wife comes upon her husband and..." Maggie looked pointedly at Miss Always while still holding aloft her invisible sheers, awash in their blood, "...her husband's lover. And in her own home."

"Ho-ho," guffawed Mr. Beveridge. "I'll testify, I will. Husband's lover. Ha-ha-ha. Jury will be in tears."

"Shut up," said Gerald.

"Dog bites faithless husband," Mr. Beveridge warmed to his fantasy. "Dog gets medal, saves wife. Newspapers go mad. Public calls for acquittal."

"Maggie, get rid of this tiresome old nut."

Maggie realized her arm was still raised, and tried to bring it down surreptitiously. She cleared her throat.

Gerald leaned on Miss Always. "I'm disappointed in you, Maggie."

"That no longer matters, Gerald." She turned to Mr. Beveridge and took Felicity from him.

"Like the little dog better now," Mr. Beveridge asserted. "But don't tell anyone I helped a dog. Not that." He sat contentedly chortling.

"Shut him up, Maggie." Gerald unwrapped the handkerchief on his wrist and daubed at the bite. "This looks really bad. Maybe I've got blood poisoning."

"Shall we go back to the flowerbed?" Maggie asked Mr. Beveridge.

"I think I'd better get on home now. Morning's been a bit more energetic than I'm used to. My arms are stronger than you'd think, though." Mr. Beveridge shook one at Gerald, who held out his wrist so Miss Always could commiserate with him.

"You were wonderful," said Maggie to the old man.

"Yes, I was. Where was that youngster with his magic? Takes a song and dance man like me to carry the day."

"Indeed it does."

Miss Always sniffed her disapproval and, high heels leaving tracks in the lawn, led Gerald to the house.

Maggie watched them go, wishing she could eliminate Miss Always as she would a mole that played havoc with her garden.

CHAPTER XXIII

Depressed at Gerald's attempt to give Felicity away, Maggie walked slowly into the mask room. Lately the masks hadn't been successful.

Then she had a brighter thought. Maybe she no longer needed any of them. Earlier it had seemed so important to try out other personalities. Maybe her face had by now taken on qualities of its own.

"Sisters?" she queried as usual.

No response.

Maggie picked up Tolerance, not one of her favourites, and tossed it aside. She looked at Cloak and Dagger. Her days of surveillance seemed so far away. Cordiality brought back memories of the first Raven Hall party.

Now only Gerald wore a mask — Inscrutable. The real Gerald, the Italian Gerald, the Gerald of energy and joy, was as invisible as her masks. Had she, many years ago, simply made him up?

"You'll let us keep the hats, surely?" Sister Orelia's voice broke through the silence.

"Perhaps you could give me the one with the grosgrain," said Sister Aloysius.

"That should go to me," said Mother Magdalene.

Maggie watched as the nuns gradually appeared, each sitting on a stool, Mother Magdalene spinning.

"I hadn't thought about the hats," said Maggie.

"You should," answered Sister Orelia, her beautiful face luminescent in the soft light. "You can't take them all away."

"How do you know I'm going?"

"You must go. You have what you came for."

"What was that?"

Mother Magdalene interrupted.

"Such useless chatter. Do let's choose hats."

"We're jealous of you," said Sister Orelia.

"Why? What do I have that you want?" Maggie questioned.

"Freedom. You were — I think the current expression is 'dumped' — here by a husband, just as we were by fathers or lovers. Yet you can leave now."

"I hadn't thought of it in that way."

"You don't know how well off you are," said Sister Aloysius, her round face sad.

"Sisters," said Maggie, "you are so... well... maybe if you could expand your interests, you could leave, too."

Sister Orelia stood and looked up at Maggie with disdain.

"You think it's terrible for us to be so wrapped up in ourselves."

"Yes." Maggie agreed reluctantly as she thought of Gerald, trapped in the trivial, in the system that had become so important in his own mind it obliterated the need to care for others.

"Well, it's just as bad to be wrapped up in a husband."

Maggie gave a little gasp.

"I agree." Mother Magdalene kept spinning. "When you came here, you didn't know who you were — couldn't separate yourself from him."

"You're right." Maggie reluctantly agreed, sinking onto the stool Sister Orelia had vacated. "I was so used to putting his needs before my own." She was reminded of the Saturday lunches, of coming to Raven Hall against her will. "As women we're taught that."

"Yes," agreed Sister Orelia bitterly. And we're taught that we must be with a man or in a religious order under men's rules."

Maggie gave a rueful laugh.

"How right you are. Without a man I'll be ostracized from most social groups. I'll be suspect at dinner parties. And because I'm divorced, I'll even be scorned by the church that's supposed to give me solace."

Sister Aloysius sighed.

"Yes, dear, women are treated as failures without a man. We realize that all too well, having had several hundred years to observe the status quo." Sheepishly she pulled from her habit Maggie's Steuben Lion. When Maggie said nothing, she held it up and examined it in the grey light. "But we think you'll handle your single situation very well."

"Have I truly changed?"

"Oh yes," said Mother Magdalene, stopping spinning momentarily to inspect her work.

"Then couldn't you change?"

"It's too — I think the expression is 'high risk'," Mother Magdalene answered.

Maggie laughed."It's my husband who's in the high risk situation. He could lose everything if his syndicate were to incur heavy losses."

The nuns tittered.

"You," said Sister Aloysius, "have been at far greater risk in searching for yourself."

"That's such a risk," said Mother Magdalene, "that almost nobody does it."

"Most people wear one mask," said Sister Aloysius. "It's so much less effort than risking being themselves. But you had so many it was rather entertaining."

"Now about the hats," said Sister Orelia, gazing longingly at the collection.

"Sisters," said Maggie, rising, "I intend to keep only one of the hats, this one." She reached up and took down Robin's favourite, the black with roses round the brim.

"Wouldn't you prefer that I send the rest to charity so women who can wear them can enjoy them?"

Sister Aloysius's eyes filled with tears. "But we enjoy them. And we look so lovely in them."

"You can't use them."

"They're pretty," said Sister Orelia. "We like pretty things. Perhaps we could keep some of the crystal as well?" She pulled the Lalique panther from her habit and stroked it with thin, artistic fingers.

"Maybe it's your interest in 'things', that ties you to the earth." As she spoke, Maggie realized they'd woven a net for themselves of little falsehoods and meanesses, like Gerald's net, trapping themselves in the voracious system of life.

Mother Magdalene sighed.

"I dare say you're right. But we can't help ourselves. Won't you please leave us the hats?"

"Oh, all right." Maggie felt cross with them.

Sister Orelia reached for the royal blue hat with red feather, while Mother Magdalene and Sister Aloysius both jumped up and grabbed for the green hat with grosgrain trim.

"I'm the Superior. It's mine." Mother Magdalene gave a hefty pull, but Sister Aloysius, her round face in a pout, held on tight.

"I said I liked it first. It's mine."

Sister Orelia donned her blue hat and gazed at herself in the Baccarat vase.

Maggie went to the door. As she opened it, the usually audible creak could not be heard above the clatter. She quickly left, Robin's favourite hat in hand.

Maggie felt exhilarated. The nuns had agreed with her that she should go. A return to California seemed imminent.

She put the hat down and started into the kitchen, but Felicity dashed past her, Robin following.

Maggie stood perplexed, then trailed after them.

Upstairs, Robin stood in the hallway, outside the guest room door. He glanced at Maggie and put a finger to his lips.

Maggie sidled up beside him.

"She's in there. I'm convinced that's where her hiding place is."

"But we'd have seen it."

"Shhh." He peeked round the door. "Come on."

They crept inside.

"She's not here!" exclaimed Maggie.

"She couldn't have got out," wailed Robin. "But she's disappeared."

They both did a thorough search under the beds, the armoire, the chairs. Felicity was nowhere to be seen.

"She's done it to me before," Robin complained. "Where could she go?"

A faint munching sound commenced.

"Mother of God, how dangerous!" Maggie rushed to the television console and with Robin's help, pulled it out from the wall.

Inside sat Felicity, one paw resting on Robin's round bone, the other, on Miss Always's handbag, open, its contents strewn on the carpet under the television. Felicity, ignoring the intrusion, continued contentedly chewing on something round and rubbery.

Maggie bent down and pulled the object from Felicity's mouth. Only when it lay flat in her hand did she realize what it was. A diaphragm. Miss Always's diaphragm.

"I unplugged the set," said Robin.

"Oh, you must leave, Robin."

"But my bone?"

"Shoo." Maggie hid her left hand, which held the diaphragm, behind her back.

"My bone!"

She reached down, grabbed the bone, and tossed it to him.

"Here. Now shoo! Quickly! You really shouldn't see."

When Robin had left, Maggie, disgusted, threw away the diaphragm, grabbed up Felicity, and hurried downstairs after him. So this is what had kept them sulking that birthday afternoon.

In the kitchen, Maggie put Felicity into her basket, then glanced at Robin's bone. "What will you do with that? Make it disappear?"

"Now that I've got all my props, I might go as well."

Maggie laughed.

"Don't disappear for too long. I couldn't do without you."

Robin grinned slyly.

"I expect you could now." He threw the bone into the air and caught it.

"Whoops," warned Maggie. "Hang onto that bone."

Felicity jumped on Robin and growled to get the bone back. Robin held it high above her, taunting her.

"Robin, don't be naughty. You lost it once doing that."

"Right." He stood still a moment, staring at Maggie. "You haven't been wearing your masks."

"You noticed! Actually, I've got rid of them all. But I imagine I've taken on the look of several now. What would you call my new expression?"

Robin pondered for a minute.

"The one you came with."

"Don't tease me, Robin."

He shrugged.

"I guess it suits you."

"But one gets taken advantage of with Kind."

Robin tossed his bone in the air again, causing Felicity to bark.

"If you say 'no' to everyone, you won't get taken advantage of."

"I couldn't do that."

Robin winked at her.

"That's what I mean." He laughed, his green eyes blazing. "I'll be off then." He picked up his top hat from the kitchen table and put it on at an angle.

"Robin?"

"Yes?" He stood in the door, looking at her expectantly.

"Nothing. Just... nothing."

He laughed again and let the door slam.

"I like Kind," he shouted as he ran down the steps, almost bumping into Mr. Dunkley.

That gentleman, dressed in a new grey suit and vest, knocked at the kitchen door and entered.

"Madam," he said, "I have news."

"It's bad, isn't it?" Maggie made them both a pot of strong tea, and they sat sipping it at the kitchen table.

"All is not ticketyboo, madam."

"Has my husband changed the title of the house to include my name?"

"I fear not." Mr. Dunkley spooned sugar into his tea.

"And I don't even understand exactly what getting a bank guarantee means."

"He, of course, is using the house as collateral for his Lloyd's membership."

"That sounds terribly risky."

"But the news gets worse, madam."

"How could it?"

"I've had Basilio and Figaro discreetly checking. If anyone can uncover another's juggling it's those two." He folded his hands and looked at Maggie. "Perhaps you know that Lloyd's has a Latin motto that means Good Faith. Even so, now and then a scandal rocks the establishment." He paused as if waiting for that idea to sink in. "I regret to tell you there are rumours in the City that several of Lloyd's prominent figures, including Mr. Featherstone, are possibly cooking their syndicates' books."

"Cooking their syndicates' books?" It sounded so terrible Maggie laughed nervously. "Whatever does that mean?"

"They're suspected of siphoning money off for a variety of independent ventures. Mr. Featherstone's name comes up with…" He cleared his throat and took a gulp of tea.

"With…?" Maggie pulled at the black fringe round the turtleneck of her tunic.

"With porno movies."

"Gerald? You must be mistaken. Surely he wouldn't do anything so vicious." She felt dizzy. This wasn't possible. Not her Gerald!

They say his backers, people who innocently contribute to the syndicates as investors, are collectively responsible for seventy million pounds."

"Then he's lost the savings of dozens of unsuspecting people?" Oh Gerald, what has happened to you?

"Precisely, madam. But some are very wealthy and can handle the loss."

"That's beside the point." She put her head in her hand, then looked up at him. "You say it's just a rumour?"

"Precisely, madam. Innocent until proved guilty. But you must be prepared for the worst."

"But if it's true, Gerald will have to make good his part in the losses."

"An admirable suggestion, madam, but not the usual

procedure. For one thing the amount is too vast. For another, the funds would have disappeared. His involvement may be impossible to prove, though I suspect the auditors will get a handle on it."

"And he's lost our house as well?"

"I dare say he may have. You see, had he been an ordinary external member, he could have underwritten for a variety of syndicates. But if I am not mistaken, he became an active underwriter on the strength of his own assets, so the house… You understand?"

"Yes. Mr Dunkley," Maggie rested her chin on her hands, "just how did he perpetrate the fraud?"

"I speak only hypothetically, madam," Mr. Dunkley added milk to their cups and poured them both more tea, "but he probably siphoned off syndicate funds by placing and paying, on behalf of the syndicate, re-insurance policies with an overseas insurance company in, say, a Caribbean country. This in turn would belong to another company, say a holding company in Panama, which in turn would belong to another holding company, say in Lichtenstein, whose shares would be entirely owned by a Swiss bank, acting as nominee for a private and undisclosed client. This client would, of course, be Mr. Featherstone."

"Oh, my." So that's what they'd been talking about that day at lunch.

"You see, Mr. Featherstone would have set up the whole chain in order to be able to place as much of the syndicate funds as possible with what appeared to be a bona fide insurance company. As soon as the policies started to be called upon, no payments would be made and the companies would collapse, bankrupt, all the money having been passed back to Mr. Featherstone."

Maggie drew invisible lines on the pine table with her

teaspoon.

"He juggled too fast for us."

"I fear so, madam."

"If he's guilty, what will happen to him?"

"If the rumour proves true, he will scoot off as fast as he can to America, living luxuriously and happily with many millions of pounds of syndicate funds in his own pocket."

"America? He'll go home?"

"Not by choice. The fraud would have been committed in Britain, and warrants for his arrest…"

"Arrest?"

"… would be issued in London. There is no extradition treaty between our two countries covering the offence of fraud."

Maggie slumped in her seat.

"Mr. Dunkley, I appreciate your telling me this, but I'm too overwhelmed to talk any further."

"I understand perfectly." He rose, gave a little bow, then departed.

Maggie stayed sitting at the table a few minutes. She tried to sip some tea, but her hand was shaking and she couldn't hold the cup steady.

She rose, went upstairs and turned on the shower. When it had heated up, she undressed and got under the warm spray, letting it rain onto her hair, her shoulders. She felt dirty, covered with layers and layers of Gerald's lies.

How ruthless he'd become, how insensitive. She should have seen that he was hardening into his worst traits. That's what people did, she supposed, if they weren't [illegible] dened into their worst selves. She could no [illegible] him because of little Sean.

[illegible] im to fear to go down alone, to take others [illegible] Lord Wizzell and Mr. Normington! They [illegible] They deserved any trouble they were in.

But her heart ached for those unsuspecting people who'd thought they were members of an honestly managed syndicate.

She longed to take action, but waiting to see if Lloyd's discovered the fraud proved to be her only option.

Mr. Dunkley was right. Gerald would have millions stashed away to save himself. Did he plan to return to Hollywood? To live on his fraudulant fortune? Only weeks ago the thought of his returning home would have given her hope. But after his attempt to give away Felicity, Maggie could no longer care.

She had a sudden vision of Gerald disguised as a woman, escaping into one of the Titanic's lifeboats.

Maggie felt desolate the rest of the day. An Emily Dickinson poem ran through her mind:

The bustle in a house
The morning after death
Is solemnest of industries
Enacted upon earth.

With the news of Gerald, Maggie felt she'd experienced a death. And why did Robin's going home today seem like a death as well? He'd be back tomorrow. Yet his goodbye had sounded so final, as if now that he had his bone, he had no reason to return.

Maybe she related Robin's leaving to her loss of trust in Gerald. Or to a feeling that she would have to stay in England, see Gerald through this, though their marriage functioned now only on a respirator.

It remained for Maggie to unplug the machine. But where would she get that courage now that Gerald was in trouble, despicable as his action had been?

Unable to dispel her despair, she wandered through the house and to her room. She didn't feel like doing anything purposeful.

The sweeping up the heart,
And putting love away
We shall not want to use again
Until eternity.

Maggie realized that putting her heart in order was a horrendous undertaking. Dickinson made it sound easy, or at least possible. Maggie knew her own love wouldn't sweep up nicely to be put tidily on some shelf in the heart. Maybe smooth, comfortable, caring loves could be dealt with like that. A bond that bridged life and death, that carried one all the way to eternity didn't break. That kind of love could be put away and taken out again in eternity, dusted off, as good as new.

Maggie's sort of love offered no solace. It was more like treacle, oozing from its cracked tin, seeping into all the crevices of the heart, bleeding on all the other passions.

She felt her heart would be permanantly sticky and stained. She knew of nothing to cleanse this stigmata.

CHAPTER XXIV

That night Gerald entered the drawing room and flopped into an over-stuffed chair by the fire. Maggie watched from the sofa and Felicity, sitting beside her, growled.

"You might at least have trained that dog to fetch slippers," he mumbled. "You wouldn't like to get me a drink, would you, darling? Make it a stiff one."

Maggie didn't move, nor did she answer immediately. "What about the house?" she asked finally. "Did you lose it?"

Gerald averted his eyes.

"My angel, I told you, I'm taking care of everything."

"Gerald, specifically what happened?"

"You seem to know so much, why ask?"

"Are you guilty?"

"All right." Now he sounded simply matter of fact. Or was it defeat she heard in his voice? He kicked off his shoes and stretched out his legs. "If you must know, we've lost it."

"That's not what I mean. Are you guilty of fraud?"

He looked at her, surprised. "They haven't proved anything. Anybody can make mistakes."

Maggie picked up a comb from the end table and ran it through Felicity's ears. "What now?"

"We'll have to move to the States. But that won't bother you," he said bitterly, "you've always hated this house."

"Yes, and I've hated Miss Always, the mistress, you flaunted in it. And now I think I hate you, Gerald."

"You're awfully cool about it."

"I've lived with loss ever since you brought me to England, perhaps even longer." She couldn't sympathize with him any more, not since he'd tried to give Felicity away. "Anyway," she added, "I'm glad about the house. I'm glad you and Miss Always won't be able to live here together. No doubt, though, you've bought a cozy hideaway for the two of you elsewhere that neither Lloyd's nor I can touch."

"What's that supposed to mean?"

"That I'm not as blind as you think. You've paraded Miss Always about, not caring how I felt. But you want the whole pie — your wife, your freedom, your mistress. Well, you can have the rest, but you can't have me. I've done all I can for you. Now you'll have to help yourself. I'm filing for divorce. Going home."

He sat up from his slouched position.

"See here, Maggie. A divorce would be disastrous for me. It would look as if you don't have faith in me, and just when my honour is being questioned at Lloyd's. And I need all our resources. Surely you don't think for a minute that I would actually marry Miss Always? She's... well..."

"Sorry, Gerald."

"And you've never told me what you did with those paintings. We'll need the money from those now."

"No, Gerald, I may need the money. Those paintings are mine. You've lost all our other joint assets."

"My angel, how can you think that of me?"

"You've hidden money somewhere. Real estate under assumed names, right?"

"I don't have to answer foolish questions."

"Investments in porno films? Really, Gerald!"

"Nothing's been proved. Nothing ever will be."

"Oh, I don't doubt that. But by now probably everyone has heard of it."

"I'll come off all right. As you say, I took precautions. But I need capital to get back on top. I need those paintings. I'm counting on you, Maggie."

"Too bad you're land poor." Maggie fluffed out Felicity's ears. "Your trust in me is misplaced."

Gerald got up and joined Maggie on the couch. He put

an arm round her.

"My angel, you're always worrying about people, helping them out." He gave her his most loving, dimpled smile. "You'll surely help me for old time's sake. Think of all your strays. You won't let me down. I know you won't."

No, she'd never let him down before. She supposed it was very American of her to rush in to help, without realizing she might be taking away another's experience.

But when does one help and when does one stand back? she wondered. She knew that if a person didn't help at a crucial time, he was at fault — letting himself down as well, losing a little of his humanity. Neglecting others was how people became cogs in the system of life, grinding down and grinding others down.

Yet now it was time to let Gerald help himself.

He pulled her hair back and kissed her on the nape of her neck, where she had longed for so many months to be kissed.

Maggie rose from the couch. Felicity jumped down and remained at Maggie's heels.

Maggie walked to the door and leaned against the frame, hugging her arms to her.

"Gerald, you remind me of Foxtrot, the stray you had put to sleep. He was covered with sores, but you've more, many more. I'd prefer his mange to your corruption."

"Maggie, really!"

"But you don't have the spirit of that little dog. He wouldn't whine and beg. He wanted only love. You want power, adoration, money and more money.

Gerald removed his horn-rimmed glasses and rubbed his eyes as if he couldn't believe Maggie stood before him.

"You know, Gerald, I can't take you on as a stray. You're too sick with greed.

She turned to go, then swung back again. "And you stink, Gerald. Stink!"

CHAPTER XXV

Gerald had left for the office, though how he had the nerve to show up there when such scandal surrounded his name, Maggie couldn't think. She walked past his room. A suitcase was on the bed and underclothes had been thrown into it helter-skelter. So he was almost ready to go. Would he take Miss Always to his hideaway, his lair?

Maggie entered the room, but Felicity remained in the doorway and growled.

Absently, Maggie folded Gerald's garments and placed them neatly in the case. She rummaged in his drawer for bedsocks, found them, and packed them. He probably didn't let Miss Always know he suffered from cold feet.

Maggie noticed two plaid wool scarves in the drawer, the two she'd given him last Christmas. She held them to her cheek to breath in Gerald's scent, but inhaled the cheap, musky odor of a Miss Always's gift.

Maggie folded the scarves and put them into the case beside the bedsocks.

She found it strange to think she'd never pack another case for Gerald. That when they'd meet in the future it would be as strangers who no longer recalled the feel of each other's bodies, the scents, the needs.

It seemed odd to Maggie that Gerald had always thought she was on the fringe of life, that he was at the center of the vortex. She saw so clearly now that it was he who had been lurking on the sidelines, refusing to commit himself to individuals rather than the system.

She looked at her watch. It was almost time to tell Mr. Dunkley and Mongoose goodbye. She'd asked that they meet her in the garden, her beautiful haven. As she breathed in the pure, cold air, scented with the sweet smell of grass, she was glad that Gerald and Miss Always could never soil that garden now, that they were forced to seek refuge in their den, that they would skulk in her mind only as shadows in no definite patch of space.

She picked up her garden gloves and trowel and walked to the flowerbed, where she knelt for the last time, digging the soil round her Canterbury bells.

Felicity, pretending the trowel was a fierce enemy, growled and lunged at it, then danced back.

Maggie sensed a movement at the bottom of the garden and looked up.

Mr. Dunkley, dressed in a new suit and waistcoat, carrying Maggie's gift, a Victorian walking stick with silver handle stepped jauntily across the lawn. Mongoose ambled behind, wearing the Caribbean turquoise shirt and large-brimmed hat, banded in chartreuse and red, that Maggie had bought him.

She rose and removed her garden gloves.

"Goodbye," said Mongoose, as he still did for "hello."

"We'll be on our way, now." Mr. Dunkley added solemnly. "We'll miss you and the little dog. It has been a lovely spot to work."

Felicity stood on her hind legs and yapped.

"Thank you both for all your help. And thank you, Mr. Dunkley, for your legal work."

"My pleasure, madam." He smiled. "It made me appreciate my present lifestyle." He tapped on the ground confidently with his walking stick.

"And Mongoose, will you be all right?"

"I t'ink I be fine, now, missy. Dis mon," he grinned at Mr. Dunkley, "don't let nobody humbug me."

"He didn't let anybody humbug me, either." Maggie shook both their hands.

"Let's not say goodbye," said Mr. Dunkley. "A very sad word that."

"You'll pick up the hamper of food in the kitchen? You've got the money and everything you need?"

"Everything is in excellent order," said Mr. Dunkley. "Quite ticketyboo."

"Keep well, missy," Mongoose said.

"And you." As Maggie watched them walk away, Felicity racing round them, she knew whom Mr. Dunkley with his jaunty, bandy-legged strut, resembled — Foxtrot.

The East Indian taxi driver loaded Maggie's cases and Felicity's kennel into his boot.

Maggie, wearing Robin's favourite hat with her winter coat and holding Felicity, took one last look about the downstairs. As she passed the oak door of the narrow room she could hear the nuns singing the *Mass of the Sixth Tone*. It was hard for her to believe that by tomorrow she'd be back in Hollywood.

She closed the outer door to Raven Hall for the last time and entered the taxi, where she held Felicity on her lap.

"Which airport, missus?" the driver asked as he slid the car into gear.

"Heathrow. But we've plenty of time." Maggie felt bad that she hadn't said a proper goodbye to Father Humphrey, but he was on retreat; nor had she said one to Robin. She hated most losing him. The last couple of days she'd hoped he'd come round but felt he wouldn't. Maybe if she just went to his house...

"Driver, stop please at the house coming up."

He shrugged and screeched to a stop. Leaving Felicity in the back seat, Maggie slipped out and ran up the weed-infested walk. She rang the bell and waited, studying the worn red bricks and listening to the idling of the taxi's engine.

She rang again.

A very old, stout woman, wearing house slippers, the cloth cut to let bunions bulge free, slouched low, leaning heavily on a black cane. Her hair was sparse and white, and what there was of it had been caught back in a bun. Thick, round glasses covered her cloudy eyes. Her grey and black patterned dress hung so unevenly at the hem it almost touched the floor in spots. Yet round her neck hung gold chains.

She raised her head from her hunched shoulders and peered at Maggie. "Aye?"

"I'm Maggie Featherstone from Raven Hall. I actually called to see Robin."

"Raven Hall! Fancy that!" She spoke unsteadily. "Come in."

As the old woman slowly led the way into a dark sitting room Maggie could hear someone in the kitchen, washing up.

The woman motioned to Maggie to take one of the threadbare chairs and sat down herself with great difficulty. The room smelled musty, and it was cold. An electric heater sat unused in the fireplace.

A faded brown and white photograph on the wall to one side of the fireplace, caught Maggie's eye. The boy in it resembled Robin, only he wore a suit from years past. He stood stiffly, grinning. Robin's grandfather perhaps? She was in the right house.

"It's Robin you want to see?" The old woman broke the silence.

"Your great grandson?" Maggie volunteered.

At this the woman gave a chortle, sending a spray of spittle into the air.

"My son, dear. My son. I'm his mother, Mrs. Macneil."

"But he's only twelve!"

"Aye!" She chuckled. "I guess he'll always be twelve."

Maggie stared at Mrs. Macneil's swollen arthritic hands and tried to gain her composure.

"My Robin's been doing magic at the Hall, that he has. Have you enjoyed it? Says lately he's been having so much trouble about a bone. Says he has to get all his props back."

Maggie cleared her throat.

"Props are important," was all she could think to say.

Mrs. Macneil struggled with her glasses, finally getting them off as if to see better with her myopic eyes.

"Used to sit in that window there and look up at Raven Hall. 'One day I'll do magic at the hall', he'd say. And to think, now he's doing it. He's a lively lad. And kind."

Maggie bent toward the window and could just make out the gables of the Hall. "Your son does wonderful magic, Mrs. Macneil." She realized she was twisting and untwisting her scarf. "I don't suppose he's here?" She glanced toward the kitchen.

"My, no. That's my companion. I'm ninety-nine, so can't manage all alone any more." She plucked at a doily on the arm of her chair. "No, Robin comes and goes. You can never tell when he'll appear."

"Say goodbye for me when he comes," Maggie said.

"Oh, aye."

Maggie shivered. She stood, and with great difficulty her hostess rose as well. Maggie shook her hand.

"I'm very pleased to have met you, Mrs. Macneil. You have a lovely son."

"Aye, that I do." Mrs. Macneil slowly led the way to the front door and opened it. "You know, he fell from the oak just outside the drawing room at Raven Hall. Watching a party he was. Imagining himself inside doing some magic, no doubt. But I expect he told you. He was gone for quite some time, so it's nice having him back."

Maggie stood for a moment, uncertain if she should ask

her question. "Can you tell me where Robin is buried?"

"Just up the road. The graveyard behind the church. I don't visit there now he's back."

"The spire I can see from here?"

"That's the one. Go safely now."

Maggie hurried down the path, got into the taxi, and told the driver to stop at the church.

"You pay me a pretty sum to be dog sitter, missus."

"Here we are." Maggie climbed out and walked quickly to where stones dotted the graveyard. Heavens, how would she find the right one? She went along the rows as quickly as possible.

Then she saw it. The gravestone was small and overgrown. It said: *Robin Macneil, magician, 1918-1930.*

Maggie smiled. Magician. What a strange thing to put on a gravestone. Somehow, seeing the actual grave made her accept that this was Robin's, that he was dead. That he had so recently worked his magic gave her hope.

"Missus, the time." The little Indian called.

Maggie wished she had flowers for Robin's grave. She turned to leave, then knew what she must do.

She knelt, took off her hat — the black one Robin loved — and placed it on the grave. She stared at the deep reds and pinks of the silk roses in full bloom, at the dark green leaves, at the bits of grosgrain that could be seen beneath the roses round the crown, at the wide felt brim, surrounded now with long blades of grass. "Another prop for you, Robin." She blessed herself. "Thank you."

"Missus," called the driver. "Any minute it will rain. Your nice hat will be ruined."

Maggie hurried up to him. "Someone's picking it up."

"But I have seen no one. It will be ruined."

"Come on," said Maggie. She ran to the taxi and climbed in. Felicity jumped onto her lap.

The driver slammed his door, then turned to Maggie. "It will be ruined."

"I think not," said Maggie. "It's been collected by now."

The man glared at her, pushed the accelerator to the floor, and sped off.

Maggie gazed out the taxi window at lanes and houses that seemed so normal. On the dual carriageway life went on at the same frantic pace. She wondered if everything that had happened to her in the past few months had been real. Had Father Humphrey truly existed? Had the nuns appeared? Mr. Dunkley and Mongoose? Miss Letterby and Mr. Beveridge? Even Robin? Or had they been nighttime figures she'd carried into the day?

Perhaps, she thought, all life is a shadow time in our eternal search for Love. And figures come in and out irrespective of time or place.

The idea pleased her. She relaxed into the cold vinyl seat.

Like a film, she thought. We're shadow figures, light-produced. We play walk-on parts and pretend we're stars.

Her mind went to the gold stars on the sidewalks of Hollywood Boulevard, glistening before adult movie houses and cheap souvenir shops. Stars scattered with rubbish, scattered with lost souls — derelicts, runaways. Stars trampled by tourists in their search for Filmland.

She felt a tremendous surge of compassion for all mankind, for all strays.

Felicity circled and pawed at Maggie's coat to create a nest for herself.

"Head up proud, Felicity," Maggie whispered, hearing as she did so Miss Letterby's shy voice.

The puppy tossed her head back and smacked Maggie on the lips. Maggie laughed.

"Felicity, we're going home."

END